BEN ADAMS

THE ENIGMATOLOGIST

by
Ben Adams

Copyright © Ben Adams 2016
Cover Copyright © 2016
Published by Devil's Tower
(An Imprint of Ravenswood Publishing)

DEVIL'S TOWER

Ravenswood Publishing
Raeford, NC 28376
http://www.ravenswoodpublishing.com

Printed in the U.S.A.

ISBN-13: 978-0692670606
ISBN-10: 0692670602

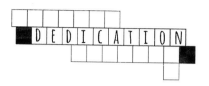

For Shelby

 CHAPTER ONE

John Abernathy watched them from behind the bushes, the man in the car wearing a rubber ducky mask, an e-cigarette between the orange and latex beak, the woman's head bobbing in his lap. John didn't know the woman's name, but the man was Randall Neilson, his client's husband. Mrs. Neilson had walked into McGullicutty and Sons Private Investigations a week earlier, needing her suspicions confirmed. Rooftop, John's boss, gave him the case, thinking it'd be easy, photographing a cheating husband in the act. John had been following Mr. Neilson for a couple of days, sitting in the Village Inn next to his office, waiting for him to leave work. Usually, he went straight home to John's client, but tonight, Mr. Neilson headed to the Genesse Mountain Lookout parking lot just outside of Denver to meet his girlfriend.

John pushed his glasses back up, adjusted the zoom lens as the couple moved to the back seat. For the first time since she got in the car, John saw the woman's face. She flipped the hair out of her eyes, tolerating Randall grunting behind her. She put her hand against the window, bracing herself. Her palm slipped on the slick glass, her fingers getting snagged in the latch. The door popped open. She tumbled out, but caught herself, skinning her hand on the ice and gravel. A can of Axe body spray rolled from the car, clinking against the frosted asphalt. The dome light glowed dull yellow, giving John a clear shot of their faces. He started taking pictures again.

She dragged herself from the car. Her navy blue skirt was bunched around her waist and she pulled it down. Randall crawled out after her, holding his unzipped pants. He tore off the mask and tossed it in the back seat. She brushed crisp ice from her palms, tears building. Randall tried to grab her, soothe her, but she twisted loose.

"Is this 'cause I asked you to wear those Care Bear pajamas?" Randall asked, zipping up his pants. "Because that was a one-time thing."

She spun and slapped him. And walked to her car, barefoot, shoes in one hand, holding her shirt closed with the other.

Randall Neilson picked up the can of Axe body spray and spritzed some on his bare chest. The wind carried the fumes to John, the gag-inducing smell of teen exasperation, moose testicles, and entitlement. He put his hand over his mouth, suppressing the coughs building in his throat. Randall tossed the can in his car, leaving the cap on the pavement, and drove away shouting at the woman through his open window.

She gripped the top of the steering wheel, rested

her head on her hands, and cried.

John stopped taking pictures.

He felt the urge to go to her, console her, but heard Rooftop's voice, reminding him that he was there to observe and record, not to get involved, that he needed to remain separate, in the shadows.

She lifted her head from the steering wheel, started her car. The car exhaled gray exhaust into the night. She backed out, paused for a moment, then revved her engine and sped from the lot, tires spraying loose snow.

John tugged his wool hat down around his ears. He wiped May snow and mud from the knees of his secondhand corduroys, and put his bare hands in the pockets of his black pea coat, drew it closer to his slender frame and slogged to the empty lot. Melted ice had seeped into the gap between the loose rubber sole and tip of his left black Converse All-Star, soaking his sock and toes, and John stopped intermittently to kick snow from it.

The lot was quiet. The only sound came from trees bending, trying to hold against the wind. And John's crunching shoes. He stooped and picked up the cap Randall had left in the parking lot and tossed it in the trash.

The breeze shifted, whispering in his ear. It chilled John through the layers of wool and cotton. Standing in the ice-covered parking lot, he felt uneasy, like someone was behind him, watching, their eyes pushing against him.

A branch cracked near the set of trees where John had been hiding, like someone stepped on it. Startled, he jumped. John tried looking through the tangled brush. Stars were starting to appear, competing with Denver's evening glow, and his eyes were only beginning to adjust to the oncoming night, but every shaded trunk and overgrown bush looked like something sinister hid behind it.

Another branch snapped.

John stood upright, stiff. Up until then, he had thought he was alone. But he wasn't. Someone prowled the forest, observing him.

John took a step back, fumbled in his pants pocket for his keys. His car was just down the road. A quarter mile of ice and slush. He'd have to run for it. He didn't think he could outrun whatever was back there, especially over tire-crushed dirt and snow. Giant trees and lack of streetlights had darkened the road. John pivoted toward it, digging the rubber tips of his Chucks into the ice.

Snow fell from the trees, crashing and breaking limbs. John sighed. That's what it must have been, heavy snow on a dead branch.

* * * *

"Well, Mrs. Neilson," John said, sitting behind a desk in the Blake Street office. She sat in a wooden chair across from him, fogged in perfume that nearly strangled him. "As you know, I've been following your husband for the past couple of days."

Rooftop stood behind him. He leaned against the

windowsill, observing his young assistant. He was a squat man, like the gravity of his profession had compressed him. His bald head, the tufts of gray hair ringing it, barely reached the window sash.

"Yesterday," John continued, "I witnessed him leaving work shortly after five. As you can guess, he didn't go straight home." He tapped the manila folder on the desk. "There's no easy way to say this." John slid the folder over to her, proud to be showing Mrs. Neilson his portrait of her husband.

Mrs. Neilson opened it, started flipping through the photos like a magazine at the hair salon.

John had witnessed Rooftop give this same speech several times over the past year. He had memorized and internalized it, knew what to expect. And right then, he expected her to start crying, disbelief and grief taking over. He dropped his arm and opened the desk drawer. Without looking, he reached for a box of tissues, readied to offer them.

"What the fuck is this?"

"Like I said, I followed your husband."

"Yeah, I heard that part. I mean this." Mrs. Neilson pulled out a picture, pointed to the woman in it. "That's my goddamn cousin! Wearing my clothes!"

"That's the first thing you noticed?" John asked, looking at the rubber ducky mask.

"In every single picture! Look at this! That trailer park bitch is soiling everything. Is she wearing my jewelry? Now I have to go home and wash that skank's stank off everything."

"I think we need to focus our attention on what's important. You now have evidence that your husband's been unfaithful," John said, trying to remain professional.

"No shit! With my slutty cousin! You know she got fired from the DMV for fucking her manager? They photographed the whole thing with the photo ID camera. An old man had a heart attack when he realized his new license photo was someone's balls."

John slammed the tissue drawer closed. Behind him, Rooftop cleared his throat.

"And you, this is how you tell me? with pictures of my husband fucking in the backseat of the LeBaron? That's where we put our car seat for Christ's sake. No wonder my baby's getting sick."

"She's probably allergic to skank stank."

"What are you, a fucking doctor? Of course she's allergic to skank stank. She's a classy baby."

"She obviously takes after her mother."

"What the fuck did you just say?"

"John," Rooftop interrupted, his hand on John's shoulder, "why don't you go make us some coffee?"

"Whatever." John went into the storage room, brewed coffee among the filing cabinets, hotplate, cot, and spare suits hanging from nails driven into the wall.

Rooftop sat behind the desk. He barely peeked above the wooden plane, his bald head like a rising moon. The storage room windows were thick and John struggled to hear the few words Rooftop said. Mrs. Neilson wiped her fingers under her eyes and started crying. Rooftop pulled the tissues from the desk and offered them.

"Un-fucking-believable." John shook his head in disbelief and ran his hands through his thick brown hair.

The phone rang.

The caller ID said the number was from California, although John didn't recognize the area code. He turned off the ringer and lowered the answering machine speaker volume.

John returned with coffee. Mrs. Neilson nodded her head, agreeing with something Rooftop had just said. She blotted her eyes, sniffling.

"Thank you, Mr. McGullicutty," she said, digging in her purse. She put a check on the desk. "This has been very enlightening."

"I'm sure it has," John said.

"And you, Mr. Abernathy," Mrs. Neilson said, "I'm definitely talking about you in my Yelp review."

She slammed the door. John and Rooftop listened to her walk away, her high heels clicking against the marble floor of the hall.

"John," Rooftop said, "what was that?"

"She was just..." John looked at the door. "It's not what I expected."

Rufus McGullicutty had been a good friend of

John's grandfather. His grandfather had given Rufus the nickname 'Rooftop' when they were kids, because 'he was so short he'd never see the roof of his own house.' When John's father disappeared, Rooftop looked after John like a son, even offering him a job as his assistant when John graduated from The Boulder School of Esoteric Art and Impractical Design, a job John always told himself was temporary.

"You're going to have difficult clients. It's part of the job. Got it?"

"This whole thing, it's not what I expected."

"I told you, this is what we do." Rooftop gripped the pictures, shook them at John. "We're paid to take pictures. That's it. This isn't anything glamorous like the movies. There are no car chases or shoot outs. You never get the girl. If you want excitement, go do something else. If you want a regular nine-to-five behind a desk, go do something else. This job is not fun. Got it?"

"It shouldn't be like this!" John gestured to the photos Rooftop held. When he started working for Rooftop, he thought it'd be easy, take a couple of pictures, design crossword puzzles in his free time. He never anticipated the reaction he'd have, the anger and hopelessness he felt when he photographed grown men taking their pants off.

"Did they teach you that in that fancy art school?"

"They never told us we'd be working some shit

job that'd make us miserable."

"We all got to do something," Rooftop said, tossing the folder onto the desk.

"That's just it. I don't think I can do this."

"You quitting on me? Is that it? What are you going to do? go back to The People's Republic of Boulder, work in a coffee shop?"

"That's where all the Advanced Pictorial Ceramics majors work. I can't work with them. They're cliquey."

"Cliquey? What the hell's 'cliquey'? Look, kid, you got a good job here. I know it's not enemagraphy or whatever."

"Enigmatology. Writing puzzles. You know this."

"Enigma shmigma, whatever," Rooftop said. "Look, you got it pretty good here, kid. The work is steady. The money's good. More than what those Ceramics kids are making, I bet."

John tapped the waste basket with his toe. The few crumpled tissues inside the can moved slightly, then settled back into place.

"You've been doing this for a long time," John said. "How do you deal with it? with people like that?"

"Heavy drinking."

"That's great advice."

"Look, some people can do it, some can't. Got it? John, you're a good kid, a little sensitive, but a good kid. Something this business needs. Why don't you backup the photos you took in case we need to send them to her attorney? Take the rest of the day off, think about it."

By the time John had backed up the files, Rooftop had listened to the voicemail. He was on the phone, swinging his stubby arms around. He got like that when he was excited, usually about a client. John put on his coat and stood at the doorway, waiting for Rooftop to look at him so he could say goodbye.

"John, come here," Rooftop whispered, putting his hand over the phone's mouthpiece. "I got a big job for us. Pays a thousand dollars a day, plus expenses. You want to go out of town? All expenses paid?"

"Sure, I guess," John said, shrugging his shoulders.

"Great, hold on," Rooftop took his hand off the phone. "Rex, I'm putting you on speakerphone. Got it?" He pushed the speakerphone button. "Rex, you're on with John Abernathy."

"Hello, John," a confident voice said. "I'm Rex Grant, the editor-in-chief for *The National Enquirer*. We'd like to hire you and Rooftop."

"I'm a little old for a paper route," John said, "and Roof hasn't been on a bike since the sixties."

"Don't worry," Rex said, almost laughing, "we already have people for that. I want to hire you to investigate a photograph, see if it's legit. A few weeks ago a woman contacted us saying she had photographic evidence that Elvis was alive. We talked to her on the phone and looked at the photo.

I've seen a lot of Elvis photos, but this picture's different. It's arguably the best documentation of an Elvis sighting to come across our desks. A once-in-a-lifetime find."

"Why are you calling us?" John asked. "Don't you have reporters for this sort of thing?"

"Normally, yes. Especially for Elvis sightings. Shortly after Elvis's death, we offered a reward for anyone who could prove he was alive."

"That sounds like responsible journalism."

"Yeah, it was great. We were inundated with phone calls and letters from people saying they'd seen Elvis. Some were obviously a waste of time, but a few seemed credible. So, we hired investigators from different parts of the country to authenticate them. Rooftop was one of the people we hired. Unfortunately, none of them panned out, I'm sure he'll tell you about that, but this photo, it's the real deal."

"Yeah, but..." The window blinds were tilted, one side higher than the other. John tugged the cord, but they wouldn't align. "Why don't you just publish it?"

"There's...there's a really good chance that there's, well, something more to this story."

The only time anyone ever called them was when something had gone terribly wrong with another person.

"You sent someone down there already, didn't you?" John asked on a hunch.

"Yeah, we..."

"Rex," Rooftop said, "you need to be straight with us if you want our help. Got it?"

Rex sighed. "When the photo came in, I thought we should send someone to investigate, but we don't have the budget we had in the eighties, so I decided to send an intern. The kid...the kid never checked in. We called his cell phone, the motel where he was staying. Nothing. A few days ago, the New Mexico State Police found his body in the desert just south of Truth or Consequences. He'd been shot. He was...he was just a kid. His parents keep calling, asking if we've heard anything. The police don't have any leads. He was only eighteen. Just a kid."

"What the hell, Rex?" Rooftop said. "You want us to risk our lives for a photo of Elvis? No. This is not what we do. We do not risk our lives for photos of Elvis. We don't risk our lives for anything. Got it?"

The kid. He probably went to a prestigious school like John, majoring in journalism, interning at the tabloid, getting coffee for people who Photoshop celebrities' heads onto obese bodies. Like John, the kid had waited for his big break. But when it came, a chance to travel to New Mexico, do some investigative journalism, his art school dream, it got him killed.

"I'll do it," John said, his voice hushed.

"This is why we have police. This is why...Wait. What?" Rooftop glared at John, his bald head

12

turning scarlet.

"I'll do it. I'll go down there."

"Like hell you will! Rex, I'm putting you on hold. Got it?" Rooftop hit the hold button, rubbed his hand on his bald head. "Jesus Christ, John. What would your dad say?"

"My dad hasn't been around for..." John did the math for an equation he'd performed every day since age five, "eighteen years, so he can't say much."

"He wouldn't want you doing something dangerous."

"This job is already dangerous. Last night, that Neilson guy, if he'd seen me, he probably would've pulled a gun on me if he had one. Besides, someone needs to do this."

"This is not what we do."

"Since I've been working for you," John said, throwing his coat on the chair where Mrs. Neilson had sat, "all I've done is help people get divorced."

"This is why we have the police."

"I need to do this."

"This is not what we do. We take photographs. That's it. Got it?"

"That kid, he was me, doing a job he hated until something better came along."

"That's everybody!"

"And he got killed for what? a photo? When he could have been..." John thought about the unfinished puzzle that awaited him. "I need to do this."

"Goddamnit, John."

"That kid was me," John said, pointing to the computer where he constructed his puzzles when Rooftop was out of the office.

"This is not what we do." Rooftop looked out the window, toward a mountain range half-forested by black and needle-bare trees, victims of a parasitic relationship with rice-sized insects.

"Don't worry. The minute I find anything, I'll call the police." John pressed the hold button. "Alright, Rex, I'm in."

"Great. We'll e-mail you everything, a digital copy of the photograph and the photographer's address."

"And our usual retainer, five thousand dollars," John said. Rooftop grinned, then quickly scowled, his anger at John being only temporarily satiated by the money.

"Of course," Rex said.

"Alright, I'll head out as soon as I get everything. Where am I going?"

"A little town in New Mexico called Las Vegas."

That night, John sat at the kitchen table in his apartment sipping a PBR Tall Boy, looking at the Elvis picture. He had reprinted it several times and uploaded it to his phone. Something wasn't right about the picture, something that struck John as odd, bothered him, made him feel uneasy. Whoever had taken it didn't know how to use a camera and hadn't focused the lens, leaving the image blurred, just an impression of the moment. And John's eyes glazed over trying to make out the details, the big hair, a bloated belly. He couldn't tell if it really was Elvis or just some guy with the misfortune of having a pompadour, but through the haze of magnification and an unfocused lens, a man stood on a deck, legs shoulder width apart. One arm in the air, slightly blurred in captured motion.

"Is he waving?"

John spent the next several hours researching Elvis conspiracies. As expected, the internet proved to be a reliable resource for contradictory and unbelievable information. There were conspiracy theories connecting Elvis to organized crime, Richard Nixon, the DEA, theories about extraterrestrials being present at Elvis's birth, Elvis helping Michael Jackson fake his death, Elvis and Michael Jackson living in Ecuador with new identities courtesy of the Illuminati. Having studied puzzles, their logical design and rules, John saw the loose connections forming these beliefs. He also recognized the places where those connections frayed and split from reality. *The National Enquirer* had a reputation for attracting believers of all ilk, people who accepted modern myths like boy bands praying to the Loch Ness Monster, Bigfoot having a Dallas Cowboys themed mancave, or Elvis being alive. John flipped the photo several times, deciding not to get caught in someone's fantasy.

He let the photo fall through his fingers. It landed on the table, mingling with a thick copy of *Merriam-Webster's Colligate Dictionary*, *Walker's Rhyming Dictionary*, a copy of *Word Squares*. The books were some of the tools John used to build his crosswords, although since graduation, they'd sat on the table, stacked and stockpiled.

The screen of John's laptop glowed. He sighed when the empty crossword puzzle grid appeared. The computer program he used, *Crossword Compiler*, had suggested several filler words, erne, Ursa, olio, all crossword clichés. And he'd deleted them.

Written along the top was his theme, 'Moving Day'. That's all John had been able to write since graduating from The Boulder School of Esoteric Art and Impractical Design. A theme. No words. No clues.

John had discovered puzzles the way most young boys do, by reading the funnies. They were the graphics-less boxes beneath *Family Circus*. He wasn't interested in Bil Keane's pudgy children and their labyrinthine routes home, or the inner demons making them break or steal. To John, their idealized family was a farce and could never exist outside of the printed world. He was drawn to the jumbled letters needing arrangement, the empty spaces needing words.

Puzzles gave him the order, logic, and stability he was missing. His father had just disappeared, leaving him and his mother with unanswered questions. But puzzles always had an answer. He just had to figure them out.

As a child, John had spent his spare time studying and solving puzzles, filling in boxes in every newspaper he found, buying puzzle books at gas stations and truck stops when they traveled, trying to finish the book before they reached the landmark or national monument or highway oddity that comprised their summer vacations.

And when it came time for him to go to college, choose a major, he only wanted to do one thing, become an enigmatologist, someone who designed puzzles. While in college, he experienced the excitement of immersion, the thrill of being completely absorbed in his education. However, since graduation, he'd only been able to stare at the screen and question why his creativity and passion were absent, whether he had traded them in for an overpriced degree or they'd been burned away by years of study. And in his darker moments, when he'd lie in bed half-drunk on cheap beer, staring at the ceiling, questioning his choices and how they'd shaped the flow of his life, he wondered if designing puzzles was something he was supposed to do, and if not, maybe it was time to do something else. But he never shared this doubt. He just kept working.

He put his fingers on the keys and tapped them like someone pretending to type on a television show, hoping movement would spur thought. When nothing came, John leaned back and put his hands in his hair. Grunting in frustration, he closed the file, asked himself why the imaginative spirit he possessed in college had abandoned him, only to be replaced by uncertainties.

* * * *

The next morning, John packed for the trip. It didn't take long. He threw three days worth of vintage sci-fi and comic book t-shirts, plaid shirts, mismatched socks, and zip-up hoodies next to his tooth brush and razor in an old hardcover suitcase he'd bought at a garage sale.

John cradled the gun in his hands. Rooftop had insisted that he take it, reminding John of the hours they spent at the shooting range when John was younger, then the Oreo Cookie Blizzards they'd have afterward. John was still reluctant to take the gun with him, but knew it would make Rooftop feel better knowing he had it. John sighed, and put it in his suitcase.

"You have everything you need?" Kristen Abernathy, John's mom, asked, sticking her head into his room. Her brown hair was starting to turn gray, and she had pulled it into a ponytail.

"Mom, knock first. I could've been, I don't know, doing something." He moved quickly and closed the suitcase so she couldn't see the gun sitting on his rocket ship patterned boxer shorts.

"Sorry. I'm still getting used to you being back. I packed a cooler with some sandwiches." She crossed her arms over her blue and faded Denver Broncos sweatshirt. She smiled, her face compressing like a concertina, folksy but dignified.

"Thanks. Oh, hey..." John pulled some cash out of his pocket. "Here, this is for you, for rent."

"No, no, no. This is your money. You save it for something." She tried pushing the money away, but John grabbed her hand and forced the cash into it.

"This is why I moved back, to help you out."

"When you said that, I thought you meant laundry or cleaning," she said, looking at the clothes on the floor.

"To help you pay down some bills. Eventually get you outta here, into a nicer place."

"John, I don't need a nicer place. I just need you

to be happy."

"Then take the money."

Kristen folded the bills and put them in her wallet, next to a family photo. In the photo, John is three. He is sitting on her lap and makes a face at the camera. John's dad has seen it and is trying not to laugh, while Kristen is smiling like a proud wife and mother, unaware of the transformations in her husband and son. Kristen loved the photograph. Every time she saw it she sighed.

"You were so little," she said. "You missed out on so much with him not being here." Her eyes swelled like overstuffed grocery bags ready to break.

"Fuck him."

"John!" She looked up from the photo, her eyes wide and wet. Since adolescence, John had expressed his animosity for his father daily. After eighteen years, Kristen was used to it, but it still disturbed her.

"I was five, Mom. You know how much that messes with a kid's head? I thought he left 'cause I broke that stupid *Cape Canaveral* glass he got at Burger King."

"He got that because it's your favorite show."

"I cried for weeks, swearing I'd be good if he came home."

"If you'd only known him…"

"I know he didn't come home from work. I know the police stopped looking for him when they found his car at his job, his wallet and credit cards still in the glove box. Christ..."

"John. Language," Kristen said, faking shock.

"You asked Rooftop to look for him and even he gave up after a while. When does Roof ever give up on anything?"

"He loved you so much. I saw it on his face every time he held you."

"Well, that must have changed."

"Something else must have happened. He wouldn't leave us."

"That's what happened. For whatever reason, he left us. And you did the best you could. No, you did a great job. Because of you, we didn't need him." A flap of t-shirt was sticking out of the suitcase and John stuffed it inside. "Still don't."

John despised his mother's infatuation with his father, her forgiving him for leaving and ruining their lives. He wished she could see his father for what he was, the type of person John was hired to photograph.

"Mom, I gotta go," John said, tired of always having the same conversation. He grabbed the suitcase off the bed and kissed her on the cheek as he left.

The suitcase sat in the trunk of his '98 Saturn sedan, the cooler filled with sandwiches in the back. John put the gun under the driver's seat. He flipped through the radio until he found a song that wasn't sung by teenagers with expensive haircuts. He backed out of their assigned parking space, started to leave the parking lot of the apartment complex, the six buildings conforming to the beige and yellow look of the outlet mall and surrounding sub-divisions, and headed for Las Vegas, New Mexico.

John pulled into Las Vegas, New Mexico around 2:00 p.m. He took his time driving down, hoping the guy in the picture had already left town and he could turn everything over to the local sheriff's department, let them deal with it. He knew the only reason *The National Enquirer* hadn't relinquished their evidence was so they could still run their story. A 'Killer Elvis' would generate headlines for years.

As he turned off the highway, his stomach tightened and twisted, like the cheese and mayonnaise sandwich he ate around Walsenberg had been a little sour. But the pain didn't last long, subsiding as he drove through town.

Las Vegas, New Mexico was a mix of old brick buildings, prefab homes, stucco covered bungalows, ranch style houses. All of them looked like they were held together by rubber cement and thumb tacks. The town was old and rough, the opposite of an expanding Denver. It was the inspiration for paintings of a fading America, or the setting for modern Westerns where the family farm is jeopardized by industrialization. It was the subject of lectures from Intro to Rural Imagery and Its Use in Word Scramble Design.

Several motels punctuated Grand Avenue, many of them newer, built as the town stretched. John ignored them, looking for something that met his art school sensibilities. Then, on the corner of Baca Avenue and Grand Avenue, a galloping centaur repeatedly shot arrows at Earth, all in neon. The sign for The Sagittarius Inn. It was a nostalgic beacon that had flashed the same message for sixty years. Charged by vintage neon, John pulled into the parking lot and checked into the pink desert motel.

* * * *

The photographer's name was Mrs. Elizabeth Morris. John had asked the hotel manager for directions to her house. She lived on the west side of town, on the corner of Socorro Street and Montezuma Street, buried in an old residential neighborhood. Addresses had faded from mailboxes like dates on weathered tombstones.

John parked in front of a small brick house with a front addition that looked like it had been done by family. Faded vinyl siding contrasted brown brick. A fallen air conditioner rested under a lopsided window. Patches of dead, brittle grass, fitful tufts on bald earth, were the leftovers of a lawn that had died years ago.

He walked up the gravel driveway, past a brown '74 Pinto and a trailer on blocks.

At the door, he heard music playing inside. '(You're the) Devil in Disguise'. A minor hit for the unmistakable voice that changed the world.

After a couple of knocks, a woman in a white blouse and tan skirt answered. She was older, aged by the desert's unforgiving sun and dirt-flavored air.

"Mrs. Morris?" he asked.

"Yes?"

"My name's John Abernathy. I'm a private investigator." He said this almost like a question, as if asking for confirmation, then handed her his card.

"You don't look like a private investigator," she said, arms crossed, looking at his dark green zip-up hoodie, its ratted cuffs stained brown from lack of washings, his faded jeans, vintage *Cape Canaveral* t-shirt, the iron-on decal of the show's cast peeling on blue cotton.

"Yeah, I get that a lot," he said, adjusting his glasses. "I'm here on behalf of *The National Enquirer*. Do you mind if I ask you a few questions?"

Her eyes widened and mouth opened. She flung her hands over her mouth, trapping her excitement. But the seal broke. She squealed. John flinched and stepped away from the door.

"I knew it! I knew you'd come!" She screamed, grabbing John's arms, jumping like a lottery winner. "This is about my photo, isn't it? Oh, please tell me it's about my photo! Please tell me it's about my photo!"

"That's right," John said.

"Oh, goodie, goodie, goodie!" She jumped, clinging to John's elbows, shaking him. He clutched her shoulders to stop her and moved his hands down, dislodging himself.

"The *Enquirer* hired me to authenticate it, see if it's legit. Now, has anyone else come around asking about the picture? any other reporters?"

"I didn't send my picture to anyone else. I've been reading the *Enquirer* for thirty years. I know it's the only paper qualified to handle this story."

"Okay, good," John said, relieved. The intern never interviewed Mrs. Morris, had never made it to town, had died before he could talk to her. His death had nothing to do with the photo. He was probably just in the wrong place at the wrong time. Or saw something he shouldn't have seen. Either way, it was someone else's problem. And John relaxed a little. The tension of investigating a murder was released, replaced with the prospect of a simple case. All he'd have to do was find the guy in the photo and prove he wasn't Elvis. Easy. But John knew better. He'd worked for Rooftop long enough to know that nothing was ever easy. The kid might have died before he could make it to town, but that didn't mean the guy in the photo wasn't involved somehow, making it crucial that John find him, ask him some questions.

He pulled his phone out of his pocket and flipped through the pictures saved in it.

"Now, just for verification, is this the picture you took?" He showed her the picture of the overweight man.

"That's my picture. Do you think it's really him?" Mrs. Morris asked, trying to contain her excitement.

"You know," as John spoke, he felt greasy, like someone who sold used cell phones at the carwash, but he thought he still needed to earn her trust, "I'm not supposed to say this, but I've done a number of these investigations, and I've got to say, your photo is the best documentation of an Elvis sighting I've seen. A once-in-a-lifetime find."

"I knew it! I knew it!" She screamed.

"I do have a few more questions I'd like to ask you."

"Of course. Please come inside."

John followed Mrs. Morris inside, but stopped at the door. The sight of the walls of her living room caused him to drop his phone.

On the wall next to him hung movie posters, Elvis in colorful shirts being rugged, a clock where Elvis's arms pointed to the hour and minute and his hips swayed to the pulse of sixty beats per minute. Against the far wall, a display case contained autographs, promotional photos, concert programs, hair clippings tied with a bow resting on a small, satin pillow. Magazines with Elvis's faded face, from the different stages of his career, weighed down the second shelf. The overburdened shelf sagged like an older Elvis waistline. Porcelain busts, large and small, some formed into salt and pepper shakers or figurines depicting movie scenes, lined the fireplace mantle. On another wall hung a series of toy guitars decorated with images of young Elvis encouraging children to learn his songs. Plates hung above the guitars, showing highlights from Elvis's life, the scene from *Jailhouse Rock,* or Elvis surfing, scenes portraying him as vibrant. On a table next to the couch was something resembling a Fabergè egg on a stand, adding an implied class to the room. The egg was open, split down the middle, revealing a tiny Elvis in a Vegas jumpsuit, like he had just hatched and was ready to do two shows a night and matinees on weekends. And of course there were recordings, shelves of 45s and 33s in plastic sleeves.

John had expected a normal southwestern home, with ceramic cacti and purple and turquoise art like the houses depicted in his Regional Home Décor 202 textbook. Unlike those homes, Mrs. Morris's place wasn't dedicated to the desert's color scheme. It was a shrine to the fallen King.

"Your home is amazing," John said, in awe of her idolatry. She was the type of person John and his art school friends would simultaneously mock and revere for the sincerity of her devotion to kitsch. He picked up his phone and walked around her living room, looking at her collection. He reached out, jerked his hand back, then gave into temptation, picking up memorabilia. He fondled a porcelain figurine, Elvis in a racecar from *Viva Las Vegas*. He ran his finger over a gold ring with a diamond-studded horseshoe and horse head. But stopped at a faded dental mold. A human incisor had been placed in the mold. Next to it, a framed letter of authenticity. John knelt to get a closer look at the tartar-covered relic. He shook his head, doubting that a modern day grave robber had ripped out Elvis's tooth, then mounted and sold it. Then again, he couldn't believe someone would buy half the memorabilia in Mrs. Morris's home, like the sombrero stitched with Elvis eating a fish taco that hung on the wall next to the window.

"Well, I'm glad you like it," Mrs. Morris said, standing in the kitchen door watching him.

"Some kids I went to school with, they would die if they saw this place. You mind if I take some pictures?" John asked, putting the stopper back in an Elvis-shaped bourbon decanter.

"Of course. I'm happy to share my collection."

John took pictures on his phone, then sent them to some friends from art school.

Mrs. Morris stood in the kitchen doorway, her hands folded at her waist. She smiled, happy that someone else appreciated her collection. In the kitchen behind her, a crumb-filled Cool Whip container sat on the yellow linoleum.

"What, no Elvis dog bowl?" John asked.

"Oh my, no. Elvis is way too pretty for the dog."

The living room couch had also received the Elvis treatment. It was airbrushed with Elvis's face. John sat on it, gingerly.

And there.

Above the fireplace.

Elvis painted on black velvet, completely naked, with an erection. John's erectile knowledge was limited to his own, when he woke in the morning, and a magazine Jimmy Rosebottom had brought to school in the third grade. He thought he was a good size, but Elvis's painted erection, the length of a kielbasa, the girth of the fat end of a baseball bat, made him feel inadequate.

"You like my painting?" Mrs. Morris asked.

"Uh, yeah." John shook his head, refocused, his attention magnetized by Elvis's painted wang. He quickly took a picture.

"Sometimes I can't stop staring at it," she said.

"I see why," John said, resting his elbow on the couch armrest, propping his head on his hand, fingers shielding him from the painting.

She sat in a chair across the room, moving a quilt made from cloth replications of Elvis album covers, and said, "Most people think I'm a little odd for filling my house like this, but I don't care. It makes me happy."

"I can see that. So, how did you get into collecting?" From watching Rooftop, John had learned that the easiest way to get someone to open up was to ask them about what they loved.

"Well, I suppose it all started with Elvis's second appearance on Milton Berle, June 5th, 1956. I'll never forget that day. We just bought our first TV and were really excited to watch a broadcast from New York City. Well, I was, anyway. Herman, my husband, was an old fuddy-duddy and never cared for that sort of thing. Well, Elvis performed 'Hound Dog'. In all my life I'd never seen anything like it, the way he moved and shook his hips. Well, when he danced something moved inside me. I jumped up and asked Herman if he would dance with me, but he sat in his chair grumbling about corrupting the youth of America. Herman turned off the TV and went and put on a Bing Crosby record. I used to love Bing, but after hearing Elvis, Bing sounded like sour milk.

"The next day, I went out and bought my first Elvis record. The man at the store looked at me funny. I was embarrassed and told him it was a birthday gift for my niece. I don't think he believed me. I was ashamed, really, not telling him the record was for me. I didn't have the confidence to be independent back then."

"You seem alright to me."

"Well, I am now. Thanks to him." Mrs. Morris pointed to the picture of naked Elvis. When John lived in the dorms, he heard passionate students tell stories about how an artist, filmmaker, or musician changed their lives. And he knew he was about to hear the story of how Mrs. Morris was reshaped by Elvis.

"Anyway," she continued, "I bought more records and would dance to them when Herman was at work, hiding them in the closet before he came home. I even secretly joined an Elvis Fan Club. Well, a few months later, Herman went out of town for work, to Los Angeles. We lived in Albuquerque back then. I discovered, through the Elvis Fan Club, that Elvis was performing in Dallas that weekend. Herman never liked me driving, but I said to heck with him and took the car anyway. I left at five in the morning and drove all day to get to the show in time. That's the program and ticket stub framed on the mantle." She pointed toward it.

John turned and was poked in the eye by the painting.

"That must have been some show," he said. The stub occupying a place of honor, sitting at the right hand of Elvis's schlong.

"Oh, it was. The show was sold out. There were over twenty-five thousand Elvis fans at the Cotton Bowl, screaming at the top of their lungs. My seat was in the back and I could barely see the stage. When Elvis came out, he looked like a tiny speck, and with all the screaming, I couldn't hear any of the songs, but you know what, it didn't matter. I was finally near him."

"Did Mr. Morris ever find out?"

"You know, I wasn't going to tell him, but then something happened on the way home. I was feeling energized and a little rebellious. Elvis's music has that affect on people. I was hungry and went into a bar in Dallas. I met a man there and spent the night with him." She folded her hands in her lap and looked down. "I hope you don't think I'm a bad person for being unfaithful to my husband."

"No, I don't." She seemed sweet, naïve. John had a hard time faulting her for something she did sixty years ago. Instead, he felt a little sorry for her.

"Thank you," she said, smiling. "That's very sweet of you to say, but Herman didn't agree. You see, Herman and I were high school sweethearts and waited until our honeymoon to be together. Our first time was embarrassing and painful. We didn't know what we were doing. We were never really intimate after our honeymoon. We'd try every so often, usually when Herman was drunk. Fortunately, and I hate to say it like that, but it's true, well, fortunately, he couldn't maintain his...well, let's just say he couldn't maintain. I doubt you have that problem, Mr. Abernathy."

"Wait. What?" John jerked his head back, unsure why she'd said that.

"The man in Dallas," she continued, crossing her legs, smiling like a super villain whose plan was unfolding, "when I slept with him it was like something awoke inside me. I'd never really experienced sex before. Real sex. And I wanted more."

"So, uh, did you ever tell your husband?" John asked He propped his elbow on the armrest, lowered it, then propped it again.

"I had to. I told him everything. I felt so relieved. It was liberating, saying everything I'd been feeling for the past couple of years. Feeling deep inside me. I was sure he'd throw a fit, but Herman didn't say anything. He locked himself in his study, listening to Bing Crosby. That night I packed some things and went to stay with my sister. She thought I was crazy. Most of my friends did back then. Although now, looking back, they tell me they thought I was brave, free to experiment."

"So, you went into science?" he asked, like a naïve kid interviewing her for his high school paper.

"I'm an expert at chemistry."

The innuendo threw John. He thought the interview was heading toward discovering the man in the photo's address. Based on the way Mrs. Morris was looking at him, John was starting to think she wanted it to head someplace horizontal. He heard Rooftop's voice telling him to remain professional, get Mrs. Morris back on topic.

"So you left your husband, then what?" he asked.

"Well, I took a job at the University of New Mexico as a house mother in the girls' dormitory. It was so much fun. The girls were crazy about Elvis.

We'd have pillow fights, wear out records dancing in our underwear." Mrs. Morris leaned in, whispering, "The girls called them panties."

John tensed, sat upright.

"And of course, the whole time I was collecting. By the 1960s you could find Elvis's face on everything. Clocks, towels, figurines. Everything."

"Even paintings."

"And more," Mrs. Morris said, punctuating her syllables with raised eyebrows.

"And now you have your own picture of him," he said, hoping that talking about the photo would get the interview back on track. He needed to find the man in the picture, solve the reporter's murder, even if that meant he had to suffer Mrs. Morris hitting on him.

"Oh yes, I'm so proud of that photo."

"About that, how did you find him?"

"Well, I was driving down South Grand, coming back from my sister's house. I visit every Saturday to play Canasta with a group of women from church. Don't worry. I only pretend to be reformed."

"Who's worried?" John said, shifting on the couch.

"Anyway," Mrs. Morris continued, "on my way home, I stopped at the Stuff 'n Pump filling station on Alamo Street and saw this man get out of a truck and start walking into a mobile home. I'm always noticing men. Well, I watched him." She leaned forward, her hands folded, she whispered, "I like to watch." She continued in her normal voice like the previous creepiness never happened. "He was acting strange…"

"He's not the only one."

"Looking around before he went in. I didn't recognize him at first, but when he turned in my direction, I knew instantly it was him. It was Elvis Presley! Well, I didn't have my camera with me, so I went back the next day to see if he was there, but he didn't show. So, I went back every day for a week, parked across the street from the lot, and waited. Well, on Sunday he came back. And you know what, I took out my camera and took that picture. Then I sent it to you. And here. You. Are."

"Did you approach him, try talking to him?"

"Heavens, no." Mrs. Morris picked up an old lunch box decorated with images from the Elvis movie *Follow That Dream*, and held it over her heart.

"Why not? You'd think with everything you've collected you'd want to at least talk to him." John leaned back and relaxed, thinking that having her focus her attention on the picture, on Elvis, was like a cup of chamomile tea and horse tranquilizers, settling her down. And later that night he could text his friends and tell them about a crazy old woman and her Elvis collection, and not a story about how he grossly underestimated the sex drive of senior citizens.

"I know some people think I'm a little odd for all my collecting, but I know enough to know that this is the Elvis I love." She gestured to the icons and idols hanging on the walls, cluttering flat surfaces. She looked at the painting, said, "What if the real person doesn't..."

"Measure up?" John said, not able to help himself.

Mrs. Morris smiled. "John, do you mind if I join you on the couch?"

"Uh, I'm sure that would be fine," he said. "It is your couch after all."

"Yes, it is." Mrs. Morris sat the far end of the couch, and removed a few bobby pins from behind her head. She mussed her silver, shoulder-length hair with one hand, her reading glasses swinging from the beaded chain around her neck.

"You are a skinny little thing, aren't you?"

"Don't be fooled. I'm bigger than I look," he said, immediately regretting it.

"That's what I'm counting on." Mrs. Morris smiled like John was a piece of hard candy she wanted to unwrap.

John cringed. When he lived in the college dorms, a kid down the hall Scotch taped magazine clippings of naked women to his own bedroom wall. The kid dubbed his room the 'The Dirty Girl's Bible Study'. Mrs. Morris's painting hinted at interests besides Elvis, and John reprimanded himself for not recognizing it. He was ready to end the interview, drive away and never return, but something bothered him about the photo, something that seemed off, unnatural. John hoped Mrs. Morris could clarify it for him.

"So, is there any chance he saw you?" John asked.

"I was across the street," she said.

"In this picture," John said, pointing to the man, "it looks like he's waving at you."

"He wasn't waving at me. He was looking up." She put her finger next to the man's head. It was tilted, the sideburns at a sharp angle.

"Like at a plane or something?" John said.

"I don't know. Why do people wave at anything?"

"To get someone's attention. To be recognized. They want to know that someone else in this world sees them, acknowledges that they exist. Mostly, they wave hoping someone will wave back."

"John," she said, "I feel comfortable with you, like I can be myself. Do you feel that way?"

"Uh, sure, I suppose," he said. When John was in college, and a girl said she 'felt comfortable', like she could 'be herself', it usually ended with her sharing her poetry about hand-knitted, penguin sweaters and alienation, and John was concerned that Mrs. Morris was going to recite poetry about Elvis and her vagina.

"Can I tell you something?" Mrs. Morris asked, unbuttoning her top blouse button, running her fingers along her neckline, playing with a sealed button. "I think we should be friends. Do you want to be friends?"

"Uh, sure. Friends is good," John lied. He thought about what he'd seen working for Rooftop and worried that Mrs. Morris wanted to be 'friends with butt stuff'.

"Good." She slid closer on the couch. "I think you and I will make perfect friends. You know what friends do, John? They share."

"Like the address where you took this picture?" he said, sliding further from her, bumping against the armrest.

"Sure. But, first," Mrs. Morris said, sliding a finger down his arm, "I have something else I'd like to share with you."

"I'm sure you do," John said.

Mrs. Morris went into the back room. John decided he'd jump through the window if she came out wearing a crotchless Elvis costume. He leaned over on the couch, peeked into the room. Mrs. Morris dug through collectibles, exhuming a small, white box.

"This is my most recent acquisition," she said, returning to the room and sitting next to him, their legs brushing.

"Here, open it." She handed him the box.

John held it, arms outstretched, head turned away. He lifted one corner of the box's lid like it was a bomb, cautious whatever crazy sex toy inside might explode in his face.

Nothing.

He removed the rest of the lid, peered in, sighed,

sank back into the couch. And pulled out a silk tie.

"I picked it up in Albuquerque last November," she said. "It's the bowtie Elvis wore during the Hawaii benefit concert in '61. It's the prize of my collection." She took it from him and bit one end. "You know, you could use it to tie me up. Or choke me."

"That's it, I gotta go." John leapt from the couch and ran to the door.

"But you just got here," she said, pouting slightly.

"I need to check out the man's trailer. Would you mind writing down his address for me?" he asked, bouncing from one foot to the other.

"I thought we were friends, John?"

"I'm not sure I understand what you're asking," he said, his voice shaking a little.

"If you want the address..." she said, sashaying toward him. She squished him against the door, one finger slithering down his shirt. "You'll have to give me something for it."

"Uh..." John groped around for the door knob, jiggling it, but it was locked.

"Oh, don't get so worked up. All I want is a kiss. Right here on the cheek." She pointed to her right cheek.

One little kiss on the cheek wouldn't hurt. And it would save him from searching every trailer on Alamo Street. He clenched his eyes shut and puckered, expecting something sour, inched closer to her.

She offered her cheek and leaned in, anticipating. When his nose grazed the thin hairs on her cheek, she turned and seized his head with both hands. And pressed her mouth to his.

John tried to yank and jerk free, waving his hands frantically like a cartoon cat with its tail caught in an electrical socket, but she held him, rubbing her sagging breasts against him. She opened her mouth and forced her tongue deep into his. It circled around the inside of his mouth, violently pushing against his tongue, teeth, and roof of his mouth. He gagged at the taste of it. She tasted like a combination of a baseball glove and menthol cigarettes. She finally let go, and John gasped for breath.

"There," she said, smiling. "That wasn't too bad."

"Fuck this," John said, unlocking and running out the door. He wiped her slobber off his face and spat on the dry earth, feeling like kneaded dough, molested by wrinkled hands, then dry humped for about an hour while listening to 'Love Me Tender'.

"Don't you want the address?" she asked as he sprinted down her drive.

He yelled over his shoulder, "The Hump 'n Pump on Alamo Street! I think I can find it!"

"Oh, do let me know what you find out!" she said from her door, leaning her chest against the jamb.

"Don't worry! I'll be in touch!" John lied, getting in his car, vowing to never return to her Elvis Museum & Fetish Den.

John plunged his hand into his pocket, feeling around for his keys. They should have been just past his wallet, next to some loose change, but something else filled his pocket. His fingers fumbled over a soft ball of fabric. Stitching and folds. He couldn't identify the object. He just recognized it as a tactile mass, and didn't remember stuffing it in there. Worried, not knowing what it was, he slowly pulled the wadded fabric from his pocket. He found the ends with his hands and tugged. The jumble of black cloth fell loose, revealing a long piece of silk that trumpeted at the ends. Mrs. Morris's bowtie.

John shrieked.

Somehow she slipped it into his pocket, probably hoping he'd return it and take her up on her bondage offer. He involuntarily imagined her hands and feet tied to the bedposts and he shuddered.

"Fuck that," he said, tossing the bowtie out the window, the silk wafting like litter into the dry gutter.

A little before five, John parked on Alamo Street, next to the gas station. He didn't park directly in front of the trailer park, but he could still see its entrance. People came and went from every trailer except one, the one in the photo. Its driveway was empty, its windows dark. He didn't know when the man would be home, so he waited.

John lifted the armrests and stretched out on the front seat. He put the gun on the floor next to him, just in case someone tried sneaking up on him. Like Mrs. Morris. The sun was setting, but he'd hear the locked doors rattling, or her licking the window.

Working for Rooftop, John was used showing up to an empty home, having to entertain himself until whomever he was supposed to be following showed. Most detectives would get on their phones, amuse themselves with addictive games, ninja birds destroying candy, Viking farmers complaining about retirement, but John tried to utilize his time, be productive.

He pulled out a pen and a pad of graph paper. He counted fifteen squares across, then fifteen down, drew a frame around them, embracing the emptiness. On the top row, he counted four squares in, then blacked out the fifth square. He did the same on the other side and at the bottom corners, making it symmetrical. Twenty-eight more squares were blacked out, continuing a pattern of balance. He wrote 'Moving Day', his theme, across the top of the page. It was a recreation of a puzzle he'd been working on since graduation.

It had a grand premise. All the definitions were going to read like standard puzzle definitions, leading the solver to think it was about moving into a new home, but once they solved the theme words, the fifteen-to-twenty-eight-box-length phrases, they'd realize that it was really about unexpected transitions, the large and small occurrences that force people to adapt and change.

Four empty squares along the top row waited to be filled and John wrote a single letter in each box. A word. He added another word underneath it. He tried writing a clue that would give them some meaning beyond the standard definition, some existential subtext that an astute crossword solver would appreciate. Tapping his pen against the pad, he found nothing deeper than what existed in the dictionary. John erased the words, leaving rubber splinters where letters had nested. He scrawled new words, new clues, but they failed to conform to his criteria, and he wadded up the paper, tossed it on the floor.

He didn't have this problem in college, the

inability to stack words, their letter arrangements creating words within words, then give them clever clues. Since leaving the purchased comfort and community of school, he'd been stuck, uninspired. 'Unable,' as his friends would say, 'to do the work.'

* * * *

Ten o'clock. Everyone had gone out for the evening, leaving the trailer park empty, no lights in the windows, vacant parking spaces.

The street lamp above John flickered out and darkness absorbed the street around his Saturn sedan. It was getting late. The Stuff 'n Pump night manager locked the front doors and pulled down the gate, closing for the night, his employees heading home.

Midnight. Trailer park residents returned home from the bars, trying to drive straight, parking at odd angles. They stumbled from their trucks, up their trailers' makeshift steps. Lights flipped on and off in each room until there was darkness.

3:00 a.m. If the man in the photo wasn't home by now, he probably wasn't coming home tonight.

John grabbed the universal lock pick gun he bought at the police supply store. He'd bought it for moments like this, but so far he'd only used it to open his front door when he'd locked himself out. He got out of his car and pulled up his sweatshirt's hood, looking around as he quietly crossed the empty street.

He walked up the trailer's homemade steps. They

wobbled underneath him like they were built with the assistance of a six-pack, not a level. He crouched down on one knee and put the pick gun in the lock. John held another pick in his right hand. He set it in the lock and started aligning the pins.

On the street, the recognizable rumble of an engine, music, and drunk driving. A truck swerved into the trailer park.

John quickly looked around, wondering where the truck might be headed. Every trailer had a car, truck, motorcycle, ATV, go-cart, or riding lawnmower parked near it. All except the trailer he were he knelt. The man in the picture was home.

John stood, lost his balance, and fell backward off the steps. He landed on his back and crawled and picked himself up off the broken gravel drive and ran and hid behind the trailer's hitch and propane tank.

The truck turned down the stretch of gravel that started at Alamo Street and ended at the trailer John hid behind.

John peered around the trailer wall as the truck's headlights panned the trailer park, its rusty folding chairs, satellite dishes loosely hanging by their cables, pieces of fiberglass insulation, sleeveless flannel shirts drying on car hoods. Finally, the lights landed on the trailer where John hid. Illuminating the dangling lock pick gun.

John spun behind the trailer. He made a fist and slowly, silently, tapped his head in penance. How he could be so stupid, so careless? How could he have let Rooftop down? If the man in the photo saw the pick gun, he'd run and John wouldn't get the answers he needed about the photo. Or the dead reporter. He breathed heavily and told himself to calm down. There had to be a way to keep the guy here, to keep him from running. John lifted his head suddenly and his eyes widened like he had been abruptly woken from a nap. He had an idea. It was a bad idea, but it was all he had.

He peeked around the trailer.

And reached for his gun.

But there was nothing.

His thumb caught on his belt as his hand passed over the emptiness where his clip holster should be. He had left his gun in the car.

The truck turned and headed down the row of trailers, coming right for him. The man would see the pick gun, would know John was there, would speed away, knocking over trashcans, waking his neighbors, leaving John trapped behind the trailer while everyone stumbled into the street, investigating the late night racket.

The truck parked in the driveway, its headlights went dark. John peered around the corner. The doors opened. Out stepped a skinny teenager with acne and an overweight older woman. They started kissing. She shoved the kid against the trailer John hid behind. She grinded against the kid, shaking the trailer, causing the lock pick gun to jiggle, almost fall from the lock. The woman grabbed the kid's shirt, dragged him to the trailer next door. They spent several minutes at the door making out, then disappeared inside. A stereo blared .38 Special's 'Rockin' Into the Night'. In between songs, odd noises, like farm animals eating, came from the trailer.

John walked back up the steps. The lock pick gun hung from the door knob. John knelt, gently pushed it back into the lock. A click. The bolt slid free of the doorjamb's plate. The door opened. It was unlocked.

The trailer door creaked open on rusting hinges. The interior screen door hung loose in its frame, broken. Most of the wire mesh was ripped, no longer protecting the trailer from insects or collection agents.

The trailer, green with a white stripe down the center, employed a thin layer of dirt to show its age. Unwashed and corroded. Dirt and rust had consumed the elegance of the antique road palace. John stuck his head inside the dark trailer and listened, but didn't hear any shuffling footsteps or drunken snores. He stepped inside, turned on his flashlight. Empty beer cans and dirty clothes. Unopened mail on the collapsible kitchen table. He flipped through junk mail addressed to 'Resident', nudie magazines in sealed, plastic bags, store bought. No bills. No address labels. Nothing that could tell him the guy's name. John was hoping for a mountain of unpaid bills, or pink envelopes stamped 'Final Notice'. But they were strangely absent.

In the living room, dirty clothes lay on the floor, couch, everywhere. An empty fish tank with a couple of trophies in it slept on the couch like a weekend house guest overextending its stay. The trophies were topped with little gold figures kicking the air in frozen Karate poses. John removed a couple from the tank, checking the engravings. 'Cincinnati, OH, March, 1998, Third Place'. 'Kokomo, IN, June, 1995, Fourth Place'. 'Spokane, WA, October, 1991, Third Place'. And a blue ribbon from Springfield, IL, for participating. The statues were all engraved with different names, not the man's name, but the names of others. His version of identity theft. John frequented garage sales on his free weekends and was familiar with trophies like these. The man in the photo probably bought them from someone's mom trying to make Diet Coke money.

John shined the light around the rest of the room. The curtains were drawn, guarding the man from prying neighbors, or protecting neighbors from seeing him walk around shirtless, slapping his gut, scratching himself.

A small, flat screen television, its wires running out the window. John moved the blinds and followed the wires to a neighboring trailer, up the side to a satellite dish. Pirated cable.

Black and white pictures were tacked to the wall opposite the couch. There were several of Elvis, but they were not the normal fan photos. In one, Elvis is standing by the front door to Graceland, surrounded by Elvis impersonators. It was easy to tell which one was Elvis. He was the focal point of the picture, standing between large columns, framed by impersonators. And he was the only one not wearing a sequined jumpsuit.

In other photos, Elvis is surrounded by armed, uniformed men, leaving hangars, boarding helicopters or planes. A white haired man wearing an Air Force uniform is standing near Elvis. They are laughing or talking, the man looking at Elvis fondly, with pride, while other officers are a few steps behind. In one photograph, Elvis is in a hangar. He is wearing earphones and holding a long range microphone in one hand and a hotdog in the other. He isn't looking at the surveillance equipment. Instead, he is looking down at a dollop of mustard on his shoe. In another, Elvis is standing next to a circus ring watching men jousting on alpacas. One man has been thrown from his mount and is lying in the center of the ring. Elvis is grumbling and handing money to the man with white hair. The man is laughing, adding Elvis's cash to a stack of bills. John wasn't sure if the picture was of military training or a wealthy man's entertainment.

Next to the Elvis pictures were aerial photos of

what looked like military installations. Buildings were circled in red ink. The names 'Area 51', 'Los Alamos', 'Dulce', or 'S-4' were written on them. Before he left Denver, John researched Elvis conspiracies and found photos like these. They were typical of someone obsessed with the perception of a hidden truth, the belief that something in Elvis's history was being kept from them.

Sitting in the car, he had wondered what he'd find in the trailer. He thought, if anything, there'd be a few pictures of Elvis, flattering images printed from websites, taped to the wall. But he didn't expect this. He looked closer at the photos, the paper stock, the edge and grain of the print. They weren't copies. They were originals. This guy had hid in the bushes and taken these photos.

Like John.

But they were nothing alike. This guy acted out of some delusory belief that Elvis had a secret past. John took pictures of naked men in the back of a Payless Shoe store rubbing latex balloons on each other, waiting until he could earn a living writing puzzles.

John kicked some beer cans out of the way and headed to the kitchen. Dirt had saturated the small kitchen's linoleum cracks, staining the floor brown and gray. When John walked, his shoes sounded like band-aids being removed. Pliers replaced the missing knobs on an electric range. The sink overflowed with dirty dishes, plates covered in food remains, chicken bones, BBQ. He shined the flashlight on them. The crusted food looked preserved, like a furniture store display of wax fruit. John sniffed the sink. No rancid food smell. He opened the cupboards. Peanut butter. Jar after jar of peanut butter.

The refrigerator door's fake wood paneling had cracked, a disguise peeling. Magnets decorated with pictures of half-naked women and beer logos had fallen on the floor. John opened the fridge door. The refrigerator was filled, crisper to fridge light, with bananas.

The pantry continued the single-item theme. It was stocked with bags of bread.

Peanut butter and banana sandwiches.

The guy's obsession with Elvis extended to his diet.

One more room, the bedroom. An accordion door separated it from the rest of the trailer. Age and lack of maintenance dulled the magnet lock. Screws stripped the holes holding door to frame. John jerked on the handle and the door came out of the wall.

The bedroom looked like the aftermath of a manmade disaster. Clothes were piled on the unmade bed. Fast food bags, junk food wrappers, plastic cologne bottles, tiger-striped bikini briefs, internet-purchased male enhancement pills, tubes of hair dye, and bubble wrap carpeted the floor. John had seen trailers like this working for

Rooftop, recognized the debris of a cheating husband. He half expected to see used condoms everywhere, but there weren't any.

On the other side of the bed, a built-in dresser and closet completed the furnishings. The dresser's drawers hung half-exposed in various stages of evacuation.

John pulled on the closet door but it stuck, the cracked mirror rattling. The plastic hook on the top left corner had broken off and only three hooks attached the mirror to the door. He put his hand on the loose corner and jerked the door, popping the magnetic latch. John shined the flashlight inside and was blinded by light reflecting back in his face. He moved the flashlight off to the side, away from the reflective surface, hoping to get a better look.

And there it was.

Hanging in the closet.

The uniform so closely associated with Elvis that when someone mentioned his name you saw him wearing it, on stage, sweating, the lights reflecting off it and into the eyes of a nostalgic crowd in a Las Vegas theater.

A white sequined jumpsuit.

"No way!" John whispered in the dark. He removed the jumpsuit to get a closer look. It had a high, stiff collar covered in shiny, gold stars. A giant, red, white, and blue eagle made of fake jewels, framed by gold stars, bedecked the back. John didn't count the stars, but he was sure there were fifty. The same pattern adorned the front of the jumpsuit, except the eagle was split by the slit that divided the suit's chest. Smaller eagles were perched on the shoulders, with several gold stars showering the sleeves, like the eagles were pooping freedom. Similar eagles flittered down the outsides of the suit's legs, ending in large flairs. A belt, easily a foot wide, decorative gold chains dangling from it, eagles flying around it, hung around the suit's waist. A giant, gold eagle glittered on the white belt buckle. The jumpsuit was the flashiest thing he'd ever seen. The flash and glitz of the Vegas Strip on polyester.

Black patent leather boots, freshly polished, rested on the closet floor.

John examined the suit reverentially, checking everything, the fabric, the sequins. It appealed to his art student aesthetics. It was old, flashy, distracting, popular. American. It was everything he was supposed to love and hate, making it the best thing he'd ever seen. He took several pictures with his phone, sent them to friends, and to Rooftop.

From the photo, John had expected the man to be the kind of person he'd become familiar with working for Rooftop, another slob cherishing and despising his own indecency. After seeing the jumpsuit, the photos tacked to the wall, John figured the man fit into two categories, an Elvis impersonator, or a fan obsessed with the speculative side of Elvis.

John hung the jumpsuit back in the closet and heard the flutter and shuffle of falling paper. He shined his light on the closet floor. A yellow piece of paper, folded over three times. He lifted it and illuminated the image of a naked woman eating a double bacon cheeseburger on a take-out menu from a strip club on the interstate, with a Truth or Consequences mailing address. Evidence connecting the guy in the picture to the reporter.

John took a step back, crushing an open bag of potato chips. Holding the menu, he felt flattened by its implications, that the guy in the photo had lured the reporter away from town with the promise of a story, meat loaf, and shaved bush, then killed him. John shivered. He spun around and looked over his shoulder, terrified by the realization that he was in a murderer's home. If he'd learned anything from his Survey of Slasher Films, 1978 to 1986, was that being alone in the killer's house never went well for anyone.

He crammed the menu into his pocket and wiped everything he had touched with one of his hoodie sleeves. He leapt over piles of dirty clothes and closed the accordion door, putting the frame's screws back in their holes. In the kitchen and living room, he scrubbed every handle and surface where he might have deposited his fingerprints, and left the trailer, trying not to knock anything over. The cluttered mobile home embodied the consequences of unpaid credit card debt, but John still didn't want anyone to know he'd been there. If the man returned home, saw that someone had been in his house, he'd run, or come after John.

Outside, John shut the door, leaving it unlocked. He heard the neighbors snoring and quickly scanned the lot and street, making sure that it was empty, that even the street lamps were sleeping.

He drove back to The Sagittarius Inn, careful not to turn on the headlights until he was beyond the trailer park. He thought about driving all the way back to Denver, calling the local police once he'd crossed into Colorado and telling them about the reporter and the trailer, but the reporter was killed doing what he loved. And all John could think was that if he were killed for one of his puzzles, he'd want someone to find out who did it.

John parked a few doors down from his room. The motel was empty except for a few bikers passing through. John crawled under the cotton comforter and thin blanket. The parking lot lights leaked through curtain cracks, highlighting peeling wallpaper.

As soon as he got comfortable, someone knocked on his door. John reached for his gun, thinking that the guy from the photo saw him sneaking from his trailer and followed him, but John remembered checking his rearview mirror, the reflection of the deserted street, no headlights, and set his gun on the table. He put his eye to the peephole. It was black. Not black like the night, but black like oblivion, like nothing existed outside his door.

John left the chain on the door, and opened it slowly, carefully.

"Yeah," he said.

It was the only word he said. The person on the other side of the door kicked it in. The door hit John on the head, throwing him across the room.

John's eyes fluttered like a bird shaking water from its wings. He licked his lips and his mouth tasted metallic. Dried blood had crusted under his nose and on his chin. His face was tight and he stretched it, opened his mouth, and the dried blood cracked. His favorite t-shirt was beaded with umber muck. Fortunately, there was a boutique in Boulder where he could get another one, managed by a friend who had majored in Faux-Vintage Silk Screening.

As consciousness slowly returned, John heard voices. He tried to speak, but could only mumble.

"I think he's coming to, sir," a cold, emotionless voice said.

"Hello?" another voice said. "Are you still with us?"

A hand lightly slapped John's face. He shook his head, fully waking to a world of blurry figures, their forms' strict boundaries made lenient by poor eyesight. He suddenly became conscious that he was sitting in a chair, his hands bound behind his back. Cold, metal handcuffs dug into his wrists, cutting him every time he moved.

"My glasses," John said.

"Oh, yes," the second person said, a slight Southern twang coloring his voice. "I'm so sorry. This must be disorienting for you. Sergeant, would you please?"

A man walked toward John, holding something in his hand. John flinched as the man reached for him, but relaxed as his glasses were placed on his face. The man didn't put them on all the way and they were tilted, the frame halfway covering his left eye. John instinctively moved to adjust them, but the restraints cut him. He grunted in pain and annoyance.

John looked around the room. He was still in the motel, sitting next to a table. Two heavily armed soldiers stood next to him, dressed in black. It was the first time John had been this close to soldiers that hadn't been in video games. He'd seen several in Denver, but they weren't young. They were the career types, officers whose responsibilities, the lives of young men, had aged them.

An older man with white hair, wearing a blue Air Force uniform, sat on the bed. His jacket and hat lay on the bed with him, next to John's wallet, phone, and gun.

"I don't really know what's going on here," John said. "But I'm pretty sure there's been a misunderstanding."

"Colonel Alvin P. Hollister, United States Air Force," the man said, a programmed formality. "You and I are going to have a conversation about your nocturnal activities."

One of the soldiers whispered in Colonel Hollister's ear, handed him John's driver's license and business card.

"Seriously," John said, "I think you got the wrong room or something."

"That's interesting. But you're more interesting, aren't you?" Colonel Hollister said, reading John's ID. "John Abernathy, Private Investigator."

John scooted against the motel chair, seeing the age hidden in Colonel Hollister's eyes. Not wrinkles or crow's feet, but the exhaustion of a true believer.

"Just let me know what you want," John said. "I'm more than happy to help out."

"That depends," Colonel Hollister said, "on what you were doing at that trailer tonight."

"That's what this is about? the guy in the trailer? I don't know him, don't know anything about him. I was just hired to..."

Colonel Hollister nodded once to the soldier next to John. The soldier punched John, knocking off his glasses again. His jaw felt like it had been crushed by a cinderblock and his mouth filled with metallic tasting blood.

"What the fuck?" John said, spitting blood on the floor. "You asked me a question, remember? I'm just trying to give you an answer."

"Now, what were you..." Colonel Hollister stopped. He examined John closely, visually dissecting him. "When I walked in, I could have sworn you had a broken nose. Sergeant, I thought you said you broke his nose when you kicked open the door."

"I did, sir." The sergeant leaned in, inspected John. As he got closer, his features came into focus, his straight jaw, close-cropped hair, the abandoned look in his eye.

"John," Colonel Hollister asked, "were you ever sick as a child? Ever have any broken bones?"

"I thought you wanted to know about the trailer."

"Why do you wear glasses?"

"What does that have to do with anything?"

"I wonder what happens when you leave your glasses off for a while." Colonel Hollister tilted his head like he was pondering John's poor vision.

"Look, you want to know about the trailer, let's talk about it. The guy's a slob. You shoulda seen the place, shit everywhere. Can I just have my glasses back? I get headaches without them."

"Well, we don't want that." Colonel Hollister leaned over, picked up John's glasses, and placed them on his head. "I normally don't conduct interrogations. I'm a scientist. I prefer the lab. Research doesn't lie. Not like people. People think they're clever. I don't have the patience for clever. Now, about the trailer..."

Colonel Hollister motioned to the man standing next to John. He pulled an iPad out of one of the many pockets on his vest. He held the screen in front of John. It showed John's car from the rear,

John crossing the street, going into the trailer park.

"Yeah, that's me, going to the guy's trailer. We established this."

"Fast forward," Colonel Hollister said.

The man fast-forwarded the video. John is running from the trailer park. He removes his hood, and unintentionally looks up, into the hidden camera. The man paused the video, zoomed in on John's face.

"You remember the trailer now?" the colonel said, his voice sounding hollow.

"You obviously know I do. I don't know how many times I have to tell you this, I'm on a case."

"I'll tell you what you were doing there. You were looking for this man." He held up a copy of Mrs. Morris's picture, a printout John kept in his bag. "Why are you looking for him?"

"Yeah, I told you that. *The National Enquirer* hired me to find him. But when I went to the trailer, the guy wasn't there."

"Then you're of no use to me. Kill him," he said, gesturing to his men.

"Wait. What the fuck? Hey…Hey, just give me a chance to explain. There's been some kind of mistake."

"Leave his body here. It'll send a better message." The two soldiers grabbed John's shoulders, slammed him back into the chair, tried to hold him steady.

"To who? the guy in the trailer?" John asked,

struggling against them. "Who is he? Who are you looking for?"

"Keep it quiet, but messy," Colonel Hollister said to the soldier standing next to John. He put the iPad away and pulled out a large knife. He grabbed a handful of John's hair, pulled his head back, exposing his neck.

"He has pictures of you," John blurted out. "Pictures of you and Elvis."

The colonel held up his hand. The sergeant released John's hair, pushed him forward. He sheathed his knife.

"You didn't know he had pictures of you?" John sat back, panting. His mind began to move laterally, skirting around obvious questions to something more obscure. "Or that he was following you? What does he have on you?"

"Tell me about the pictures."

"You were friends, weren't you? you and Elvis? That's what the pictures show. The two of you."

Colonel Hollister stood. He walked to the window and drew the curtains back.

"We were friends. Not many people can say that," Colonel Hollister said, putting his left hand on the window. He didn't drop his head, look to the place where the carpet joined the wall. Instead, he looked at the black parking lot, the barely lit street. At something in the darkness.

"In the pictures, he seemed happy, comfortable, like he enjoyed talking to you."

"There's never enough time to..." Colonel Hollister took his hand from the window and held it behind his back.

"He knows you're watching him, doesn't he? That's why you haven't gone in the trailer. He's smart. Sneaky. Knows where you have your cameras. That camera angle," John said, motioning to the soldier with the tablet, "it's not from the gas station. I'm guessing it's from a lamppost or telephone pole, maybe a junction box. I bet you even have a satellite over it right now. He probably knows about that, too, and knows how to avoid them both. That's why you haven't found him yet. Who is this guy? Why are you looking for him?"

"An old acquaintance," Colonel Hollister said. "Someone I need to talk to."

"He has something you need? information? I can find him for you."

"I thought you already had a client," Colonel Hollister said.

"*The Enquirer*? They don't care about finding this guy."

"You're just a kid." He looked down at John.

"And that's a bad thing? I can go places you can't, talk to people you can't."

"And I imagine this will cost me?"

"Right now," John said, thinking about how Rooftop would negotiate with someone who had handcuffed and punched him, "my client's paying me two thousand dollars a day."

"Two thousand dollars a day?" Colonel Hollister said, startled by the expense.

"Take the cuffs off and we can negotiate."

Colonel Hollister nodded. The sergeant uncuffed John. The handcuffs had cut off the circulation to John's wrists and left them white with red and raw rings around them. John rubbed his wrists and fresh blood flooded them, waking them. He flexed his fingers.

"My fee," John said, "fifteen hundred a day, plus expenses."

"One thousand," Colonel Hollister countered.

"And my five thousand dollar retainer. Up front, of course."

"Your confidentiality does have a price, doesn't it?" Colonel Hollister picked his jacket up off the bed. He pulled a money pouch out of his pocket, unzipped it, and removed a stack of cash, all hundreds. The colonel counted out fifty, left them on the bed, and slipped the pouch back in his jacket.

He picked up John's business card, wrote on the back. "This is my number."

"I'll contact you when I find something," John said.

Colonel Hollister motioned his men out.

"You know," he said, stopping at the door, "I'm usually pretty good at anticipating the unforeseen, but, I must say, I did not expect you."

"What, a P.I.?"

"No, an Abernathy." And he walked out.

John ran to the door, tried to catch him, find out what he meant.

"Wait! Wait!" John shouted, running into the parking lot as the colonel was pulling away from the motel, his taillights already down the road.

John chased them down Grand Avenue, heedless of the loose pebbles and broken glass that were scattered across the street, gouging his bare feet. He lost sight of them when they turned onto East University, heading to the interstate.

Standing in the middle of the road, the stomach pains from earlier returned and John clutched his bloodstained shirt. A breeze picked up, blowing dirt across the road, a desert visitor. The air was fragrant, not the normal smells of trash, diesel exhaust, dead skunks, the slow decay of a small town, but with something that made John remember his childhood, sitting in the park reading comic books with his mother. It sedated him, made him feel content.

He walked back to the motel, holding his stomach, the pain dwindling as he approached his room.

In the motel bathroom, John rinsed caked blood from his face and blew blood clots from his nostrils. He calmly went to bed, knowing the Air Force wouldn't return. They might return some night, waiting in the room for him again, but not tonight. Tonight, John fell asleep, unaware of the eyes peeking just above the bottom of his window.

CHAPTER SIX

The next morning, a key turned in the lock. The sound snapped John from his sleep. He sat up in bed, reached for the gun on the nightstand. He was not the same angry kid Rooftop used to take to the shooting range, envisioning his father's face on the targets. He hadn't been to the shooting range in years, and art school had changed his Old West views. But the Air Force spooked him. The broken chain rattled as the key turned and there was nothing stopping someone from forcing their way into his room. John pointed the gun at the door and his hand shook as the door creaked open a crack and the morning and the routines of the small hotel imposed themselves upon him.

"Housekeeping," a woman said in a thick, Mexican accent. It was just the maid, not uniformed men armed with guns and iPads.

"Still sleeping. Come back later," he said, collapsing into the bed. He clutched the gun to his heart.

She apologized in broken English, and quickly shut the door. A cart, heavy with cleaning supplies, creaked to the next room on worn, uneven wheels.

John put the gun on the nightstand. The clock. It was a little after eleven. Six hours of tossing under starched sheets and synthetic blanket. The sun burned through the cracks in the curtains. He tried to fall asleep again, but lay there, feeling sticky from a stressful snooze. John rubbed his throat where the soldier had held the knife. He could have died last night, been killed just like the kid, on his own for the first time, unprepared. What had he gotten himself into? He could pack up, run back to Denver, but the kid had died alone in the desert, unable to fulfill his journalistic aspirations, while John clicked away at his computer, searching for the right words. He rubbed his wrists, noticed the abrasions from the handcuffs were gone, his skin fresh and healed, and decided to get up, to keep looking for the guy in the photo. He owed it to the reporter.

A phonebook hid in the nightstand's only drawer. It was thin, a small-town phonebook containing yellow and white pages. He flipped through the yellow pages to the bar section. There were bars around New Mexico Highlands University. John shuddered, remembering boorish University of Colorado-Boulder parties and DJs playing songs about doing shots. He couldn't think of an Elvis song about shots, so he ruled out the college bars. The rest of the bars were in the plaza. That's where he'd start.

* * * *

Everything spread from the plaza, the town center, like cracks in a windshield. At one end stood brick and mortar history, the stately Plaza Hotel, a grand hotel predating statehood. The plaza extended into the downtown, a desolate blend of brick and tumbleweed. It seemed empty but watchful, like old, Colorado ghost towns, restless. Mud brick walls dissolved and intricate facades deteriorated under sun and time.

Rooftop used to say, 'Pueblo's the armpit of Colorado.' Driving through town, John thought Las Vegas might be the armpit of New Mexico.

Several restaurants and bars inhabited the older buildings surrounding the plaza. At least one person had to know the man in the picture.

John walked into a neon-lit hole occupied by a couple of retired cowboys riding bar stools. He asked them about the photo, but they couldn't make anything out in dim lights. And the daytime drinking didn't help.

The bartender was bearded and overweight. The sleeves had been cut from his black t-shirt, exposing hairy upper arms. John asked him about the man in the photo. The bartender didn't even look at it. He pulled out the biggest handgun John had ever seen, a Colt Python with an eight-inch barrel. John recognized it from the first-person shooters he played in high school, the type of gun that would blow the head off a zombie or alien. The bartender stared at John, a preamble to a showdown. John didn't say anything. He bolted out the door and across the street.

Collapsing on a bench, John collected himself, tried to catch his breath. He'd been threatened twice in twelve hours. Making puzzles wasn't nearly this dangerous. All he had to worry about was high blood pressure from sitting all day, maybe developing restless leg syndrome. And John swore on his puzzle notebook that everything would be different when he returned home. He wouldn't take his time working on puzzles for granted. He'd be fully engaged in the creation of each clue. He'd put everything he had into finding filler words that would supply subtext for his theme words. When he returned home, things would be different. But he had to finish the case first, find the man in the photo. He had to check out the other bars. Sitting on a bench, John wondered if the other bars were run by gun-toting bikers, and thought maybe he should start by asking if they had any meth, then ask about the photo.

An open door next to him. The neon sign in the window said, 'The Watering Hole', and he heard music playing somewhere inside. It sounded like the type of band he'd like, low energy rock not played on the radio.

The bar was dimly lit. Most of the light came from the window's neon beer sign and a glowing hula girl lamp. Bottles lined the back wall, blocking the mirror. The walls were dark green but obscured by framed pictures of old buildings, trains, forgotten men and women, old liquor ads, and three movie posters for films starring Annette Funicello and Frankie Avalon. John recognized the titles from his Surf Movie Appreciation class, *Madam Groovy's Wondiferous Bongo Bikini*, *Dr. Surfenstein's Robot Bikini Babes*, *The Surftacular Rock Waverider on Bikini Planet X*. The classics. A ceramic Dalmatian sat by the door.

A couple of barflies displaced their day on stools. They didn't turn when John walked through the door or look up when he sat next to them. Instead, they continued gazing into their glasses, completely consumed by their bourbon encouraged meditations.

"Sup." The bartender flicked his head, his tattooed arm throwing a square coaster in front of John.

"Sup." John flicked his head. He motioned to the iPhone plugged into the sound system behind the bar. "Who's this playing?"

"Pinecone Strip Mall," the bartender said, irritated by people who weren't familiar with his favorite band.

"Aren't they the side project of The Harvesting Radiators?" John asked, adjusting his glasses.

"Yeah," the bartender said, looking back at John, surprised.

"I saw HR in October at the Boulder Ballroom."

"No way," the bartender said, his handlebar

mustache quivering when he talked. "I was just listening to that podcast the other day. The second set was killer." He walked back over to John. "What can I get you?"

"PBR," John said. He motioned to the two barflies. "Their next round is on me, too." The two men raised their glasses.

"Sure thing. You from Boulder?" He set the beer can on the coaster.

"Denver. In town a couple of days. How much?"

"For yours and theirs? Twelve bucks."

John tossed a twenty on the bar. "No change."

"Since you're new to town," the bartender said, "I oughta warn you, Clem over there, now that you bought him a drink, he thinks you wanna take him home with you."

Clem smiled, exposing gums and missing teeth. The teeth he did have were stained yellow and brown by tobacco. Clem put his hands on the bar, started to push himself up.

"Sorry, Clem," John said, waving his hands. "I'm here on business, not pleasure."

Clem slumped back down, staring into his now empty glass.

"Hold on a sec," the bartender said. He poured Clem another drink. Clem nodded courteously toward John, then watched the ice melt in his glass. "So, what brings you to town, other than Clem?"

"Actually, I'm looking for someone. You know this guy?" He slid the photo across the bar with a folded twenty-dollar bill on top.

The bartender rolled his eyes, but still pocketed the twenty. He looked at the picture for a couple of seconds. "Ha, you're looking for this piece of shit?"

"So, you know him?"

"Yeah, it's Al Leadbelly."

"Leadbelly, you sure?" A rockabilly name to match the blurry pompadour, the beer can littered trailer, the jumpsuit.

"Yeah, he works for my uncle. Comes in here trying to get free drinks. Had to kick him out last night. Hold on a sec." The bartender refilled the other barflies' drinks.

"Why did you kick him out?" John asked.

"He started a fight with some kid."

"Over what?"

"No idea. It was pretty busy. I was taking care of some customers, next thing I know, Al and this kid are going at it, beating the shit outta each other. I had to run over and break it up. Had to kick them both out."

"About what time was that?"

"I dunno, ten thirty?"

"You know what happened after they left?"

"Nope, don't care either." The bartender wiped the bar with a rag.

"Did you call the cops?"

"What are the cops gonna do? give Leadbelly a ride home?"

"Uh, yeah." John thought about what would have

happened if the cops and Leadbelly had crashed into the trailer while he was reattaching Leadbelly's bedroom door, and was suddenly grateful for the latitude small towns give their residents. "So, what about this kid, what'd he look like?"

"I dunno, young enough for me to card him. He'd just turned twenty-one. I'd never seen him in here before"

"You think maybe you'd seen him around town?"

"I grew up here, know pretty much everybody or at least their families. I'd have recognized him."

John thanked the bartender. He got up to leave. At the far end, Clem was slumped over his drink. John threw another twenty on the bar.

"Whatever they want, it's on me. Thanks again for your help," John said, patting the ceramic Dalmatian on the head as he left.

#

The sunny street, cloudless sky. The heat was coming.

Across the street, someone leaned on John's car.

"Friend, I say, can I talk to you for a moment?" he asked, getting off John's car, walking toward him. His chest shined with the badge of the local sheriff. The sheriff was a real cowboy, leather-faced and pearl-buttoned, with a cowboy name, Sheriff Lee Masters III.

"Sheriff," John said, "what's up?"

"Word is you're going all over town asking questions, looking for someone."

"Yeah, sorry about that. I should have come by your office, introduced myself when I came to town. Name's John Abernathy. I'm a P.I. from Denver." John handed him his ID.

"A little young to be a P.I.," the sheriff said.

"I get that. Anyway, I'm looking for this man." John showed the sheriff the picture. "A woman, Elizabeth Morris, took it. Thinks he's Elvis. A newspaper down in LA hired me to see if it's legit."

"LA, huh? Los Angeles is the armpit of the United States."

"Everyone has a favorite armpit."

"Huh?"

"Never mind. So, Sheriff, maybe you can help me out. Bartender inside said it's a guy named Al Leadbelly. You know him?"

"Well, the picture's kinda blurry," the sheriff said, holding it close to his face, "but that looks like Al Leadbelly."

"You know where I can find him?"

"I hope so," the sheriff said. "He works for my brother at the lumber yard. Tell you what, let me buy you lunch and then we'll head over there together. Rosa's Restaurante makes the best smothered burritos this side of the Rio Grande."

"You want to keep an eye on me or something?" John asked, regretting not going to the sheriff's office first.

"Something like that," the sheriff said, putting his hand on John's shoulder, leading him across the street to a pink adobe building with tinted glass windows.

"Ah, smell that," the sheriff said, when they opened the glass door. "Just like Heaven."

"If the smell of Heaven is burning meat."

A high school kid sat them at a table by the window, with a perfect view of parked cars. The sheriff rested his cowboy hat, a sweat-stained Chesterfield Stetson, on the seat next to him. His hair was matted down like carpet under furniture legs. A line circled his forehead, the boundary for sun exposure.

From the outside, the restaurant promised to be like most Mexican restaurants in Denver, either a greasy hole-in-the-wall or a franchise Tex-Mex restaurant decorated with sombreros and old pictures, making a foreign country seem like an amusement park, but looking at the menu, John got excited. It was the type of place he'd expect in Boulder or Lower Denver, labeled '100% Organic, Locally Sourced, Free Range'.

A woman walked up behind John, but he didn't see her. The stomach pains he'd been feeling since arriving in town returned. He felt like his body was about to implode. He grimaced and, dropping his menu, clutched his stomach.

"Are you alright?" she asked, putting her hand on his shoulder.

"Yeah," he said, the pain gradually subsiding with her touch, "I ate a bad sandwich yesterday and I'm still feeling it."

A beautiful, young, Mexican woman stood over John, her hand on the back of his chair. She appeared to glow naturally, overpowering the mid-afternoon sun and florescent lights. John looked up at her and shook in his chair, but was calm, experiencing the excitement and tranquility that come from seeing beauty.

"Lee," she said, "I think we need to get some food in your friend."

"Rosa," the sheriff said, "this here's John Abernathy."

"Oh, uh, hello," John said, embarrassed by his stammering, his inability to convey his thoughts, the main one being that Rosa was the most beautiful woman he'd ever seen.

The simple, black dress that draped her body, protected by an apron tied around her waist, flowed to black stockings and green Chucks. The hem of a tattoo peeked from under her right sleeve at her elbow. John wondered if other ink decorated her body. Or if she had any hidden piercings.

"You seem awfully young to be running a restaurant," John said.

Her bangs ended above her trimmed eyebrows and two strands of hair hung on either side of her face. Rosa tucked a strand behind her ear. The rest of her hair had been pulled into a raven ponytail. A dyed blue streak. John smiled, hoping it meant Rosa was artistically inclined. He learned in college he had a greater chance with artsy girls.

She smiled back playfully. "I'm older than I look."

"What are we talking here? thirty-five, forty?"

"I'm not that old," she said, laughing and slapping his shoulder.

"Hey now," the sheriff said. "A person's age don't mean nothing."

"I graduated from college a couple of years ago."

"Yeah? Me too," John said. "What school?"

"University of New Mexico. You?"

"The Boulder School of Esoteric Art and Impractical Design."

"Wow, that's a mouthful."

John's cheeks turned slightly pink.

"What did you study?" he asked.

"A little bit of everything. Psych, Business Administration, Sociology, Biochem, Medieval Studies, but nothing really resonated with me. So I went the easy route. New Mexico History."

"That's the easy route?" All John had ever wanted to do was study puzzles. It never occurred to him that some people didn't have a concentrated vision, that they tested everything until they discovered something they loved. "So, the restaurant, how did that happen?"

"I was going to go to grad school," Rosa said, "get a PhD, do the academia thing, but I found that what I really wanted to do was help people. And the best way for me to do that was with food."

"So you went to a culinary academy?"

"You don't need a degree to make your grandma's recipes."

John tore the edge of his paper placemat, shearing away a fragment of green paper that protected the table from lunch falling from a fork.

"What about you? What do you do?" she asked.

"John's a private investigator," the sheriff said.

"You seem awfully young to be private investigator."

"I get that," John said, feeling slightly inadequate. Rosa was a small business owner, had studied multiple disciplines. He wanted her to know that he was more than a guy who photographed cheating husbands sitting naked on chocolate cake in front of a room full of Civil War re-enactors. "It's just my day job, though. I'm really an enigmatologist."

Sheriff Masters squinted, like the word 'enigmatologist' was sandstorm in a desert of spelling bee vocabulary, but Rosa smiled and nodded like enigmatology was something she talked about all the time with her guests.

"You design puzzles," she said.

"How did you..." He looked up at her, surprised, eyebrows furrowing behind the frames of his glasses.

"Like jigsaw puzzles?" the sheriff asked.

"Like crosswords," John said, "logic puzzles. What I want to do is create puzzles that change the way people view their world."

"Like those pictures folks look at till they go all cross-eyed?" the sheriff asked.

"Crosswords are like form of meditation, something you do when you're alone. You're trying to recall everything you've learned, being flexible enough to fit your accumulated knowledge into the right amount of squares. That's what I love about puzzles. They can alter us, stretch our thinking, expand our awareness, push us to become something more." John prepared this quote years ago for when someone asked him about puzzles. He thought it was an impressive line and had been waiting for the right time to use it. Looking up at Rosa, he thought it worked.

"I think people just like to fill in boxes," Rosa said, giving John a slight shove.

"Well, there's that, too," John said, blushing but grinning.

"I have a riddle you can answer for me," Rosa said. "What brings a young enigmatologist to Las Vegas?"

"John's on a case," the sheriff said, leaning in, putting his elbows on the table. "He's looking for Al Leadbelly."

"Really?" Rosa started laughing. "Why him?"

"Show her the picture."

John rolled his eyes and pulled the picture from his hoodie pocket, unenthusiastic about having to explain. He thought Rosa would think less of him if she knew why he was in town.

"My client thinks he's Elvis," John said, trying to sound indifferent, "wants me to check it out."

"Al? Elvis? He's like forty," Rosa said. "Although, I've heard him do karaoke down at the bowling alley. He does do a mean Elvis."

"Have you seen him lately?" John asked.

"Yeah, I saw him last night at this bar, El Borracho Feliz."

"The Happy Drunk?"

"Sí." She smiled, putting one hand on his chair back. "¿Cuánto tiempo ha hablado español?"

"Uh...," John stammered, bewildered. "Uh...yeah,

I really..."

"That's what you get for trying to talk Spanish to someone named Rosa Jimenez," the sheriff said, laughing.

"So, you saw Al Leadbelly last night?" John asked, quickly trying to conceal his banter misstep.

"I hope he's alright. He looked pretty beat-up."

"Not everyone likes karaoke."

"About what time did you see Leadbelly?" the sheriff asked, suddenly sounding professional.

"Well, I went there after we closed," Rosa said. "So, around eleven thirty."

"You were there by yourself?" John asked.

"I was with Jose. We go there for a drink sometimes after work."

"Jose, your husband?"

"My brother," Rosa said. "He's a sous chef here." She thumbed over her shoulder, toward the kitchen.

"Your husband or boyfriend meet you there?"

"I'm not seeing anyone, if that's what you're asking." She put her hand on John's shoulder, shook her head. "You just can't catch a break."

"Actually," John said, flustered by his transparency, "I was just wondering if I needed to talk to anyone else."

"Nope, the only person you need to talk to is me." The strand of hair fell from her ear. She re-tucked it.

"That's what I was hoping." John gazed at Rosa,

absorbed by her smile.

"Do you know how long he was there?" the sheriff asked.

"He was still there when I left, but he was talking to Brandi Cartwright." Rosa tilted her head and looked at Sheriff Masters.

"I'm sorry, I don't understand," John said.

"Brandi Cartwright," Sheriff Masters said, "is...how can I say it...notorious around town for having many boyfriends, especially for one night."

"Gotcha."

"Anything else?" Rosa asked.

The women he talked to were usually clients, bitter and flirting with divorce. Or, when he hung out with friends in Boulder, art school graduates who had just figured out that the real world didn't care about their macramé yoga pants or their short film about toothpaste, and that they'd have to work in a fair trade coffee shop selling lattes to the next generation of art students to support their craft, this knowledge putting them on suicide watch. But Rosa was different. She exuded a soft vitality, a mellowed, youthful exuberance. It injected every movement, gesture, phrase with her love for this world, this town. John felt refreshed being around someone who was genuinely happy.

He heard Rooftop's voice, lecturing him about the necessary distance required of P.I.s, the fact that he couldn't get close to someone, but John didn't care. It'd been a while since he'd enjoyed talking to someone. He was surprised at how good he felt and knew it was because of Rosa. And he didn't want it to end.

"Oh, here," he said, reaching into his wallet like it was something he just remembered. "This is my business card. You can call me whenever you want, if you think of anything else, or, you know..."

"So if I need a seven letter word for oceanographic that starts with 'a', I can call you?"

"Aquatic. Or maybe even abysmal. Depending on the clue. Sorry, it's part of my...Anyway, yes, you can call me for anything."

They gazed at each other for a while. Rosa smiled at him, content and delighted, like she'd been waiting several years for him to walk into her restaurant. John hoped that Rosa was interested in him and not that she was waiting for him to order.

"Oh, lunch," John said, opening and pretending to read the menu. "We came here for lunch."

The sheriff ordered the combo platter: an enchilada, a flauta, and a chile relleno. John ordered ala carte: one enchilada con mole and a tamal. When Rosa walked away, John turned and watched her hips sway. They moved gently, like willow branches in a March breeze. When she reached the front counter she turned and caught John staring. She smiled and laughed a little. John blushed, quickly looked away.

He wanted to spend more time with her and regretted having to be on a case, having to track down some jerk who dressed like Elvis, did karaoke, and picked up loose women. Rosa glided between the register and the kitchen and John outlined their future, starting with coming back to her restaurant once his case was wrapped up, talking to Rosa, asking her out, charming her somehow, doing the long distance thing, becoming more serious, then moving in together, John working on puzzles while she ran the restaurant, his numerous awards hanging from the walls.

John shook his head, stopping his thoughts. He knew from experience how dangerous fantasies could be. When he was a child, he would sit next to the door and imagine his father walking through it, hugging him and his mother. His father would explain that he'd gotten lost coming home from work, something that happened to John once when he was at a neighbor's third birthday party. So, John sat by the door waiting for something that never happened. Once he realized his father wouldn't be walking through the door, John learned to control his fantasies, only dreaming about outcomes he could control, his puzzles, his future.

Rosa brought them a couple bottles of Negro Modelo. John leaned forward, his mouth slightly open. He thought of something funny while she was getting their drinks, but she left to check on other lunch guests before he could say anything and he slumped back into the red vinyl chair. He held his beer bottle with both hands, almost in his lap, and picked at the label.

"About Leadbelly, anything I need to know?" John asked.

"Nah," the sheriff said, sipping his beer. "He's just one a those characters we have here in town. A good natured type, jokes around a lot. No one really takes him seriously."

"Someone took him seriously enough to take his picture."

"You wanna go by his trailer?" The sheriff leaned over the table, perking up. "I know where he lives."

"How long you been sheriff?" John asked, the bottle almost slipping from his grip.

"I've worn this badge the past fifteen years. My pa was sheriff before me, and my grandpa before him. I guess you could say being a lawman's in my blood."

"So you like it, then?"

"Sure, I like it. I like this town. The people. Honestly, I don't really have that much to do, just the occasional domestic disturbance, but nothing that can't be handled by talking things out. These are good people here. Most of the time I don't even wear a gun, only when strangers come around asking questions." He slapped John's arm, laughing.

Forcing fake laughter, John watched the sheriff for signs that he was either joking or about to arrest him.

"What about you, how'd you get into the P.I.

business?"

"It's a pretty long story," John said. "I graduated school, needed a job. My boss, Rufus, was a friend of my grandfather, kind of an unofficial uncle. He needed an assistant, said he'd take me on. Really, he was doing it as a favor for my mom."

"What does your dad do?"

"Not sure. He hasn't been around for a while."

"He run out on you?"

"That's the way it looks. Truth is, we don't really know. He disappeared when I was five. He went to work one day and never came home. We filed a missing person's claim. There was an investigation and everything. Police told us he clocked in at his office, but never came back from his lunch break. He just disappeared. It's one of those unsolved mysteries, like you see on TV."

"I'm sorry to hear that, John."

"Don't be. My mom and I got on fine without him. We didn't need him after all. Never did."

John picked at his beer label, peeling it away from the bottle. He didn't drink during the day and the beer was starting to affect him, loosening his reserve.

"The crazy part is," John continued, "I still have dreams about him, ever since he left. We'd do all these father-son things, play catch, he'd give me advice about girls, shit like that. All the stuff we would have done had he stayed, the stuff I missed out on as a kid, I get to experience when I sleep.

Messed up part is, after all these father-son moments, I tell him to fuck off. Every single night. It's like my subconscious or whatever is letting me say what I'll never get a chance to say. But those dreams, they seem more like memories, like it actually happened. It's weird."

Rosa brought their food and another round of drinks. When she placed the plates, she leaned over and John saw the top of her bra, black lace. He cleared his throat.

After they were done eating, Rosa came over to check on them. "Do you need anything else?"

"I think we're good," the sheriff said, slapping his gut. His gut wasn't big, but it did hang over his belt a little.

"Just the check, please," John said, wanting to ask Rosa for her phone number, address, shoe size, anything that would help him be able to spend time with her.

"Lee, I can't believe you didn't tell him?" she said, her hand on her hip. "Well, John, don't worry about it. You just have a nice day." She put her hand on his shoulder and slid it across his back as she walked off.

"What was that all about?" John asked, watching her walk away.

"Oh, a few years back," the sheriff leaned back, his hands folded across his belly, "Rosa's brother was taking classes at the college. Got jumped walking to his car. Got roughed up pretty bad. Rosa asked me to help. We found the kids, took care of them. They won't be bothering anyone anymore."

"You mean..." John formed his hand into the shape of a gun.

"No, no," the sheriff said, laughing. "The DA's a fishing buddy. I talked him into charging the kids with attempted murder. Since the judge on the case is a cousin a mine, he found them guilty. Now they're serving fifteen with no parole."

"Small town justice."

"It's got its perks. The DA and I get free food whenever we come in here."

"Dang."

"Rosa's good people. Her brother's a good kid, a bit of a fuck up, but a good kid. The plaza was a ghost town before she showed up. This here restaurant pretty much revitalized the downtown. The town owes her. You see, we're a small community here. We look out for our own."

The sheriff stood and pushed in his chair. He set his Stetson back on his head, into the erosions of a lifetime of hat wear. John dug into his pocket, dropped a twenty on the table next to the wadded and stained napkins, salsa-smeared plates, and empty beer bottles. Sheriff Masters wrinkled his forehead, making his hat move slightly.

"I gotta leave something," John said. "Besides, it's on the *Enquirer*."

"You sonuvabitch! You're buying dinner."

The afternoon sun moved across the sky, expanding awning shade, creating the perfect hiding place from heat. John and Sheriff Masters moved slowly, sleepy from well-cooked Mexican food and beer. They crossed the street, walking to the sheriff's car.

John took one last look at Rosa's Restaurante. Inside, Rosa flowed between tables. She wiped a table next to the window, looked up, and waved. John waved back, his hand at his waist, like he was trying to hide his gesture. He wished he was still inside, sitting at a table, working on a puzzle, talking to her between coffee refills. He wanted to be near her, cracking jokes, waiting for the moment when he could ask her out. Instead, he was standing in the street about to get into a cop car.

He slid into the front, onto a hot Pleather seat, the metal cage rattling behind the headrest. The sheriff picked up his CB and started talking.

"Shirley? Shirley, you there?"

"Yeah, Lee. You find that newcomer yet?"

"Yeah," he said, chuckling. "He's here with me now."

"Oh. Hi, there."

Sheriff Masters stuck the CB under John's mouth, motioned toward him as if to say, 'Say something.'

"Uh, hi," John said.

"So, what brings you to town? You know, we've been getting an awful lotta calls about you. Well, only two, but still."

"Shirley," the sheriff interrupted, "I'm going out to Jeremiah's for a bit. Gotta have a talk with Al Leadbelly."

"Al Leadbelly? Is he in some kind a trouble? Let me talk to that stranger again. This has something to do with him, don't it?"

"Don't you worry about that none. You just let Jimmy know where to find me if he needs me." The sheriff turned to John, said, "Jimmy's my deputy, not too bright."

"Roger that." The CB went silent.

They drove to the lumberyard, passing houses verging on collapse. A tarp covered one roof, held down by bricks, ready to blow away at first wind. Another's roof sagged, waiting to snap with the next snow. The town was crumbling to dust, becoming desert.

"So, how many of these...what'd you call them, sightings have you been on?"

"This is my first one."

The sheriff groaned. The route to the lumberyard devolved from potholed roads into dirt and loose gravel.

"Look, Sheriff, this might be my first Elvis sighting," John said, sensing the sheriff's apprehension, "but I can tell you for a fact this Leadbelly guy isn't Elvis. Unless Elvis has been frozen the past thirty years."

"I'm more worried about that paper a yours, wondering what they're gonna do with that photo when they find out he's not Elvis."

"They'll probably publish it anyway," John said, the beer and Rosa causing him to be careless.

"They'd do that?" The sheriff looked at John, angry and aggrieved.

"This guy, Rex Grant, the *Enquirer's* editor, he only cares about selling papers."

"What do you think'll happen when they publish it?"

"Well, you'll probably have a bunch of Elvis super-fans running around looking for Leadbelly."

"Quite frankly, I don't want that to happen," the sheriff said, twisting the steering wheel as he drove. The town was a quiet place full of dead grass and slowly dying people, and the sheriff didn't want fanatics disturbing decay.

John understood the need for quiet and stability. It's how he worked best, late nights, his mom sleeping, the harmonic hums of computer and fridge. His investigation conflicted with tranquility. Its outcome meant screaming groupies, hotel riots, and several generations of Elvis fans treating this town like their personal souvenir stand. John knew this was unavoidable, that Rex Grant didn't care if the photo was a hoax, that he'd publish it regardless of John's objections. They drove past two men hosing down a septic tank, and John knew it was time to tell the sheriff about the other part of his investigation, his other reason for needing to find Leadbelly.

"Sheriff, about Leadbelly. I'm not the first person the *Enquirer* sent looking for him. A few weeks ago, they sent a reporter down here. He was found outside Truth or Consequences, shot. They hired me to find Leadbelly, find out what happened to the kid."

"Holy shit!" The sheriff almost skidded off the road. John put on his seatbelt. "You're on a goddamn homicide investigation. You lucky sonuvabitch!"

"You're a little too excited about a dead body."

"Sorry. This here's a quiet town. It's been about five years since our last homicide," the sheriff said.

"You might have to wait a little longer."

"You don't think Leadbelly did it, do you?"

"Not sure," John said, thinking about what he'd found in Leadbelly's trailer, the menu from the strip club in Truth or Consequences.

"Hold on a sec." Sheriff Masters picked up the CB again. "How old'd you say this kid was?"

"The *Enquirer* said he was eighteen, just an intern," John said.

"Shirley, you there?"

"I'm here, Lee."

"Can you call the Sheriff's Department down in Truth or Consequences, find out about a case they got going? Something involving a male, late-teens-to-early-twenties, found outside a town a couple of weeks ago."

"Does this got something to do with Al Leadbelly? Or that stranger?"

"Just make the call, Shirley."

"Alright. Will do," she said.

"She sounds disappointed," John said.

"Yeah," the sheriff said, "Shirley's got an appointment at the hairdresser's this afternoon. She's gonna be sitting under a cone dryer for a while, wants to talk about the case."

"How do you know that?" John asked.

"'Cause I married her," the sheriff said, laughing.

The sheriff turned off of 7th Street, pulled into the lumberyard parking lot and rolled down his window. "There's that sonuvabitch! Leadbelly! Leadbelly! Get over here! This fella's got some questions for you."

The lumberyard consisted of a small retail building covered in rough, red paint, like the wind had sprayed dirt on it when the paint was wet. Behind the building, cut timber was stacked according to size in a maze of home improvement material bordered by a chain link fence.

Leadbelly disappeared into the lumber stacks.

95

"Leadbelly! Leadbelly!"

Sheriff Masters and John stood at the entrance to the lumber stockpile, an opening wide enough for a truck to back into.

A man who looked like the sheriff, but shorter and fatter, his belly hiding his belt buckle, office life having faded his cowboy hat tan line, stomped out of the retail building.

"Lee, what are you going on about?" he asked.

"We're here on police business. This here's John Abernathy," the sheriff said, pointing to John. "He has some questions for Leadbelly."

"Questions? What kinda questions?"

"Don't you worry about it none, Jeremiah. We won't be disrupting your business."

"Just as long as you're not. And...and I'm gonna be here for the questioning." Jeremiah poked himself in the chest, like he was confirming his own importance.

"What are you, a goddamn lawyer now?"

"Gotta look out for my employees is all."

"Yeah, that's who you're looking out for."

John had seen situations like this with Rooftop, two people with long and complicated histories fighting for dominion over the past and the present.

"Sheriff," John said, trying to calm everyone down, "I don't mind Jeremiah sticking around."

"Alright. Just remember, Jeremiah, this is official police business. So, don't go interrupting."

They watched Leadbelly return from the stacks

of cut timber. He walked out with saw-bound one-by-sixes on his shoulder. The stomach knots John withstood since coming to town returned, although they weren't as gnarled. His lunch helped. Or maybe it was Rosa's enduring influence. But the tangle fully loosened as Leadbelly got closer.

The sheriff called him again. "Leadbelly! Leadbelly! Get over here! This fella's got some questions for you!"

Leadbelly put down the planks and strutted over, the sun being absorbed by the black and green bruise around his eye and cheek. He shared many striking similarities with Elvis, height, eyes, jaw, black hair, sideburns crawling down his face, but as he walked closer, John instantly knew the man was not Elvis, just an imitation. His black hair color looked like it was courtesy of a box bought in a pharmacy, and he needed to re-dye. Gray roots were growing along his temples. Despite the indications of age, Leadbelly was still considerably younger than Elvis. If Elvis were still alive, he'd be in his late seventies. Leadbelly looked like he wouldn't reach that mark for another thirty years.

But there was one thing that was the same. The voice.

"Al Leadbelly?" John asked.

"Man, I wouldn't be coming over here if I weren't. Sheriff, what's this all about? I got work to do, man."

"Leadbelly," the sheriff said, "this here's John

Abernathy. Now, he's got some questions for you and you're gonna answer them. That's just how it is."

"Alright then, ask away. But be quick with it, man. I got some ladies meeting me at the Whataburger after work."

John put his hand in his pocket, felt for Mrs. Morris's picture. His fingers rubbed its glossy surface, then grazed the rough edge of the folded menu from the strip club. He pulled it out, swatted it against his hand. Leadbelly's arrogance reminded John of everything he hated about his job, the late hours, the miserable people, having to photograph a client's husband putting on clown makeup while a dominatrix, dressed like the man's mom, told him all the ways he'd disappointed her. And the fact that it kept John from doing what he loved.

"I know how you got those bruises," John said, pointing to Leadbelly's face with the menu.

"This?" Leadbelly pointed to his purple eye. "Man, this is nothing."

"Tell me about the kid, the one you got into a fight with."

"Nothing to tell, man. He just came up, started talking shit. Wouldn't shut up."

"What was he saying?"

"Nothing really, man. Most a the time when people talk shit to me it's 'cause I slept with their sister or something. This kid, he just said he knew me's all. I ain't never seen him before." Leadbelly shrugged, like the kid and the fight were insignificant.

"But he knew you, didn't he?" John said, thinking about the people Colonel Hollister had watching Leadbelly's trailer. "That's what he told you, that he knew you. That he's been following you. Why was he following you, Leadbelly?"

"How the hell should I know, man?"

"He knew your secret, didn't he? That's what he said to you."

"He was just some drunk kid, man. That's all."

"A drunk kid you felt the need to beat up," John said, pointing at Leadbelly with the menu like it was Leadbelly's signed confession.

"It wasn't like that, man," Leadbelly said, shaking his head, his pompadour swaying.

"When was the last time you where in Truth or Consequences?" John asked, shifting directions. He unfolded the gentleman's club menu, showed it to Leadbelly.

"Oh, man. Fuzzy Beaver's? I go there every couple of weeks. They have a great all-you-can-eat buffet."

"You couldn't have thought of a different way to say that?"

"They got really good chicken wings, too, man. Although you gotta wash your hands before you get a lap dance. The girls don't like greasy fingers messing up their glitter."

"What about this?" John said, taking Mrs.

Morris's picture from his pocket. "Is this you in this photo?"

"Well, man, that looks like me, and that's my place. So, it must be me. What's this got to do with Fuzzy Beaver's? It's a hell of a place. You really should check it out."

"I was hired by *The National Enquirer* to investigate it. But they already sent someone down here. Here's what I'm thinking, the kid they sent found you and followed you down to Truth or Consequences on one of your excursions."

"They got this girl there, man," Leadbelly said, eyes empty with daydreams, "you know how strippers are all named after cities?"

"The kid follows you," John continued, "asks you some questions, like the kid from the bar."

"Her name's Old Detroit. She's gotta be like seventy, man."

"It gets a little heated. He makes some accusations."

"She brings you your lunch butt naked and you pay her to put her clothes on. It's outta sight."

"And since you obviously don't like people asking you questions, you kill him and leave his body in the desert. Am I close?"

"Whoa, whoa, man," Leadbelly said, waving his hands, warding off the accusations, taking a couple of steps back. "Hold on a second. I don't know nothing about no kid in Truth or Consequences. I swear. And I certainly didn't kill nobody."

"And you would have killed that kid from the bar if you still had your gun. What did you do with it? Where did you hide it?" John asked, taking a couple of steps toward Leadbelly. Jeremiah tried to step between them, and opened his mouth slightly, about to defend Leadbelly. But the sheriff held up his hand, backing him off.

"Leadbelly," Sheriff Masters said," if you did this thing, now would be the time to tell us. We could help you out, work with you."

"Sheriff, what the hell is this, man? You know me. I might do some crazy shit every now and then, but I'd never shoot nobody! Hell, everybody knows I'm all about the ladies."

"The DA's a buddy a mine," the sheriff said. "If you give up the gun, I'll make sure he goes easy on you."

"Hell, I don't even have a gun," he said, pleading. "On top of that, I ain't even been out to Fuzzy Beaver's in, like, two months, man. Call down there, ask."

"Two months?" John said. He flipped the calendar back in his head and knew Leadbelly was innocent. The reporter had been murdered last week. Leadbelly couldn't have killed him. But it wasn't just Leadbelly's alibi that convinced John of his innocence. John believed Leadbelly because his fear appeared to be genuine. It possessed the distress and dismay of someone being falsely accused.

"Goddamnit, Leadbelly," the sheriff said. "This is your last chance."

"Sheriff," John said, "he's telling the truth."

"What? How can you be sure?"

"The only thing he's guilty of is..." John thought about what he'd found in Leadbelly's trailer, the jumpsuit, the photos. He knew Leadbelly was guilty of something, he just wasn't sure what.

"Living life on my own terms," Leadbelly said, finishing John's thought.

"Sure, living your life or whatever," John said, crumpling the menu in his fist. He was the one living on his own terms, a struggling artist trying to build a career in puzzles. Leadbelly looked like he borrowed every aspect of his personality from a drive-in movie.

"You had me scared there for second, man," Leadbelly said. "Thought I was about to get locked up for sure."

"Sorry for coming at you so hard," John said.

"Man, that's what I say to the ladies at Fuzzy Beaver's."

"I just have one more question," John said, scowling, "if that's alright with you, Jeremiah?"

Jeremiah nodded.

"Leadbelly, you ever been to Las Vegas? Nevada, I mean?"

"No, sir. The only Las Vegas I been to is right here, man." He pointed to the ground with a defiant finger. John thought this action seemed artificial and forced, and knew Leadbelly was lying.

There were stories on the internet, conspiracy theories about Elvis and business dealings with the Mafia that would scare anyone with enough knowledge of Elvis folklore. John bet Leadbelly was the type of guy that knew these stories.

He held the picture in front of Leadbelly, flapped it. "In twenty-four hours this picture will be in every major news outlet with the headline, 'Elvis Lives'. And you'll have a lot of people down here looking for you. I'm guessing some of them will be a whole lot meaner and tougher than that kid you beat up. Right now, the only thing stopping that from happening is a phone call from me. So, you'd better be straight with me. Got it?" John heard Rooftop in his voice and accepted it as the natural influence of a surrogate father.

"Okay, okay." His voice changed, making him seem smaller. "My name's not really Al Leadbelly."

"Really?" John said. "Al Leadbelly's a made up name? Never would have guessed."

"My real name's Steve Johnson. I was an Elvis impersonator. That's why I look like him. I ran a chapel in Vegas for twenty-three years. I had an opportunity to buy the building the chapel was in. Unfortunately, I bought it at the height of the housing bubble. When it crashed, I couldn't make payments. I had to borrow some money from some very serious people."

"The mob?" the sheriff asked.

"The Slot Machine Repairman's Union. They loaned me some money to stay afloat."

"And this kid you fought, he was from the Union?" John asked.

"That's what he said. Scared the hell outta me. They have their hands in everything in Vegas. A casino can't be built without their approval. Anyway, I took their money. I saw an opportunity and went to the blackjack table."

"Don't tell me you blew everything in one hand," John said.

"What do you think, I'm stupid? It was three," he said, grinning, proud of his gambling abilities.

John shook his head. "So, you lost all your money in blackjack and moved down here?"

"First, I burned my chapel for insurance money."

"I'm guessing that didn't work out," John said.

"The arson investigator figured it out. So, I ran. That was four years ago."

"But you kept the sideburns?"

"I was an Elvis impersonator for twenty-three years. I've been pretending to be someone else for so long, I've forgotten how to be Steve Johnson."

"John." The sheriff tapped him on the shoulder. "A word?"

"What do you think?" the sheriff asked as they walked to his car.

"He's hiding something," John said, glancing over at Leadbelly. "If he was trying to reclaim his identity he would've shaved and cut his hair."

"You don't believe he's out here trying to find himself?"

"Most people trying to find themselves go to Europe, write a memoir, not hide in the desert working in a lumberyard."

Leadbelly put his hands in his back pockets and rocked on his boots, heel to toe. There was something off about his story. It was unnecessarily complex, like it was meant to entertain, not convince. It conveniently placed the blame for his situation on external factors, making him a victim of a corrupt city where the house always wins.

"Yeah, he's definitely hiding something," John said, "but I have my answers. What about you? He just confessed to insurance fraud."

"I'm willing to let that slide as long as we can wrap this up," the sheriff said. "You gonna tell the *Enquirer* Leadbelly left town?"

"I thought about that. They can just make some phone calls, turn him into a fugitive, make this whole thing bigger than it needs to be."

"Sonuvabitch." Sheriff Masters kicked the dirt.

"Don't worry about the *Enquirer*. I'll take care of them," John said, wondering what he'd tell them, and the Air Force.

They walked back over.

"Alright," John said, "I need to make a phone call. Jeremiah, can I use your office?"

"Sure thing. It's the second door on the right."

The lumberyard office window's metal blinds

were open. Outside, Jeremiah tried to say something to his brother, but Sheriff Masters kept brushing him off. Even though they were talking about him, Leadbelly wasn't watching them. He looked at the window, at John sitting behind Jeremiah's dinged, metal desk. John thought for a moment that Leadbelly wasn't concerned about the phone call or its outcome, but about John, and some secret hardship that awaited him. It made him feel awkward, having an Elvis impersonator concerned for him, and he quickly looked away and called *The National Enquirer* from his cell phone.

"Yeah, Rex Grant, please? Tell him it's John Abernathy."

"John," a voice said after making him wait a couple of minutes, "what do you have for us?"

"Well, for starters, it's not him," John said, leaning back. "He was an Elvis impersonator for a while. That's why he looks like him. But it's not him. This guy's in his forties."

"What about our reporter?"

"He doesn't know anything about that either."

"You sure?"

"I grilled him pretty good. So, it looks like you don't have a story here," John said, his voice rising in false optimism.

Rex was silent for a moment.

"I wouldn't be so sure about that. We can print the photo with the headline, 'Elvis Impersonator in New Mexico May Hold Secret to King's

Whereabouts', or something like that. This is great, John! Better than we expected."

"Are you serious? There's no story here. Just some guy in a trailer park who happens to look like Elvis."

"Yeah, isn't it great? This is how we did it in the eighties. Damn, it feels good to be back."

"But there's no story." John pushed away from the desk, hit the wall behind him, rattling plaques from the Chamber of Commerce, the Association of the Lumber Retail Specialists, the International Association of Belt Buckle Enthusiasts, the New Mexico Chapter of the Global Coalition for the Advancement of *Who's the Boss* Cosplayers.

"It doesn't matter," Rex Grant said. "People want a distraction. And we give it to them."

"What about your reporter? Did you think about him? You run this story and you'll chase away anyone who might know anything about his death."

"If you say he doesn't know anything, what can we do? We have to move forward. We're publishing the photo. End of discussion."

"You..." John put his hand on Jeremiah's desk. It wobbled on uneven legs. "You don't care about the reporter, do you?"

"Of course I do."

"What's his name?"

"What?"

"The reporter, what's his name? The kid who died, the one you sent down here, what's his name?"

"John, that's hardly…"

"You don't know, do you?" A calendar on the wall showed a calico kitten holding a circular saw, a word balloon above its head saying 'The first cut is the deepest.'

"We'll send you a check as soon as we get your expense report. You've done a great job."

"Yeah, whatever."

John leaned back in Jeremiah's chair and took a deep breath. He swiveled the chair side-to-side, moving only a few degrees in either direction. He knew before he called that Rex Grant intended to run the photo regardless of what he'd found, that it'd appear at supermarket checkouts next to other impulse buys, breath mints, chocolate pudding, 3-for-1 action-adventure DVDs starring aging, European martial artists. But John needed to try anyway. He felt an attachment to the town, a comfort he hadn't experienced in Denver or Boulder, and he wanted to insulate it from Rex Grant and his scant journalistic standards. John set his elbows on the desk. He took off his glasses and rubbed his eyes. He needed to call another number, be disappointed by another client.

"Colonel Hollister. It's John Abernathy."

"John, have you found him?" Colonel Hollister sounded chipper, hopeful.

"He left town. I'm at his job right now. His boss said he quit yesterday then took off." John knew lying to Colonel Hollister was a calculated risk.

He'd been watching Leadbelly's trailer for a while, would have seen Leadbelly packing up, moving on. If Leadbelly returned home, the colonel would know that John had lied to him. Colonel Hollister could still break into John's hotel room, fulfill all the implied threats of a knife to the throat, and John hoped his tenuous story would convince Colonel Hollister that he no longer had a reason to stay in Las Vegas.

"That's too bad. Did he give a reason why?"

"I know he was in a bar fight last night. Did one of your guys run into him? Maybe they went looking for him when he didn't come home."

"I can't discuss ongoing operations."

"So, that's a yes." John heard Colonel Hollister breathing on the other end, a silent admission. "So, we're done now. You paid me to find this guy and he's not here. I did my job. It's over."

"John, it's never over."

"Whatever." John hung up, frustrated at the obstinance the two men shared. He decided he'd write a puzzle about self-important people, a scathing commentary set in squares.

Outside, the sheriff had his arms crossed like a man not accustomed to waiting. Jeremiah watched his brother peripherally. They pretended not to notice each other. Both were obviously concerned, but for different reasons. Even though the sheriff and his brother were concerned about him, Leadbelly wasn't watching them. He was looking east, toward the desert.

"Leadbelly!" John said, sprinting from the building. "Those tabloid douches, they're gonna publish the photo anyway! They actually think it's better you're not Elvis. They think they can sell more papers telling people you know where he is."

"Goddamn Los Angeles sonsabitches!" Sheriff Masters said, slapping his Stetson against his thigh. "They think they can take advantage of us 'cause we're small town folk. I have half a mind to drive out there and have a word with them."

"I apologize, Sheriff. I tried talking them out of it."

"I know it's not your fault, John. It's just big city folk thinking they're better than everyone."

"What do you think I should do?" Leadbelly asked John.

"Well, for starters, cut your hair and lose the sideburns. Then get outta New Mexico. Go someplace like Canada, where they don't give a shit about Elvis."

"I'd listen to the man if I were you," the sheriff said.

"And Leadbelly. Don't go back to your trailer," John said, thinking about what he'd told Colonel Hollister. "That kid's got friends." John pointed to Leadbelly's bruised face. "If I can find you, so can they."

Leadbelly closed his eyes and tilted his head toward the sun. He breathed deeply, inhaling a desert breeze carrying the smell of cut lumber. The sound of an electric saw slicing measured wood. Leadbelly turned to them, smiling, his secret burden removed.

"Jeremiah, thanks for everything. Sheriff, it's been nice knowing you. John, thanks for the advice."

He shook their hands and ran to his truck. Before he jumped in and drove away, Leadbelly spun around, got in the Elvis stance, legs parted wide, knees bent, weight forward. He pointed fingers on both hands, curled his lip, and committed his final act as King, saying, "Thank you. Thank you very much."

CHAPTER NINE

Leadbelly's tires kicked lumberyard parking lot gravel, and dust clouded his exit.

John took out Leadbelly's picture, folded it in half, image upon image, creasing it with his thumbnail.

The sheriff patted John on the shoulder and smiled. John didn't smile back. Instead, he dropped his head and rubbed the back of his neck. He didn't accomplish anything that merited commendation. The *Enquirer* was still going to publish the photo, and the Air Force was still going record every car, truck, and dirt bike swerving in and out of Leadbelly's trailer park. He gazed into the cloudless sky. Above them, the flash of something in orbit, and John mouthed the words, 'It's never over.'

The dust gradually settled on their shoulders and shoes.

"Lee, what the hell was that?" Jeremiah said, coughing and spitting dust from his mouth. "Leadbelly was one of my best employees. Employee of the Month three months running. What the hell am I gonna do now?"

"Put an ad in the goddamn paper for all I care. You're a smart guy, you'll figure something out." The sheriff waved at his brother with the back of his hand.

"Family problems?" John finally asked when they were standing by the car. Behind them, Jeremiah plodded into his office.

"You could say that. I got three brothers and a sister. We all serve our community in different ways. Since I'm the oldest, it fell upon me to follow our dad, become sheriff. Jeremiah, he's the youngest. And the smartest. He coulda used his gifts to better this town. Instead, he went and opened this place, making a little money. Our dad was always disappointed that Jeremiah, with all his smarts, didn't become a doctor or something."

"Why didn't he, if he's so smart?"

"You see, Jeremiah always doubted himself. After high school, he saved his money, took out a loan, bought this place."

"Doesn't sound like he doubted himself to me."

"There's different kinds a doubt," the sheriff said, backing out of the parking lot. "You did good work back there. You got a real knack for this stuff."

"I hate this shit, talking to people that way. It feels like it's not me."

"What the hell are you talking about? You should feel good. You ran the bad guy outta town, saved the day."

"I think the bad guy might still be here." John

hung his elbow out of the open car window. "Christ, I just want to make puzzles."

The case was a calisthenic of futility. The *Enquirer* didn't care about the reporter, or the truth, and John doubted that Colonel Hollister would give up his search for Leadbelly. John was frequently disheartened by his clients, their lack of sympathy, their utilizing John and Rooftop for a quick and profitable retribution. His two current clients, two people interested in an Elvis photo, were the same as the clients seeking divorce, twisting the outcome of his investigation into something sordid for their benefit. He wanted revenge, to show them what happened when someone tried to manipulate him. Regrettably, his vengeance was limited and could only take one form. Fortunately, it was one a for-profit business like the *Enquirer* would understand.

"You know, the *Enquirer's* covering my expenses," John said to the sheriff, his mischievous streak awakened.

"Hell, let's get something to eat."

Julio's Diner was on Bridge Street, across from the Grand Plaza Hotel. They sat on red vinyl bar stools at a Formica counter, drinking beer while Julio, the heavy set chef and owner, cooked their food on an old griddle and stove in front of them. The diner smelled of old grease and cigarette smoke that had burrowed into the pores of the cracked vinyl and the foam underneath.

John swiveled often, unconsciously, toward the large window at the end of the counter. Rosa's Restaurante was a block away. It was getting dark, but John could see the light coming from her window. He'd thought about her all day, the way she touched him and how, when she did, it made his skin feel like lightening was shooting through it. He thought about the way she walked and smelled and how she was the only woman he'd met since graduation who knew what enigmatology was. Spinning toward the window, he wondered how he'd be able to see her again.

"You gonna wear out that stool, you keep turning like that," the sheriff said.

"What?"

"You got a thing for Rosa, don't you?"

"What? No. What?" John said, denying it like a grade school crush.

"You know what? I think she's got a little something for you, too. She's usually pretty cold to guys, like she's got something more important to do. It's this restaurant a hers, it takes up all a her time. I always tell her, 'life is short'. She needs to have some fun. You know, she closes up every night." The sheriff checked his watch. "We'll probably get outta here just in time."

"In time for what?"

"For you to go talk to her."

John sipped his beer and turned again toward the window. The diner had emptied. Julio shredded potatoes for the breakfast hash browns, getting ready to close. John leaned back against the counter, peeled the label from his beer in thin strips. He would be returning to Denver in the morning, to his job, to the unfinished crossword puzzle, and all the puzzles he had yet to struggle with at the kitchen table in his mom's apartment, head in his hands, a half-finished PBR Tall Boy leaving a ring on his scratch paper, another night of questioning why his inventiveness had dissolved. That was what waited for him, the bleak and vanishing prospects of the frustrated artist. But across the street, Rosa's Restaurante glowed invitingly.

"Fuck it." John stood and chugged the rest of his beer. He threw a twenty on the counter and jogged to the door.

The sheriff laughed, clapping his hands. "Hey, Julio! Look at this sonuvabitch."

"Be sure to get me a receipt," John said, backing out the door. He flipped the sheriff off with both hands, then ran across the street.

Outside, the sun was setting. A slight breeze coming off the mountains blew thin dirt. Dust reflected light from street lamps like a thin layer of dirty fog.

Everything in the plaza was closed or closing, but a couple of the restaurants were still seating. John sprinted across the empty street to the only restaurant that mattered.

Rosa's Restaurante.

CHAPTER ELEVEN

The paper work, the files needing to be read, the forms requiring an authorizing signature, were organized into neat piles on Colonel Hollister's particle board computer desk. The desk had been hastily assembled using Scandinavian instructions and an Allen wrench, and wobbled when he would put his weight on it, used it as a crutch to help him rise from his padded folding chair.

Colonel Hollister rubbed his eyes. He was exhausted, running two operations, being the senior administrator at the Los Alamos research facility and overseeing the investigation into *The National Enquirer's* photo. This wasn't a problem when he was younger, when he was constantly invigorated by his charismatic apprentice. White haired and past retirement age, he now wished there was someone else who could take over the field operations and he could go back to his lab and tinker and experiment with everything he'd collected. There had been someone who could have succeeded him, but that person had been taken from him.

How long had it been? almost forty years since

Elvis died? And there were still so many questions. He hoped that when they found this impersonator, and they would find him, it was just a matter of time, that he would be able to answer some of them.

Colonel Hollister had suspicions about him, who he really was, where he came from. His suspicions were deepened by the fact that the impersonator didn't exist four years ago. Since Elvis's death in 1977, the Air Force had been compiling information on Elvis impersonators, looking for people with a specific connection to Elvis. They had extensive dossiers on every Elvis impersonator that either was or had been professionally employed. And when they intercepted Mrs. Morris's photo, they discovered that the man in it was not in their registry.

Colonel Hollister picked up a picture that sat on the edge of his desk. He and Elvis had just come from a meeting with the Joint Chiefs. The meeting, like all their meetings, was held in secret at an undisclosed location, which was usually a barbeque joint in midtown Memphis. It was one of Elvis's favorite restaurants. He would sit at a large table, elbows on the red and white checkered vinyl table cloth, a plastic bib around his neck, slurping pork off rib bones, nodding and talking through his barbeque-sauce-covered face. In the picture, Elvis and Colonel Hollister are leaving the restaurant. Colonel Hollister is carrying a to-go bag and Elvis is teasing him about not being able to finish his meal while asking for the leftovers. A tourist from Iceland happened to be walking by and had taken the picture. He was arrested, his camera seized. He died in a secret prison in Tunisia. His family searched for him for years, but all records of him had disappeared. The restaurant had closed since then. It was a shame. They really had good barbeque.

Someone knocked on his door, bringing him back from his dry rubbed and hickory smoked memories.

"Uh, sir," a young analyst said, sticking his head in the door, "we have a hit, sir."

Colonel Hollister brought a skeleton crew, two analysts, two Special Forces officers, and his personal assistant to Las Vegas, the idea being that Los Alamos was only a few hours away, and if needed, a small, armored platoon could be there quickly. They had set up their command center in a foreclosed house on Delores Street, a block and a half from the Elvis impersonator's trailer. The house had been purchased through a shell bank they used to fund their black ops. Colonel Hollister had claimed the master bedroom for his office. He spent most of his time there, even sleeping on a small mattress and sleeping bag in the corner. The living room had been transformed into a command hub by the analysts who'd filled it with computer screens that showed images from around and inside the trailer park. They had also placed cameras all around the block, and were close enough that if the Elvis impersonator came home, or anyone snooped around his trailer, they could mobilize in seconds.

"Well then, Private Ramsey," Colonel Hollister said, standing and pushing his chair under his desk, making sure its cushioned back was perpendicular to the mahogany-finished plane, "alert the men. Put them on standby."

"Yes, sir." Private Ramsey ran to his station and sat next to another analyst, Private Mulworth. Both men were interchangeable, same close-cropped hair, same pink, eager faces.

Colonel Hollister tried to hide his grin, striding into the room. He had wondered how long it would take for the impersonator to return home. He trusted John to be like a typical Abernathy, accepting an assignment, then inexplicably sympathize with the enemy. So he wasn't surprised when John lied to him, had said that the impersonator had quit his job, left town. Despite John's attempted deception, Colonel Hollister was confident the impersonator wouldn't leave just yet. He had known many impersonators while Elvis was alive, and none of them knew when to get off the stage.

Colonel Hollister stood behind Private Ramsey, leaning over, one hand on the desk, the other on the back of Private Ramsey's chair. The curtains were drawn and their faces glowed green from the monitors.

"What's the sitrep?" Colonel Hollister asked.

"It's a truck, sir," Private Ramsey said, "registered to a Steve Johnson. The same Steve Johnson that the trailer's registered to."

"And now he's come home," Colonel Hollister said, crossing his arms. "You've been tracking his movements, I assume."

"Yes, sir. You asked us to reposition the satellites, follow the Abernathy subject. We tracked him to a lumberyard. This truck left several minutes after your phone conversation with the subject ended. Per your orders, we followed the truck."

"That was a half an hour ago. Where's he been?"

"Liquor store, sir."

"Of course."

"We have surveillance footage of him leaving Harry Mann Liquors with a thirty rack. That's thirty cans of beer, sir."

"I know what a thirty rack is," Colonel Hollister said, thinking of long nights at Graceland, body doubles passed out on couches, empty cans and half crushed diet pills on the coffee table.

"And he was carrying a sack, possibly of some hard liquor."

"He must be planning on sticking around. Can you verify it was him? Credit card transaction?"

"No, sir. We're assuming he paid cash."

"Of course he did. Trying to be clever, staying off the grid. If I didn't know better I'd say this Steve

Johnson didn't exist," Colonel Hollister said, sharing a rare joke with his men. He knew that the analysts, to pass the time, created back stories about the trailer park residents, speculating about their jobs, whether they'd ever been arrested for stealing airplane glue, if their first sexual experience happened at the same time as their first DUI arrest. It was their favorite game. They continued it after they'd vetted everyone who lived there, their fantasies being more interesting than the truth, that the trailer park was occupied by dull and uninspired people.

Private Ramsey laughed uncomfortably. He wasn't sure if Colonel Hollister knew they played that game about him as well. The current bet was that their colonel was assigned to show Elvis around Area 51 and was demoted when Elvis was caught having a three-way with some prostitutes on an alien spacecraft, Elvis having asked them to wear glow-in-the-dark alien masks. That's why he had been assigned to work in Los Alamos, and why they were in Las Vegas, New Mexico watching a trailer park. Being new to the unit and not having the proper security clearance, the analysts didn't know that this story was actually true, except Los Alamos wasn't Colonel Hollister's punishment, it was his promotion.

"Where is he now?" Colonel Hollister asked.

"A couple of blocks away. Alamo and Chavez, sir."

"Perfect. When he gets into camera range, I want

a close up, a nice picture of this Steve Johnson."

Colonel Hollister stood back and crossed his arms, satisfied. Soon they would have him, whoever he was, and Colonel Hollister would get answers to questions that had kept him from sleeping soundly for forty years. He never understood how Elvis could just die like that. One day he's a vibrant, vigorous man, the next he's dead with his pants around his ankles. It didn't make sense. Someone must have learned what Elvis was really doing, why he had all those body doubles performing for him, why he let himself be perceived as a drug-and-woman-crazed lunatic, and decided he was a threat to their machinations. Someone assassinated Elvis. There was only one group Colonel Hollister could think of that would be threatened by Elvis. The same group Colonel Hollister had been hunting his entire life, the same group he recruited Elvis to hunt alongside him.

"Sir," Private Ramsey said, "we have the truck coming into range."

Colonel Hollister stepped closer to the monitor. He squinted at the pixilated image of a truck driving up Alamo Street. The image on the screen was in black and white and he couldn't tell if it was the same truck he saw in satellite images or just another one of the beat-up pick-ups that seemed to infest this town.

The truck drove past the expertly-placed lens, but the driver's face was blurred. Private Ramsey switched angles to a camera that was attached to a telephone pole across from the trailer park. The night before, it had captured the image of a hooded man leaving the park, a perfect view of his face. It helped that the guy had looked right at it. Private Ramsey hoped that the driver would look into what he was starting to call his 'lucky camera'. But the window was up, and they saw a faded reflection of the gas station where they bought microwaveable jalapeño poppers and energy drinks.

He switched to a camera attached to the gate leading into the trailer park. They had to replace this one every few weeks. Some of the local kids discovered it and ripped it down, using it to film homemade zombie movies. Private Ramsey routinely changed its positions and camouflage, hoping it would remain undetected. Now it hung from a tree growing next to the mailboxes, hidden in a birdhouse shaped like a 1920's Craftsman home with purple walls, white roof and trim. Private Ramsey had found it at a yard sale and hoped none of the neighborhood kids would think to look for one of his cameras in it.

The truck turned into the trailer park and stopped in front of a row of mailboxes. The driver pulled some mail out of a box, flipped through a few bills, junk mail, a pennysaver, and tossed them on the truck's floor. He shifted into drive, but waited, his hands on the wheel, like he was thinking about something. He backed up until he was even with the birdhouse and stared at it like he was contemplating its existence. An open beer can sat in the cup holder. The man took a sip, leaned back, sighed. Then he hurled the half-full beer at the birdhouse. The coat hanger holding it to the tree rocked and slipped off the branch, and the birdhouse fell to the ground and shattered.

The camera feed stopped.

"Rewind a couple of frames," Colonel Hollister said.

Private Ramsey tapped at his keyboard. The birdhouse rose from the ground. The beer can flew into the driver's hand, and his slightly blurred image stared into the camera. Private Ramsey outlined the window and cut away everything else. He zoomed in and adjusted the resolution. The image resembled different colored blocks, but, with a few key strokes, Private Ramsey smoothed it out, revealing the man's face.

When the truck turned down Alamo Street, everyone had certain assumptions about the driver's appearance, that he would look like an Elvis impersonator, but what they saw failed to fulfill those expectations. He had short, gray hair, no sideburns. His skin was wrinkled with red splotches, like he had been drinking in the park and passed out under the sun everyday for most of his life. His nose was large and thin veins spread across it. And he was short. Elvis was six feet tall, without platform shoes. This man appeared to be

5'5", his seat pulled close to the steering wheel.

"Goddamnit," Colonel Hollister said, hitting the desk with his hand. He turned his back to the monitor, hands on his hips.

"That was a waste of time," Private Ramsey said.

"Excuse me?" The colonel turned his head.

"Sorry, sir. I'll, uh, I'll tell the men to stand down."

"You do that."

Colonel Hollister paced the living room. He had been at this for forty years, searching every town, city, and suburb in the country, and just when he thought he was getting somewhere, a sixty-year-old alcoholic had to go and throw a beer can into his plans. And Private Ramsey, being so glib. Did he understand what it meant to dedicate one's life to something? sacrificing everything for the mission, family, friends, a life outside of service? He could never perceive the world, see the full scope of it, know the classified knowledge, the hidden dangers, understand that the awareness of those mysteries eliminated choices, compelling the individual to dedicate their life to finding and stopping threats that disguised themselves as friends, ultimately betraying that trust by taking the most beloved person in the world, the son that sacrifices had denied. Private Ramsey couldn't understand what that was like. No one could.

The Abernathy boy would be able to. But he didn't realize it. Not yet.

"Sir," Private Ramsey said, "your orders?"

"Monitor the truck. Let me know where it goes."

"I'm sorry this didn't pan out, sir. I know how much you wanted this to lead to something." Private Ramsey spun his chair, faced Colonel Hollister.

"Do you now?" Colonel Hollister stopped pacing, glared at the private.

"Yes, sir. It's frustrating, spending you time looking for someone, only to…"

"I've been at this a long time, Airman. Longer than you've been alive. And I've learned that patience wins the day. So we'll wait, wait until the man we're looking for shows."

"What if he never comes back? What if he disappears, assumes a new identity, and it takes us another four years to track him down?"

"If this man is who I think he is, it'll take another forty years for him to reappear."

"But…" Private Ramsey put his hands in his lap, studied at them. The last time he Skyped his girlfriend they talked about their future, she'd become a school teacher, he'd work whatever he could while he went to college. Anything was better than a life in Los Alamos. Unfortunately, that's what they'd get, a lifelong assignment in a town of secrets where you needed security clearance to cross the street.

"Don't worry, Private," Colonel Hollister said, with disingenuous interest, "we won't be here long."

In the monitors, the truck parked in front of the trailer from the photo.

"Our enemy is playing a longer game than we are. They've been at it for centuries. So we have to play the long game, too. Whether we want to or not."

The old man stepped out of the truck, carrying the open case of beer. He fumbled with his keys, dropped them and hit his head on the door as he bent over to pick them off the ground. The door popped open. He swayed and laughed and stumbled inside.

"And one of the virtues of playing the long game is that you see each move for what it is, a short step one way or the other. Do you know why this is important, why seeing the world like this is really a beautiful thing?"

"No, sir."

"It means that you have more than one piece in play at all times."

Two men walked up the basement stairs and into the living room. They were the Special Forces operatives that had served as Colonel Hollister's security when he confronted John Abernathy. In a failed attempt to look inconspicuous, they had traded their black uniforms, the vests holding ammunition and other tools of urban soldiering, for windbreakers, jeans, tennis shoes. One man pulled out a gun, checked his clip, and returned it to his shoulder holster.

"So don't worry, Private Ramsey, if our surveillance didn't pan out. It's just one operation, one piece on a very large board."

The drunk slipped on the top step. He tumbled forward, almost falling into the trailer, but caught himself, dropping the case of beer on the floor mat. Three cans popped out, like they were expelled from a malfunctioning vending machine. One Slinkyed end-over-end down the steps, landing on the gravel. The other two rolled across the pitched floor, into the living room, and under the removable coffee table. He swayed for a moment. The closest piece of furniture in the small trailer was a cabinet next to the stove and he flopped against it and yanked off his boots, flipping them. They caromed off the cupboard and sink, landing on the dirt-stained linoleum.

He slapped his cheeks, then looked up at the off-white acoustic tiled ceiling. He shook his head from side to side. He bounced, building momentum, and shook his arms and hands like he was drying himself after a swim. He exhaled three times, rapidly, emptying his lungs of air. On the last breath, he inhaled deeply, filling his chest and stomach, then grunted, loud and painful, like he was giving birth to a walrus with diamond-studded tusks.

His legs stretched and grew until the hem of his pants ended at his calves. His arms grew out of the sleeves, and his torso expanded, untucking his shirt. The thin, gray hairs on his head blackened and thickened, growing several inches on the top, until it formed a perfect pompadour. Sideburns grew from the pores along his jaw, ending just below his ears. The skin and the wrinkles around his eyes, the visual representation of his guzzled and seldom remembered life, tightened. The skin on his body that sagged, his chin, man boobs, the undersides of his arms, retracted until they resembled the semi-freshness of middle-age. His bulbous nose, the physical sign of his alcoholism, reverted, the veins disappearing, the extra cartilage vanishing. He unbuttoned his shirt and pants as his stomach inflated into a small gut, and he wiggled his toes underneath it.

"Thank you. Thank you very much," Al Leadbelly said, finally returning home.

He hadn't used his 'Gus' disguise in years. Leadbelly was grateful John had warned him about the Air Force, giving him an excuse to become the old alcoholic for an afternoon. He knew they were watching him, even before the bar fight. Over the past week he'd been careful, drifting between the blind spots of their inefficiently placed cameras. He also knew he'd have to leave town eventually. He'd even prepared for it. But John showing at his job meant Leadbelly had to accelerate his plans, or as he liked to say in moments of drunken cheesiness, 'Get the Lead out.'

He opened the cabinet under the sink, the thin, brown door. He took out the trashcan, spilling SpaghettiOs cans, candy bar wrappers, empty, cheese-filled hot dog packages, and empty tins of cake icing. Behind where the trashcan rested, a hole had been drilled into the wall. Leadbelly stuck his finger in it, pushed the button inside it. The floor popped open, a false bottom. Among fake passports, stacks of cash, and a copy of *Elvis, Live in Nöbsak, Germany*, was an encrypted cell phone, bedazzled with the image of a naked woman.

"He's here, man," Leadbelly said. "I, uh, I talked to him a couple a minutes ago."

The voice on the other end sounded shrill, berating him. He rolled his eyes. He'd spent his entire life working for them, helping them achieve small objectives, miniscule pieces of a larger goal, and they still didn't trust him.

"Yeah, I know what to do. I, uh, I won't let you down... Seriously, man, you're gonna bring that up? That was just that one time...It won't...If you woulda seen her. The way she was shaking her...Shit, you're really gonna...Jesus Christ, it was just that one time...And that time in Atlantic City. But that was it. I swear...Alright. And in New Orleans...Calm down. I got this...You don't got…You don't got nothing to worry about, man…I know that's what I said last time, but this time I mean it…Alright, I love you, too, Momma. See you soon."

All the work he did, hiding and documenting, it was against his nature. Leadbelly was born for greatness, born to entertain thousands of people, sweating under the lights, getting women's panties tossed at him on stage, partying all night with devoted female fans. Not this covert business. It was enough to make an Elvis impersonator start drinking.

Leadbelly snatched a beer from his fridge and chugged half of it. He broke the phone in half, removed the SIM card. The phone clanged against the dirty dishes and basin as Leadbelly tossed it in the sink. He put the card in his pocket, his unbuttoned pants hanging loosely around his hips. He couldn't believe they thought he was careless.

He had spent the past four years living in the trailer, a home away from home. At first he resented being sent there, viewing it as a punishment. He had lived most of his adult life in the real Vegas, the one with the showgirls and cheap, all-you-can-eat buffets and lax public drunkenness policies. Then he was unexpectedly sent back here, back to where everything started. He didn't understand it at first, but when he saw John at the lumberyard, he understood why he'd been sent there, why he had to wait. He just wondered when the others, the ones who exiled him, would let him tell John the truth.

The shirt and pants clung to his body like plastic wrap on an old ham. They smelled like stale booze and baloney. His regular clothes lay in piles on his bedroom floor. Leadbelly yanked on the accordion door, trying to get to them. It popped out of the wall and its runner, screws, and small, plastic wheels flew across the room. He stumbled back a few steps, the door in his hand. Laughing, he tossed it onto his unmade bed, brown sheets wadded at its foot. His room was just as he left it, clothes covering his bedroom floor, his closet door shut. He pulled a pair of pants and a shirt from one pile and sniffed them. Clean enough. And tossed the smaller clothes against the wall.

He'd be going home soon. He'd have to answer a lot of questions, what he'd been doing all this time, why he only called when he needed money, why he never married or settled down. He didn't like the idea of moving home. He'd be around friends, but it wasn't the same as being on his own. No one to answer to, staying up as late as he wanted, playing his music whenever he felt like it. Moving home just seemed like a step backward.

His stomach growled like he hadn't eaten since lunch.

"Beer munchies," he said, rubbing his belly.

In the kitchen, he slopped together some sandwiches, peanut butter and banana, while singing a song about how much he loved sandwiches and wished he had some hot sauce to put on them. His trailer smelled like suntan lotion spread on the back of giant, monocle-wearing peanut. He shoved a couple in his mouth, choked a little, then washed them down with another beer, and Ziplocked the rest, setting them on the counter.

His trailer was full of trash accumulated through neglect and indifference. And even though he was moving, he knew he couldn't leave it like that. Leadbelly opened his cupboard and pulled out a long knife.

In his living room, the aquarium and karate trophies. A girl he met in a bar in Tucson told him should get a pet. He found the aquarium at a rummage sale and inadvertently killed the first three fish to swim in its green and slimed waters. Not wanting to see any more two-dollar fish float upside down, it became a convenient place to store his karate trophies. He tossed the empty aquarium onto the floor, breaking it. Karate statues tumbled to the ground. He never really liked the aquarium. Foam stuffing spilled from the couch cushions as he slashed them. He flipped his coffee table and kicked his chair, breaking both. He emptied the cupboards in his kitchen, sending pots and pans skidding against the ground, and dumped the drawers. Utensils, coupons, and a rubber band ball crashed, floated, and bounced on the linoleum.

In his bedroom, he jerked his drawers out of the

built-in chest and dumped out the few clothes, socks, wife-beater t-shirts, underwear with stretched out elastic. He picked up a red gym bag that lay in the corner. A light traveler, he liked to pack the essentials. He took a deep breath and opened his closet. When he saw the jumpsuit, he smiled.

"Oh, baby, it's good to see you again," Leadbelly said.

He gently took the sequined jumpsuit off the rack. He hadn't worn it in four years. But every night he opened his closet and dreamed of a time when it was all he wore and longed for the day when he could wear it again. He held the jumpsuit in both hands, one hand on the back of it, tickling the sequins with his fingers. Light danced across the eagle's chest. The gold stars shimmered around it.

He lowered it on the bed and slowly slid the zipper down, exposing the white interior of the suit. The hanger flopped in the shoulders and he tossed it like a Frisbee. It hit the bedroom window, landing on a pile of clothes. He scooped up the suit and folded it neatly, legs underneath, arms behind the back, and nestled it into the gym bag, finally putting it on the closet floor.

His room was a pile of dirty clothes, food wrappers, and cheap cologne in plastic bottles. Leadbelly felt it sent a certain message to anyone who visited, that he was too busy loving life and the loving the ladies to clean up, but this wasn't the message he wanted to send anymore. He plunged the knife into his bed, slashing it. He lifted the mattress and heaved it against the far wall and cut large, diagonal gashes into its back. A hole had already been cut in the box spring. Leadbelly leaned over and pulled out a book and a stack of three-hundred and twelve photos. He flipped through the photos, sighed, and set them next to the book, its cracked leather back barely holding the cover together. The people who sent him to the trailer park thought it was lost, but Leadbelly had kept it hidden for years like it was a once-in-a-lifetime find.

He took the book, closed his eyes, and kissed it.

"Shame I never got to know you, man," he said to the book, "but you never gave me the chance. You were right, I know that now. It was the right call. But still..." That sonuvabitch abandoned him, sent him away to be raised in the desert. Even though it had taken him years to understand why it had to happen, when he thought about it, it still hurt.

He wiped a tear from his eye. He set the photos on the edge of the box spring. Next to the knife.

The book that he'd protected for all those years was his father's journal. Leadbelly's heart almost exploded when he first read his father's thoughts and words, his love and hopes for the son he kept. And just a few sentences about Leadbelly, nothing more, coldly describing his thought process in deciding which child to keep. Leadbelly's mother tried to explain to him why his father chose another son, but Leadbelly was young and angry and didn't understand. He wanted to hurt his father, to make him feel what it was like to lose something you loved, but his father died before Leadbelly had a chance to meet him. When he was alone in his trailer, a tipped-over bottle of whiskey spilling on the floor, Leadbelly often wondered how his life would have been different if he had been allowed to stay. He wouldn't have become an Elvis impersonator, he knew that much. Sitting on the box spring, he felt the anger building, urging him to lash out, to destroy something. He touched the book to his forehead, set it on the photos. He picked up the knife, his face reflected on the blade.

And slashed at the mattress again.

Leadbelly panted and wiped the sweat with his sleeve. He opened another beer and grabbed the sandwiches in the kitchen.

The clock, now resting on the floor, the image of a beer spokesmodel on its face, her arms gradually moving to beer-thirty.

The jumpsuit lay neatly packed on the closet floor. He loved it more than cheap beer, an open mic, or a middle-aged woman with questionable morals. It needed to be protected, remain clean and unsoiled for his travels. He layered the gym bag with Saran Wrap and tossed in a couple of beers and the other peanut butter and banana sandwiches. He picked a couple of black socks off the floor and sniffed them. They smelled like rotten fish, but he shrugged his shoulders and slipped them on, zipping the black patent leather boots over them.

Dressed, packed. Cameras were aimed at his front door. This didn't bother him. One thing he learned working in Las Vegas was the headliner always leaves by the back door. He stepped over the piles of clothes, the empty cupboards, the Styrofoam barbeque takeout boxes that blocked his way to the closet. Leadbelly tapped the closet floor with his foot. A spring-release trapdoor popped up. He caught it with his foot before it closed again and propped it against the wall. The brown and gray gravel of the trailer park lot floated underneath him. Leadbelly dropped the gym bag onto the New Mexico dirt. There was a foot and a half between the bottom of the trailer and the ground. Leadbelly lowered his legs through, until he was sitting on grease-stained earth, the upper half of his body still in the closet. He sucked in his belly, slid out, and rolled from under the trailer.

He emerged behind the trailer, between it and a chain link fence that had chunks of green plastic woven throughout. He sat up and started to rise, but stopped. He slapped his head, having forgotten something, and rolled back under, hearing the same critiques, that he was careless, forgetful, selfish.

A pile of clothes was underneath the mattress. Leadbelly pushed it aside and searched for the jeans he wore when he was pretending to be a drunk. Needing a safer place for incriminating evidence, he dug the SIM card out of the front pocket and opened his wallet. The compartments were full of gas receipts, small images cut from porn magazines, and an old condom. He threw the condom across the room. He didn't use them anyway, couldn't feel nothing with them on. He slipped the SIM card into the empty slot and rolled out of the trailer again.

He stood in the gap between the trailer and fence and lifted a panel that had been built into the side of the trailer. Underneath it was a keypad. Leadbelly entered a sequence into it and heard a noise coming from inside the trailer. It sounded like his trailer had been converted into a large toilet and someone had just flushed it. He entered another code. A timer appeared on the screen, counting down. He closed the panel, his hand lingering on the side of the trailer. It had been his home for the past four years, the place he slept, ate, snuck to when he tip-toed out of women's bedrooms late at night. Leadbelly sighed. He'd actually miss this place, the town, the trailer park. But it wasn't the only town out there. The country was full of towns, trailers, and women. Maybe they'd let him go back to Vegas. Do it up, Elvis style. Leadbelly scooped up the gym bag by the strap. He patted its underside and heard the jumpsuit rustle. He grinned, his lip curling up.

He shimmied between the trailer and the fence, heading to the back of the trailer park, staying in the camera's blind spots. The chain link fence that separated the trailer park from its neighbors had been by cut by kids, a potential escape route from bottle rocket fights. Leadbelly slipped into someone's backyard. He stepped over rusted tricycles and a small swimming pool shaped like a turtle, and through the front gate.

In the street, dogs behind fences barked with aggressive insecurity. Children somersaulted and cartwheeled out of minivans while moms carried grocery bags, three in each hand. Dads parked their trucks, eyed their neighbors' boats. Leadbelly stood in the middle of family activity, needing to find something to do for the next fourteen hours. In front of him was the town where he'd had four years of small exploits. He thought about where a man of his tastes could feel welcome, relax, and find some entertainment. He smiled wide and strutted down Silva Avenue, heading toward Brandi Cartwright's house.

Away from the last four years of his life.

Away from his father's journal, still sitting on box spring's edge.

CHAPTER THIRTEEN

As he got closer to Rosa's Restaurante, the feeling John had been carrying in his stomach all day moved upward. It wasn't the same intestinal twisting he'd endured earlier. His chest pulsated and, despite the cool evening, he began to sweat. He laughed at how unglued he was becoming, and knew it was because he was anxious about seeing Rosa again. The last time a girl shook his nerves he was in high school, standing by the lockers waiting for Alison Mayhew to get out of her eighth-period art class. He intended to ask her to the prom, but when she walked by with a group of friends, John panicked. He stood with his back to the lockers, awkwardly waiting for the bell to ring while the group of girls giggled and collected their books. John was technically an adult now, had outgrown his teenage insecurities. He'd overcome his fear of rejection, and tonight he had another advantage, something aiding his courage. He'd been drinking most of the day.

The sign on Rosa's glass door said she'd be closing in an hour. John exhaled and opened it. The bell above him rang, the smell of cooking meat and peppers hit his nose.

Food sizzled.

A wooden lattice with fake vines separated foyer from dining area. A girl who looked like she was in high school, menus in hand, asked, "How many?"

"Um, I was wondering if I could talk to Rosa for a minute, if that'd be alright?" John asked, stepping side to side.

"Uh, sure. Let me see if she's around," she said, and walked into the back.

In the foyer, carry-out menus fanned on a table. Maroon vinyl covering stackable chairs. The local newspaper reporting football scores, weekend sales. In the dining area, two tables had customers.

The restaurant was mostly quiet. The background music had been turned off, although music came from a small radio in the kitchen. It was soft and John heard Rosa's footsteps. She walked toward him, wiping her hands on a towel hanging from her apron. John grinned. When he crossed the street, he wondered if he'd still feel the same excitement he felt at lunch, still want to be near her. And watching her glide toward him, all he could think was how lucky he was that he had another chance to see her again, and he wondered if she felt the same way.

Rosa kept a straight face at first, professional, but when she recognized John, she blushed and tucked a loose strand of hair behind her ear.

"Are you back for dinner?" she asked, putting her

hands in her apron pockets.

John's face warmed. He looked away, adjusted his glasses, suddenly reticent.

His drunkenness vanished, as did his confidence. He wondered had what compelled him to run across the Plaza and into the restaurant. There was no way she'd want to hang out with him. All he could offer her was an encyclopedic knowledge of puzzle history and the proper aperture for photographing a grown man's back hair. But there she stood, smiling at him, waiting for him to say something.

"No, I already ate."

"Cheating on me already?" she said, tilting her head to the side.

"What? Uh, no, I..." John said.

"I'm just kidding." She touched his sleeve.

"Oh, okay," John said, blushing. "The reason why I came over was, well, I was wondering, um, Rosa, I know this might sound kind of odd, but I was, I was wondering if you wanna have a drink with me? After you got off work, I mean." Then added, "If you're busy or something, I understand. I just thought it'd be a nice way to spend the evening, spending time with you, I mean."

"Aw, John, you're sweet. Of course I'll have a drink with you. Sometimes I like to go to the place across the street." She pointed to the scene of Leadbelly's bar fight.

"You want to meet there when you're done?"

"I should be done here around nine."

"Okay," he said, relieved. "I'll see you around nine."

Still looking at Rosa, John pulled on the door. It stuck. He laughed and looked away, embarrassed, then pushed on the door. He faced his flustered reflection in the glass. Beyond his image, Rosa watched him, smiling. His small victory created new warmth, insulating him from the cold night air.

She wanted to see him again. John bounced into the street, slapping the trunks of parked cars, feeling confident, validated. It was like when he was in his senior year and one of his puzzles won the award for 'Most Ironic Use of 1980's Television Show Titles'. That night, award rolled in his hand, he felt like he could accomplish anything, like he was on the four-letter word for 'narrow walkway' to crossword stardom. He felt the same way leaving Rosa's, only this time there was the potential for nudity and adult situations.

Sheriff Masters leaned against a light post.

"So?" he said, sticking out his hands, raising his shoulders.

"She's meeting me for a drink at nine. Wanna get something to drink, keep me company till Rosa shows up? The *Enquirer's* still buying."

"Hell yeah."

* * * *

The same bartender from earlier was still working, wiping pint glasses, pouring brown liquor into small glasses. John nodded toward him. He nodded back.

The sheriff and John grabbed a couple of barstools. Sheriff Masters put his Chesterfield Stetson on the seat next to him. Some old-timers and a few people close to the sheriff's age in dirty jeans and sweat-stained, straw cowboy hats hovered around the bar or sat at small tables having drinks. In the back, sitting silently at a table, two men nursed their beers. Lines of intense focus creased their foreheads and led to empty eyes staring into full drinks. They frowned at something invisible, their mouths tight and severe. John recognized the men as two of the soldiers who'd broken into his hotel room the night before. He'd been thinking about Rosa most of the day, imagining scenarios, conversations, and had forgotten all about them. The interactions he invented pushed them from his mind. But seeing them sitting in the back of the bar brought him out of his fantasies, and he felt the knife on his throat and heard Colonel Hollister's words right before he'd hung up the phone.

"Oh shit," John said, sitting down. He patted his hands on his legs. "You see those two in the back?"

"Yup."

"They came to my room last night." John didn't turn around, hoping that by not looking at them they'd vanish, a thought reflex from childhood.

"You know prostitution's illegal in New Mexico,

but, hey I don't judge."

"They're with the Air Force."

"Some people just love a man in uniform."

"They handcuffed me to a chair." John rubbed his wrists.

"Bondage, huh? You pay extra for that?"

"They're looking for Leadbelly. Their boss asked me to find him for them. I called them, told them Leadbelly left town."

"Think they're looking for you?" the sheriff asked, suddenly alert.

"They haven't come over yet, so probably not," John said, hoping that Colonel Hollister had sent them here to find Leadbelly, suspecting he hadn't left town, that they would eventually leave to look for him elsewhere, and John could have a quiet evening with Rosa.

"Uncle Lee." The bartender came over, threw some coasters on the bar.

"Levi, this here's John Abernathy. John, this is my nephew Levi."

"We met earlier."

"Levi," the sheriff said, leaning over the bar, "don't look, but those two men in the back, you recognize them?"

"They were in here the other night, talking to the kid Leadbelly beat up. They were only here a couple of minutes. Didn't even order anything. Just talked with the kid for a bit and left."

"How long have they been here tonight?"

"They showed up a couple of hours ago, asking about Rosa."

"Rosa? Not Leadbelly?" John asked, wrinkling his forehead.

"Yeah, Rosa. They've asked everyone in the bar about her."

"What did you tell them?"

"Nothing. Told them I didn't know her," Levi said, wiping the bar with a towel. "The way they were acting, trying to intimidate my customers, like they'd kick some ass if they didn't find her. They even tried slipping me some cash."

"Douches," John said.

"I told them to save their money and order drinks. Now they're just sitting there nursing their beers, taking a table from my regulars."

"Yeah," the sheriff said, "sitting by the window."

"With a good view of Rosa's," John added, turning to the window, the seated men.

"John, you see those bulges on their left sides? That's usually a sign they're packing."

"When they came up to the bar," Levi said, "one leaned over. His jacket was half zipped up. He had a gun in a shoulder holster."

"I'm gonna get my service revolver outta the car." The sheriff started to get up.

"Wait," John said, grabbing his arm. "We don't wanna tip our hand."

"Levi," the sheriff said, "you still have that Walther PPK I gave you behind the bar?"

"Yeah. And Ol' Bonethumper."

"You still got that? I remember making that with your dad." The sheriff turned to John and clarified, "It's a sawed-off ax handle, about a foot and a half long." He held his fingers apart, showing its size. "When they make their move I want you to slip me Bonethumper, okay?"

John had never been in a fight before, but the thought of saving Rosa from the same men who had broken into his hotel room electrified him. His legs vibrated under his skin and he rubbed them, trying to settle them down. He imagined Rosa's reaction when he saved her, the way she'd look at him, with gratitude and desire. And he knew what he had to do.

"I'll take Bonethumper," John said.

"You sure?" the sheriff asked.

"If one of us is gonna go all Whack-a-Mole on these guys, better it's not the sheriff. I don't want anyone accusing you of police brutality." That's the excuse he gave, not wanting to tell them that he was energized by the prospect of a fight.

"You expecting trouble?" Levi asked, re-wiping an already dry glass.

"Probably not," the sheriff said. "It's just in case. They'll probably just leave, then we'll follow them, see what trouble they're up to."

"Levi," John said, pointing toward him, "if something does happen you gotta pull that gun, cover your uncle. Got it?"

"Got it." The rings on Levi's fingers rattled against the pint glass he was wiping.

"Here, have a shot on me." John's hand shook as he pulled some cash from his wallet. "Looks like I better have one. I'll take a PBR Tall Boy, too."

"Get me a whiskey on the rocks, with a splash of water," the sheriff said.

The adrenaline that eclipsed John waned. He slouched, elbows on the bar, and questioned why he was so anxious for violence. He'd avoided conflict most of his life, hiding in puzzles instead. This urge to communicate rage through violence felt foreign, like a part of him was changing. But the two men in the back were looking for Rosa. John sat up and took the shot Levi poured him, swearing he wouldn't let anything happen to her.

The bar slowly filled while John and the sheriff sipped their drinks. Several men talked to the sheriff, registering small town complaints over pints of cheap beer. The sheriff introduced John as a friend from Denver. John smiled, nodded. He used it as an opportunity to watch the men in the back. They took small sips every time John turned.

He also watched the clock behind the bar. The hands appeared to be frozen, unable to reach nine and twelve, the cue for Rosa's entrance. He wondered if she regretted agreeing to meet him, if she'd changed her mind and decided to head home and forget about the skinny kid who awkwardly asked her out. He couldn't blame her. She barely knew him, and he was only in town for a couple of days. Still, he didn't think he could take it if she didn't show. The sheriff would make some joke and John would have to sit at the bar longer than he wanted, pretending he was too cool to be dejected, trying to judge the right time to leave.

And if she did come out, that'd be worse. He'd have to be interesting, funny, charming. The last time he had to impress a girl he was at a student art show, glass of boxed wine in his hand. His roommate had fixed him up with a fashion design major, a student award winner, whose work was comprised of evening gowns made out of restraining orders and Ed Hardy t-shirts. He charmed her for the first hour, but when he ran out of conversation material he reverted to talking about his favorite *Cape Canaveral* episodes and puzzle theory and she left with another artist, also a student award winner, who constructed sculptures out of mummified pigeons. By the time he started working for Rooftop, he was out of practice, had forgotten how to be interesting. And sitting on the barstool, he kept telling himself, 'Don't talk about *Cape Canaveral*, don't talk about *Cape Canaveral...*' repeating it mantra-like.

Then he saw Rosa standing at the door, radiant, glimmering, and his thoughts evaporated, were forgotten.

She stood at the door, looking around. John half-stood and waved exuberantly, childlike. He quickly dropped his hand, embarrassed. Rosa waved gracefully and floated over, otherworldly. She wore a dark green leather jacket, and a green, gossamer scarf was wrapped several times around her neck, hanging loosely around the neckline of her black dress. Soft and black, her hair was down, brushing her shoulders as she glided toward John. She ran her hand through it, her fingers piercing the dyed blue streak.

John stood as Rosa reached out to hug him. He hugged her with one arm and held the bar with his free hand for support, like the moment had made him lightheaded.

"Hello, John," she said releasing him. "Lee, are you keeping John company for me?"

The sheriff took his hat off the barstool next to him and slid over. "Rosa, why don't you take this seat? I've been keeping it warm for you."

Rosa sat between them.

"Uh, Rosa. Hey?" Levi glanced toward the men seated at the table by the window. "What are...what are you doing here?"

"John invited me out for a drink. Can I get a bourbon neat, please?" She put her hand on John's arm. John smiled and leaned in.

"Uh, yeah. Okay." Levi brought Rosa her drink, staring at the men in the back.

"Is he okay?" she asked John.

"It's nothing to worry about," John said, sipping his drink. He wanted to relax and forget about the men in the back and everything they promised. He wanted to focus on Rosa, enjoy the moment with her. She made him feel alive, like he could fill out a crossword with his left hand while arm wrestling a polar bear wearing a luchador's mask.

Rosa smiled, sweet but guarded, hiding what really made her happy. John hoped it could be him.

They talked for a while. He told her about puzzles, *Cape Canaveral*, made bad jokes. She laughed and touched his arm. John reached out to touch her, but pulled back. Instead, he smiled and leaned in closer, until there was almost nothing separating them. Their legs brushed. John laughed, jerked his leg away, then moved it back. Rosa put her hand on his knee. John inched his fingers over to touch her hand, excited to feel her skin under his fingers.

Then he heard a thunk.

And quickly turned to the bar.

Ol' Bonethumper lay on the bar in front of him. The words 'Ol' Bonethumper' had been burned into the ax handle with a magnifying glass, a technique from Sun Burnt Portraiture 202. Levi motioned toward the back. John swept Ol' Bonethumper off the bar with his left hand, holding it so it was hidden behind his forearm.

The two men moved toward them, bumping and pushing people out of their way, causing drinks to spill. Those with wet and boozy hands spun around, started to say something, but stopped at the sight of the two men walking with the gait and disposition of men willing to do anything.

"Rosa, get behind me," John said.

The men stood in front of them. Sheriff Masters and John slid around, forcing the men to press their backs to each other, trapping them.

"Rosa Jimenez," one of them said, looking right through John, "please come with us. We have some questions we'd like to ask you."

"What do you want with her?" John asked, surprised by the authority in his voice.

"That's none of your concern," he said, not looking at John. "Ms. Jimenez, I'm not going to ask again. You need to come with us."

He reached past John with his left hand and clutched her arm, exposing his gun in its shoulder holster.

"Let's go. Now," he said, squeezing.

"Hey! Ow!" Rosa cried, as he yanked her arm.

John was always irritated at something. Rooftop would tease him, saying it was art school snobbery, but his outward irritability hid a suppressed rage, fueled by the twice-held-back grade school thug who made fun of him for not having a dad, the editors that sent him rejection letters, having to photograph a cheating husband getting dry humped by a mega-church pastor wearing an inflatable Sumo wrestler suit. He never expressed his frustrations through violence, instead opting for snide remarks or a misdirected tantrum, usually when discussing his father, but when the man grabbed Rosa, John erupted.

He grabbed the man's wrist and reared back to hit him with the handcrafted baton.

John woke on the barroom floor. His mouth was wet and the liquid tasted like iron and he knew he was tasting his own blood.

"Is he dead?" Levi asked, pointing the gun at the other man. He leaned over the bar, glancing down at John.

"Keep your gun on him," John said, pointing to the sheriff's man. He reached for the barstools and lifted himself up. His legs swayed and an older, bearded man helped him stand. John gripped the bar for support. He wiped the blood from his face with some bar napkins. His perception seemed compressed and he heard a faint but constant tone. The concussion symptoms quickly vanished and the world around him glared with the acute sensitivity of an exposed nerve.

The stench of liquor. The whispers from the drunken crowd in the bar. A man lay on the floor, his limp body bleeding between empty barstools and broken bottles. John remembered him grabbing Rosa. He remembered trying to step in. Then darkness.

John leaned over and said, "Jesus Christ. What happened?"

"That fella knocked you out," the sheriff said, pointing to the man on the ground. He pointed to the older, bearded man. "Then Charlie and the boys went all 'Whack-a-Mole' on him. You'd better search that sonuvabitch, if you can."

The sheriff grabbed the conscious man, spun him against the bar, and began searching his pockets.

"I'm a federal agent," the man said.

"Mister," the sheriff said, shoving him into the bar, "look around. You think anyone here gives a shit about the federal government?"

The man on the floor was lying on his back, one arm knitted into the legs of a barstool. John knelt by him. Blood ran down the man's face, staining his collar. John put two fingers against the man's neck, checked his pulse.

"He's alive. Just unconscious."

Some of the man's blood was on John's fingers and John rubbed his thumb against them, smearing the blood.

The man's jacket was open, the gun exposed. John put it in his hoodie pocket. Another gun was in a holster around the man's ankle, a smaller one. The man the sheriff searched had the same guns on him. Neither of them had any ID.

"Where's your ID, G-man?" the sheriff asked.

"I'm undercover."

"Sure. And I'm the King of Las Vegas."

"Sheriff, this guy's got a thousand dollars on him," John said, counting the cash.

"Same with this here fella."

John handed his money to the sheriff. Sheriff Masters put half in his pocket, threw a thousand dollars on the bar. "Looks like drinks are on these fellas tonight."

Everyone in the bar laughed, their mouths watering for their next drink.

"Charlie," the sheriff said to the older, bearded man, "I'm gonna call the station, have them send Jimmy out here to get these fellas. Keep an eye on them for me would you."

"I already called," Charlie said.

Within seconds they heard sirens. A deputy was followed into the bar by a couple of paramedics with a gurney. The deputy was in his early forties. His hair was short, spiked on top and long in the back, reaching his uniform's collar. The sides of his head were shaved. Gray whiskers lit his Fu Manchu mustache.

"Levi, bro, what's up?" He extended his fist toward Levi. The bartender rolled his eyes, but gave him the fist bump. "Rosa, what's up, mamacita?"

"Jimmy." She folded her arms and took a step closer to John. Her jacket grazed John's sleeve, and for a second, he was happy.

"Uncle Lee, what's up?" he said, then saw the man on the floor. "Fuck! Dude, what happened?

"A bar fight, Jimmy," the sheriff said. He gripped the back of conscious man's shirt and shook it. "I need you to cuff this fella, take him to the station for processing."

"Bro, that guy got fucked up," Jimmy said, pointing to the injured man. The sheriff grabbed handcuffs from Jimmy's belt and put them on the standing man. "That the guy that did it?"

"That would be your Uncle Charlie's doing."

The paramedics put a neck brace on the man, rolled him onto his back. The man on the ground, it wasn't like it was in video games, where battered bodies vanished, became points earning you weapons upgrades. They never showed everything that resulted from the blunt force trauma, the blood, the surgeries, hospital bills, physical therapy, a lifetime of replaying the moment in your head and editing it slightly each time, trying to figure out how the violent confrontation could have been altered or avoided.

John touched his jaw, wiggled it, then his nose, searching for some sign that he'd been a participant in the fight. But he was unmarked.

"Are you alright?" Rosa whispered.

John didn't respond, unsure of what to tell her, that he was fine? was unexplainably uninjured after being punched in the face? that he felt guilt, fear, and shame that the other man was being hospitalized? Instead, he shrugged and watched the man being wheeled out.

"Let's go outside." Rosa took his arm and gently led him toward the open door. Her hand on his arm was warm and he let her guide him.

"Dude, who the fuck's this guy?" Jimmy asked, stepping in front of them. "Rosa, this guy bothering you? Bro, you bothering Rosa?"

"Goddamnit, Jimmy," the sheriff said. "Stop Mickey Mousing around and do your job."

"Sorry, Uncle Lee." Jimmy grabbed the handcuffed man.

"When you're done booking him, I need you to head to the hospital. Make sure you cuff that sorry looking sonuvabitch to the bed. These boys are ornery."

"Dude, what do you want me to book them for?"

Sheriff Masters grabbed a drink off the bar and threw it in the handcuffed man's face. The man flinched as booze and melting ice hit him and soaked his collar. "Book them on a 'drunk and disorderly'."

Everyone laughed.

"You can't do this. I'm a federal agent," the man said.

"Yeah, yeah, keep talking," the sheriff said.

Jimmy seized the man's neck, started to lead him outside.

"You're dead!" the man shouted over his shoulder. "Next time I see you, you're dead!"

Jimmy took him to a squad car. The paramedics strapped the other man to the gurney and wheeled him out.

"Lee," Charlie said, "me and the boys'll follow. Make sure they make it to the station and hospital."

"Thanks, Charlie."

A half dozen men left the bar, following Jimmy. A rush of fresh air from the open door caused John's thoughts to move quickly, like they were unimpaired by the violence, and he connected the sheriff to the bearded man leaving the bar.

"Charlie's your cousin?" he asked the sheriff.

"Yup."

"It must be nice to have a big family," John said, thinking about his mom and how it had always been the two of them, and how, for the first time, he wished that there was someone else.

"You have no idea. You have no idea," he said, hands on his belt, smile as wide as a dried-out river bed. "You want the paramedics to take a look at you real quick?"

"I'm fine," John said, feeling his jaw and the other places that should have been sore. He couldn't explain it. He had taken a beating, had been knocked unconscious, probably hit his head in the fall. There should have been some swelling or loose teeth. But his jaw didn't ache, his nose wasn't broken. He really did feel fine.

Sheriff Masters finished his drink in one gulp.

"Well, I'll leave you kids to it. I gotta check all this into evidence." He swept the guns into his hat.

"Then head home. Shirley's probably worried sick. John, good working with you. You got my number. Give me a call if you need anything."

John dropped the guns he removed from the bleeding man into the sheriff's hat. He held the door for Rosa as they followed the sheriff outside and watched him leave.

Bridge Street traffic cleared for the paramedics as they drove away, sirens chirping, red lights slicing dirty air.

The crowd went inside, but John stayed on the sidewalk, staring at the empty space where the ambulance had been parked. Wanting to comfort him, Rosa put her hand on his shoulder. John flinched, not because she touched him unexpectedly, but because he was surprised that after all the violence, she was still there.

John sat on a park bench in front of the store next to the bar. A green plank along its back was missing, and wrought iron ends bolted it to the concrete. His mind drifted and he studied the pavement, the places where the tree roots stretched underground and cracked the concrete. Rosa put her hand on his thigh. It was supposed to console him, but her touch only reminded John of everything that had happened.

"I'm sorry you had to see that," he said. He leaned over and stared at a flattened cigarette butt.

"That man was hurting me," Rosa said, rubbing her arm.

"I'm not a violent person. I just reacted."

"If you hadn't, I don't know what would have happened. Then Charlie and the others…"

"It's just, ever since I left school, I haven't been doing anything for myself."

"The look in that man's eyes…"

"Working for Roof, coming here, this isn't me. It doesn't feel like me. It feels like someone else is walking in my skin."

"If you hadn't been here, there's no telling what they would have done."

"I feel like there's something missing from my life."

"I think we're all missing something."

"I'm not a violent person." John rubbed his jaw, the places where he'd been hit. "I guess I'm not much of anything."

"The guys in town are…they're like Jimmy. They're crude versions of middle-aged men, going to high school wrestling matches, the demolition derby. And the guys that come through town, the ones going skiing in the mountains, they act like a night with them would be the best thing that ever happened to me. Or they look right through me, don't see me at all, but you, when you look at me…I don't know, it just…it makes me feel special. No one's ever…"

"I've never been in a fight in my life. That man…Everyone standing over him like that. Now he's in the hospital." John's fingers still had blood on them. But it had dried. He ran his hand over his head, checking for lumps, signs that he'd hit it against the bar or floor when he fell, but all he felt were the natural contours of his cranium. And he wondered if he'd suffered at all during the fight.

"John, it's okay." She put her hand on his forearm, rubbed her thumb against his sleeve. With each thumb stroke, John felt himself relaxing. He reclined in the bench and placed his hand on hers, felt her soft skin, the warmth beneath it, a warmth that the two men tried to take from him.

"Rosa, I gotta ask, what did those men want with you?"

"I don't know. I've never seen them before."

"Those same men, they were here last night looking for Leadbelly. Now they're looking for you. What kind of trouble did Leadbelly get you into?"

"Nothing." She looked away. "There's nothing to tell. I don't even know Leadbelly. I just see him around town every now and then."

"Rosa, I can't help you if you're not straight with me."

"John, there's nothing to tell," Rosa said. She leaned closer to him and lightly caressed John's fingers, sending a jolt through him. He shook his head like he was waking, and forgot what he was going to ask her.

"What do you think they wanted?" Rosa asked.

John didn't tell her everything, that the two men were with the Air Force, had broken into his hotel room, were spying on Leadbelly because of the photos hanging in his trailer. Instead, he said, "Those two men, they probably think you know where Leadbelly is. Wait, you seemed awfully concerned for Leadbelly at lunch. You and he weren't...you know..."

"Oh, God! Gross," Rosa said, laughing. "Al's...No. Definitely no."

"Okay. That's good to know, 'cause that guy..." John shook his head. "But, you need to level with me. You could be in real danger here. I can't help you unless you talk to me."

"John, you're sweet." She put her hand on his. "There's nothing to tell. It's probably a case of mistaken identity. Lee will figure it out tomorrow."

Rosa was hiding a secret world from John, one involving herself and Leadbelly and the Air Force. And John knew it. But right then he didn't care. He should have been worried, suspicious, but he wasn't. He was just happy to be with her, sitting next to her, inhaling her intoxicating scent.

And as he breathed in, the smells of the street, the cooling asphalt, the ashtray next to the bench disappeared. Even the sounds coming from the bar faded away and John heard his breath and nothing else, like a bubble had formed around them, isolating them from the evening. And all he could smell was Rosa.

His mind became cloudy, unfocused. Everything blurred. Images became soft shapes. Everything except Rosa. She glowed. A red aura surrounded her perfect frame. For a second, John froze, staring at her, and everything felt right. Then the moment passed. His vision returned. Suddenly he didn't care about Leadbelly, the Air Force, the bar fight. He just wanted to be as close to Rosa as possible.

"Yeah, you're probably right. What do you say we get a couple more drinks?"

"I have a better idea." She leaned closer to John, her lips near his ear, and whispered, "What do you say we get out of here?"

* * * *

Rosa took the key from John and opened the door. Pink and green lights from the motel's neon sign mingled and blended on the carpet, forming a new shade that would exist until the door closed.

It could have been the alcohol, or the nerves, or something showing them the humor in two people who just met stumbling into in a motel late at night, but they laughed as Rosa led him into the room. She turned her head to her shoulder, giving him a smile that made him want to grab her. John had sobered up a little, but not enough to feel self-conscious, and he kissed her.

Rosa tossed her jacket and scarf on a chair. She slipped off her shoes without untying them, kicking them away. She wore black stockings, but wiggled her toes, gripping the carpet, playing with its tight pile of fibers, moving her toes between them. She reached behind her back and unzipped her dress. It fell to the floor, landing gracefully around her ankles. She slipped her thumbs into the elastic bands of her black, thigh-high stockings and started rolling them down her legs, exposing her smooth skin and defined calves. She tossed her stockings over her shoulder like a basketball trick shot, and stood before John in a black bra and matching underwear.

John grinned and giggled. Seeing Rosa in her underwear, he was tempted to raise his arms, jump up and down, but restrained himself. It was something he'd thought about all day, the shape of her body under her dress, the way her skin felt. He thought about what he'd have to say to get her into his motel room and out of her clothes. He kept thinking about the things they'd do, but more importantly, he thought about how it wouldn't be like the people he'd photographed, the cheating husbands. He'd try to make it special. He'd try to make it mean something.

She stood in front of the bed, her hands on her hips, waiting for him to undress.

He lifted his leg and grasped his shoe with both hands, trying to pry it from his foot. John lost his balance, hit the table, and collapsed against the window. The lamp on the table rattled and almost fell. He pulled off one Chuck, then the other, bobbling it. His shoe slipped from hand to hand like a fish fighting to return to the water, before it flopped to the floor.

Rosa smiled and shook her head.

She lifted John's shirt over his head and ran her fingers over his chest. Her hands found their way to his pants and she kissed his chest and neck while she unbuttoned them.

John grabbed his pants waist with both hands and tried to take them off while standing. His left leg got caught in bunched denim and he fell forward onto the bed.

Rosa laughed and shrugged her shoulders as if to say, 'That's one way to do it.' She tugged on John's pant legs, helping him out of them. She threw them behind her against the chair. John sat on the bed. His feet didn't dangle, but he shuffled them against the ground.

She reached for his boxer shorts, but started laughing at the images of superheroes printed on them. Comic book characters flew into action, looking for evil to thwart, damsels to save.

John told her they were his lucky boxers.

She agreed and straddled him.

He wrapped his arms around her, kissed her. He moved his hands up her back, feeling for her bra clasp. He fumbled with it, trying to remove the hook from the loop. It moved and folded and slipped from his fingers, snapping against Rosa's back. He apologized as she brushed his hands away. She unhooked her bra on the first try. The straps slipped from her shoulders and her bra dropped to the floor, getting lost with the rest of her clothes.

Her breasts were everything John expected them to be. Perfect. They were just the right size, not too big, not too small. One didn't hang lower than the other. The nipples weren't pointing in divergent directions or at odd angles. Stray hairs weren't growing around her areolas. John's eyes grew wide and he smiled like a little kid getting his first bike at Christmas.

His hands moved toward them on their own, free of his control, like hands were just drawn to breasts and must squeeze them in order to fulfill something embedded deep in their genetic code.

Seeing John's hands trapped in slow motion, Rosa laughed at the power breasts have over men.

John wrapped his arms around her and rolled her onto the bed, onto her back. Rosa stopped laughing.

He kissed her neck and she moaned. John felt her moving underneath him. She battled with his superhero underwear, like she was trying to uncover his secret identity, but struggled to pull them to his knees, and John kicked them free. He took off her underwear, black and lacey, and gently tossed it to the floor.

John slid himself inside Rosa. They moved together, almost naturally, like they'd been together for years and instinctively knew the rhythm of each other's bodies.

When they were finished, he lifted the covers over them. She faced him, smiling, and John scooted nearer and wrapped his arms around her.

His first year in the dorms, the other guys talked about sex in the fanciful notions of teenage boys, spoken in horny breaths in whitewashed, cinderblock rooms, untenanted by mother and father. The dreams accompanying a year's supply of condoms, ribbed for her pleasure. Then he had sex, once during his sophomore year, and then with a different girl on graduation night, and it wasn't what his friends said it would be. There was the shame and guilt that came from a random hookup, the fear that he was bad in the sack, that he wasn't big enough, that she didn't enjoy the awkward thrashings of his skinny frame on top of her, but mostly he was afraid that these two emotionless nights were changing him in some way, turning him into someone distant and unrecognizable, the type of person who gave high-fives when he came home Saturday morning wearing the same clothes he wore Friday night, bragging about what he'd done to women, using terms found exclusively on the internet, too raunchy for cable TV.

Lying next to Rosa, he heard those voices. But something was different.

He didn't feel the shame or guilt or fear. He felt peace. Holding Rosa, her naked body pressed against his, John felt a level of comfort and joy he'd never experienced before. It felt perfect, the skin of his legs and feet touching hers, bellies brushing, arms wrapped around shoulders, dangling across and gripping torsos, like pressing against each other under low-thread-count, cotton sheets was the secret purpose of two naked bodies.

He held her tighter, feeling her heart beat against his chest, her rib cage expand then contract. He kissed her forehead and she sighed, nestling her head into his shoulder. Her body twitched, the involuntary muscle spasm of sleep. She woke up for a second, lifting her head. John brushed her hair with his fingers, lightly scratching her temple. Rosa, her eyes closed, smiled and dropped onto her pillow.

He didn't question why this time was different, what it was about Rosa that made him feel this way. He just accepted it. And closed his eyes, matched his breath with hers, and fell asleep, thinking he must be in love.

* * * *

John woke the next morning to the sound of someone pounding on the door, followed by a pounding in his head.

"John! John! It's Lee. Open up. C'mon, John! Open the goddamn door!"

"Hold your horses!" John shouted, sitting up. He rubbed his eyes with his palms, trying to wake up. Next to him, Rosa lay on her side, the sheet barely covering her back. She grumbled something and rolled over, draped her arm around John's waist.

"Tell him to go away. Let's just spend the day in bed," she mumbled.

"Goddamnit, John! Open the door!"

"Let me see what he wants," John said.

John grabbed his jeans and slipped them on. The chain had been repaired while he was out and John opened the door as far as the new, thin, aluminum security chain would let him. "Jesus Christ, what's so fucking important?"

"It's Leadbelly. He's been murdered."

A thin sliver of Sheriff Masters's cracked, leathery face, highlighted by morning sun, anxiously peered through the opening of the chain latched door.

"What do you mean Leadbelly's been murdered?" John asked, groggy from sleep and a hangover. "We just saw him yesterday."

"John, just let me in," the sheriff said.

Rosa scooped her clothes off the floor. John turned to warn her about the sheriff, but smiled, her naked back disappearing as she closed the bathroom door.

"Hold on. I gotta put some clothes on."

He grabbed a wrinkled t-shirt, unfastened the door chain. The sheriff rushed past him, a dust devil depositing earth in carpet.

"Oh shit, John! I went by...What the hell happened here?" The comforter and sheets were pretzeled on the floor, kicked off and twisted together during the night. A tall floor lamp leaned against the window. John's hoodie was half-draped over the barrel-shaped paper shade. Clothes lounged across the floor. The sheriff bent down at the foot of the bed. He picked up one of Rosa's green

Chucks, laughed, asked, "Aren't these a little small for you?"

"What's up with Al?" Rosa poked her head out of the bathroom door.

John remembered her moving above him, her hair dangling in her face. She flips it aside and smiles, almost laughs, before rolling over and pulling him on top of her. That look in her eyes that is both remote and immediate.

Rosa floated from the bathroom, tying her hair back. John put his hands in his jean pockets, smiled and sighed.

"Oh, morning, Rosa." Sheriff Masters touched the front of his Stetson, a Western gentleman. "Don't you worry about it none. We'll figure it out. I just need to borrow John from you."

"Well, then I should definitely be going, let you two get to work."

"Wait? Going?" John hoped they'd get breakfast somewhere, that she'd take him to her favorite diner and they'd get to laugh at how awkward they felt as they ate their hash browns, eventually discussing how to extend what they started last night.

"Yeah, John, some of us actually have jobs to get to."

John narrowed his eyes, a little startled by her coldness.

Rosa put one hand on her hip, the other outstretched, saying to the sheriff, "May I have my shoe, please?"

"Oh, yeah, sorry," Sheriff Masters said. "Here you go."

Sitting on the bed, Rosa tied her shoes, the final act of dressing, transforming back into a cook. She wadded her stockings and scarf into her jacket pockets.

"Sheriff, it was good to see you." She glided over to John. "John."

"Let me walk you to your car," John said, wanting a final moment with Rosa. He hoped that the reason for her change in attitude was because of Sheriff Masters and his news about Leadbelly, and not something he had done.

"Sorry about the sheriff," he said. Sheriff Masters stood in the doorway, pretending not to watch.

"That's alright, John. I understand. I need to get ready for work anyway."

They stood by Rosa's car. The hot air dried the inside of John's mouth and he wished for something to drink and instantly remembered all the beer he drank the day before and his head ached and stomach turned. The taste of a bad hangover coated his mouth. And there was the guilt.

"Rosa, I kinda want to apologize for last night." John adjusted his glasses.

"For what?"

"Well, I'm leaving town soon and I feel like..."

"You don't need to say anything."

"I just wish things were different. That we were,

I don't know..."

"John, it's fine." She wrapped her hand around his elbow, started to massage his bicep, then turned toward her car. Her windows were down a few inches, mitigating the morning sun.

John sniffed the air around her. He couldn't help it. It was his second favorite part about last night, becoming intoxicated by her aroma. John hoped it would send him to some wonderland where he'd forget about Leadbelly and puzzles and would only think about being with Rosa. But her scent was different, like their damp bodies, resting adjacent, had diluted her aroma. Standing next to Rosa, John stuck to the asphalt parking lot and suffered the heat from the sun, the responsibility to his job, the conflicted dedication to his craft, and his desire to be with her.

"Maybe I could come visit you sometime. I could come down on the weekends." His hand twitched, about to reach for hers, but he suddenly felt self-conscious and stuffed it in his pocket.

"You really are a sweet one, aren't you? I made a good choice with you. What happened last night was wonderful. So, stop worrying."

"But what about us?"

"What about us? We're both adults. Last night was something we both wanted. Anyway, I need to go home before the big lunch rush. Have fun playing with the sheriff," Rosa said, tapping him on the chest with the palm of her hand.

"Rosa, wait. I still feel like…"

Rosa clenched John's shirt and kissed him. It was soft and tender, reminiscent of the way she kissed last night. He felt eighteen years of anxiety and frustration over empty puzzles, an absent father, and his stuttered life melt away. Her kiss, the earnestness of it, made him feel like she was the only thing that mattered. He melted into her, and wanted to be with her again.

She lingered for a moment, her face near his, lips slightly parted with an almost imperceptible tremble. She released him, turning her head and exhaling, her hand skimming his shirt.

She got in her car, rolled down the window, and said, as if reading his thoughts, "Stop worrying, John. Besides, who says I didn't take advantage of you?"

As Rosa drove down the street, John touched his mouth, rubbed his fingers together, awakening the memory of their night, the places their bodies had pressed together, where he'd held her as they fell asleep, her body twitching as she dreamed.

He'd probably never understand her sudden change. Maybe that was just the way she was, passionate when it suited her, and distant the rest of the time. But it didn't matter. They had one wonderful night together, one John would always remember. And suddenly the day seemed tolerable.

"John, you old dog, you!"

"What did you hear?" he asked, turning.

"Not much, but I saw her plant that number on you. I ain't never seen Rosa act like that towards a man."

"Really?" John said, unable to hide his excitement.

"Yeah, really. Lotsa fellas tried asking her out, but she turned them all down. You shoulda seen Jimmy tripping all over himself when she first came to town. So, tell me, how was it?" Suddenly, John was back in the college dorms and his friends were asking him for details, wanting to imagine themselves in his experiences.

"What? It was...I dunno," he said, walking back into the room, replaying his night and questioning his morning.

"What the hell does that mean?"

"It means what it means."

He wanted to say it was one of the most amazing nights he'd ever had, that he understood terms like 'the one', and thought Rosa might be 'it', that he understood every love song ever written, especially the ones from the seventies, played on late night radio shows, and how he might call one of these shows and dedicate a song to her. He wanted to say that he felt empty and agitated now that she'd left, and that he was worried that he wouldn't see her again and that his half-drunk memories of their night might fade. He silently stared at the spot where she'd slipped off her shoes, thinking that the sheriff didn't want to hear how he felt, that he was only interested in the explicit details.

"You're not gonna say anything about it, are you?"

"Nope," John said.

"Well, just don't go breaking her heart," Sheriff Masters said.

John smiled and looked away. The sheriff didn't care about the different positions they tried or whether or not John 'hit it right'. He only wanted Rosa to be happy.

But Rosa had left abruptly, like she'd realized sleeping with John was a mistake.

"Might be the other way around," John said. The bed where they had slept was vacated, the sheets were wrinkled. "So, are you gonna tell me about Leadbelly or not?"

"Oh, yeah, Leadbelly. Well, I drove by his place this morning, just to make sure he'd high-tailed it outta town. I saw his truck was parked out front. So, I walked up to his front door, started knocking. As soon I hit his door, it went flying open. I started calling, but nobody answered. It was all dark inside, so I turned on a light and almost had a heart attack. Goddamn place was covered in blood. It was everywhere, the walls, floor, everywhere. I ran back to my car, called Jimmy. Told him to come out, secure the crime scene, that I was coming out here to find you. This might have something to do with your dead kid."

John didn't want to get involved. Rosa was gone.

He'd never see her again. She only wanted to be with him for one night, nothing long-term. He didn't have any reason to stick around. As far as he was concerned, the case was over. He just wanted to go home and work on his puzzles.

"This probably has something to do with the two guys from last night. The reporter was probably getting close to finding out something about Leadbelly they didn't want him to know, so they killed him. Go talk to them."

"Alright, let's go talk to them."

"Sheriff, I'd love to help, but I gotta get back to Denver, check in with Roof, file my expense report, do some other things." John pictured himself at his kitchen table, designing a crossword about heartbreak, listening to songs about the emptiness of life.

"Now, look, I've been mighty kind to you, driving you around and whatnot, treating you like a real high-flyer..."

"Sheriff, I appreciate that, but..."

"Let me finish." Sheriff Masters stepped forward, straightened himself, his presence filling the motel room. "Now, you caused quite a commotion in my town, scaring Leadbelly, putting that fella in the hospital. Now Leadbelly's dead. Whether you like it or not, you got some responsibilities here. You got a mess to clean up. Now, I can't force you to stay. But this is one a those moments, John. My dad used to call them character moments, where we get to see what kinda man you really are."

"What do you expect me to do? I just take pictures."

"I expect you to put on your goddamn shoes and get in the car," Sheriff Masters said, pointing toward the open door, his car parked outside.

When Leadbelly sped away from the lumberyard, John assumed it was to a gentleman's club in another part of New Mexico, and John could go back to Denver, to his mom's apartment, and build puzzles at her kitchen table, ignoring her theories about his dad's disappearance. But someone had murdered Leadbelly. And now the sheriff stood in John's motel room, the scene of the best night of his life, asking him to stay and help. He didn't want to admit it, but part of him was curious, and part of him was terrified. This wasn't a video game or a movie, the places where he'd encountered violence in the past. It wasn't entertainment. The violence was real. The two men last night had proven that. And it scared him. He wanted to run back to the safety of his old life, to the comfort of his routines and frustrations. It was one of the major patterns of his life. He ran to puzzles when his dad left, he ran back home after college, living with his mom, working for Rooftop, instead of penciling out his own path, and now he wanted to run back to Denver. Aware of the urge to return to someplace comfortable and easy whenever he became overwhelmed by the prospects of hardship and growth, John made it item number seven on the list of things he chided himself for during late-night reflective moments. However, since checking into the Sagittarius Inn, something had shifted in him. He noticed it just before the bar fight, and when Colonel Hollister had restrained him in his motel room, the itch to act. Now he was feeling this impulse again, compelling him to investigate Leadbelly's murder. Besides, Sheriff Masters was right. It was his mess, partly. John ran his hand through his hair, groaned at being forced to grow up.

"Alright," John said, half-whining. "Let's go."

"Hot damn!" The sheriff slapped his hands together, eager as a kid with a handful of Mexican fireworks ready to lose some fingers.

John, hand on the door knob, turned back to the empty room. "Hold on a second. I forgot something."

He grabbed his gun out of the nightstand and clipped it to his belt. He hoped he wouldn't need to use it, but knew, after last night, he needed to be prepared.

The unmade bed, the room smelling of sexual toil. The next time John walked through the door, the place would be clean and spotless, aerosoled and aromatic. John went to the side of the bed where Rosa had slept. He bent over, picked up her pillow, buried his face in the poly-cotton blend, breathed deeply, inhaling what remained of Rosa from the room. Even if he'd never be with her again, he wanted to remember her scent.

Outside, John pulled the door a couple of times, making sure it was locked.

"You got everything?" Sheriff Masters asked.

"Let's go," John said, putting his gun in the glove box. They drove down the road. In the side mirror, heat waves blended the motel into the other buildings, another motel, a fast food restaurant, a self-storage facility. Everything eventually melted together.

CHAPTER SIXTEEN

The house stank of bachelorhood, stale beer, body odor, and the general filth of young men who were ill-equipped to live on their own. Rosa stood in the doorway to Jose's house, amazed that her brother could live that way, not caring that his house smelled like a toilet full of bong water. She wiped her feet on the mat she bought him as a housewarming present and stepped inside. She shook her head in disgust and hurried past the coffee table littered with plastic sandwich bags that were dotted with green flakes and seeds, past the pink-tiled bathroom and the stacks of *Maxim* magazines next to the toilet, not wanting to think about the magazines Jose and Jed didn't leave lying around, to her brother's room.

"Jose! Get up!" She said, pounding on his door, the thin wood almost cracking.

"What?" Jose said, the door muffling his voice.

"Get up! We have to go."

"What the fuck. I don't gotta be in until...Shit, it's still early."

"Get. The. Fuck. Up. Now."

Rosa heard shuffling and collisions as Jose stumbled over piles of clothes and bumped into cabinets and an end table. He cracked the door.

"Are you alone?" Rosa asked. "Do you have a girl in there with you?"

"Damn, woman. What kinda question is that? You know this ain't Las Vegas, it's Las Vaginas."

"Are you alone?" she asked again.

"Yeah. Come in," Jose said, rolling his eyes, rocking his head. He was wearing light blue boxers and a wife-beater that was sweat-stained around the collar and arm pits.

Rosa crossed her arms, stared at the brown, circular water marks on the popcorn ceiling. She was always amazed that they were related. She was organized, motivated, driven. Her restaurant had become the star of the plaza. She intended to capitalize on her success, spread out, franchise, grow her business, bring jobs and money to town, make a difference. Jose was interested in growing other things. Every time she visited him, Rosa was reminded of this. It started when she helped him move in. Jose had refused to unpack until he had smoked a blunt and covered the walls of his room with posters of cannabis leaves and large-breasted women.

Jose plugged his phone into a set of speakers, nodded his head to a reggaeton track about the singer and his friends smuggling weed across the border in underground tunnels, stopping periodically for blowjobs.

"Pack a bag," Rosa said.

"How's about I pack a bowl? I don't gotta be at work for, shit, I don't know, a while." Jose plopped onto a beanbag chair. The bag wheezed and little Styrofoam bits spewed out of tiny holes. He picked up a red, plastic bong, a foot long, and poked the bowl with his finger, checking to see if there was something in it he could smoke.

"Hold on. I gotta hit this shit. Wake and bake, beotch." Jose grabbed a plastic lighter, the childproof metal band pried off, from his dresser and lit the bowl, inhaling. The dried grass and resin sizzled. Gurgling water. The red tube filled with smoke. Jose slid the bowl out, clearing the chamber, and the foot long column of smoke was vacuumed into his lungs and stomach.

He coughed.

"It's Leadbelly."

"That pendejo?" he said through his coughs. He exhaled the gray fog, polluting the room with the smell of burnt herbs, light and pungent. "You want some?"

"I'm trying to have a serious conversation here," Rosa said, fanning smoke from her face.

"Didn't think so," Jose said. He took another hit. The embers in the bowl glowed then died.

"You remember the other night when we saw him? He said someone was after him." She crossed her arms and leaned against the door.

"You can't take anything that guy says seriously." Jose's voice was high-pitched from holding in the smoke.

"Well, he was right."

"Shit, he's a walking ad for herpes cream." He exhaled, coughing.

"Last night..."

"Let me tell you about last night." Jose grabbed a large plastic cup of water and drank. "Me and Jed went over to Dawn's house. You remember her? She used to work at the Conaco by the airport."

"These two guys came up to me at Levi's."

"Why you hanging out there? That place sucks. You shoulda come with us to Dawn's. She was having people over."

"They tried to force me to go with them."

"This guy Nick pulled out this bag of Purple Kush." Jose pantomimed holding the bag. "You shoulda seen that shit. Nugs all covered in these red hairs. Nothing we could do but smoke that shit down."

"I think they were Air Force."

"What the...How did they..." Jose leaned forward. "What did they say?"

"They tried to make me go with them. Nothing happened, though. Fortunately, John was there and stepped in."

"Who's John?"

"He's kind of my boyfriend," Rosa said, shrugging one shoulder, tilting her head to the side.

"Is this that asshole kid from Denver?"

"He's nice," she said, putting her hands on her hips.

"Rosa, did you..."

Rosa blushed and looked at her shoes.

"You did! Holy shit! You fucking did!" Jose leapt from the ground, the beanbag chair still holding the imprint of his body. He dropped the bong, spilling the brown water on his stained carpet. "Why did you...Did Louisa ask you to do this? You know we don't have to do what she says. She's out there, sitting in the desert, we're here. We can do whatever we want."

"He's sweet. I like him. And...I don't know..." Rosa looked at the posters on her bother's wall, the bikini clad women sprawled across sports cars or dangling on young men like platinum jewelry. Her brother wouldn't understand that John made her feel loved enough that she could wipe away the barriers and disguises she used to protect herself from the leers of the men in town, that with John she could be herself.

"She doesn't get to tell us what to do. This is a new world, our world. She wasn't born here. We were. We don't owe her anything."

"You let those college kids beat you up because she asked you."

"That was different. You needed to get the sheriff to...Doesn't fucking matter why I did it. I ain't doing shit for her again. Fuck her. She can rot in that trailer park. From now on, I'm doing me." He picked up his bong, then added, "I coulda taken those frat boy putas."

Her brother was right, that she was only responsible for herself. She had always been loyal to the old ways, to the plan. When she was younger she understood it, embraced her role, was excited about living a double-life in New Mexico. She even anticipated the future, the end of everything. It had comforted her. For the past several years, she'd been operating on her own, building a life independent of oversight. She'd grown to enjoy it and was scared by the possibility that she didn't believe anymore. Then she received her latest assignment: John Abernathy. It was supposed to be simple reconnaissance, find out everything she could about him. She would smile, thinking about him, the puzzle-related puns he'd make when he hung out with his college friends, how he worked on his puzzles for hours every night after his mom went to sleep, how he believed in true love and felt ill printing photos of men covering other women's feet in Nesquik strawberry powder, cheating on their wives, and how he always gave half of his roast beef panini to Doug, the homeless guy who lived in the alley next to his office. And she was surprised when she realized that she was in love with him. Now all she wanted to do was see him again. Only, she wasn't sure he'd want to see her if he knew the truth.

She wasn't alone in her apprehension, and she knew Jose wasn't alone in his thinking. There were countless others like him who just wanted to kick back, coast for a while, delight in the indulgences of this world before everything became really complex.

But that didn't matter now. Leadbelly was dead and they needed to run, leave behind everything they loved. Rosa would never see John again, explain how she felt. She knew her brother wouldn't want to leave, knew she'd have to convince him to give up the parties, drugs, bad music.

"You enjoy this life? hanging out with your friends, smoking weed all the time?"

"What the fuck do you care?"

"I always..." she started, hands on her hips. She composed herself, folded her hands and ran them over her nose and mouth. "Jose, the Air Force knows about me. I don't know how, but they do. That means they know about you. What do you think's going to happen when they find you?"

"Putamadre," Jose said, grabbing a pair of jeans off the floor. "I was just starting to like this place."

He reached for his wallet and cell phone on his dresser.

"No phone," Rosa said. "We don't want anyone tracking us."

"No reception where we're going anyway."

Rosa waited for him in the living room, surrounded by pizza boxes, video game consoles, wondering how upset he'd be if she came over and cleaned when he wasn't home. If they had a home to come back to.

"Jed," Jose said, knocking on the bedroom door across the hall. "We need a ride."

Jed opened the door. He was naked except for a pair of mismatched tube socks and a brown baseball cap decorated to look like a designer handbag. Marijuana leaves replaced the logo that dotted the cap. The cap was turned backwards like he'd put it on right before answering the door and reverse was its natural state.

"Damn, son. You got really fucked up last night, huh?"

"Huh? What?" Jed squinted. He rubbed his left eye and half of his face with his hand. Someone moaned and tossed on the bed.

"Is that…Holy shit. You got Dawn in there? You better get your ass to the free clinic, son. Get your shit tested out."

"We don't have time for this," Rosa said.

The aroma of lavender and strong coffee hit Jed. He was suddenly awake and aware of Rosa, his boss, standing in their living room. Jed worked in the restaurant's kitchen with Jose as a line cook. He was usually late, and smoked weed on his breaks, but Rosa kept him around because he was Jose's friend. She knew Jed had a crush on her. He was barely able to get through the job interview without blushing. And when he saw her standing in his kitchen, his first thought was, 'Oh crap, I'm naked. With Rosa here,' and his second thought was, 'Damn, I hope I don't pop a woody.' He put his hand over his crotch and slammed the door.

Almost immediately the door reopened. Jed was fully dressed. Khaki pants, a short-sleeved, buttoned shirt, untucked, with a clip-on tie. He stood stiff in the hallway.

"I'm sorry about that, Ms. Jimenez, you having to see me all naked and shit," Jed said, trying to sound professional, and not hung over. He wished he had flowers.

"Don't mention it," Rosa said, crossing her arms, tapping her foot on the bong-water, stained carpet.

"Dude, we need a ride," Jose said. "We're..."

"Taking a vacation."

"Yeah, a vacation."

"I thought you had to give, like, two weeks notice, or some shit," Jed said.

"I'm the boss's brother, son," Jose said, in a developed bravado. "I don't gotta do nothing. You know this."

"Seriously?" Rosa said. "This is what you say when I'm not around?"

"So, you gonna give us a ride or what?"

"Uh, yeah, sure," Jed said. "Where you going?"

"Just drop us off at the bus station," Rosa said.

CHAPTER SEVENTEEN

They were a couple of blocks from Leadbelly's when they saw it, a tent of clouded plastic, its white canvas peak rising above the black shingled roofs, a snowcapped mountain in the New Mexico desert.

"That wasn't there when I left," the sheriff said.

"Yeah, I'd hate to think you missed a clue like that," John said.

The displaced trailer park residents clogged the street, blocking traffic on South Grand. Sheriff Masters turned on his siren. People parted, clearing a path for the squad car. The sheriff rolled up his windows and drove through slowly. Muffled shouts. A crowd in robes and tattered pajamas pointed toward Alamo Street. Large, armored vehicles blocked the intersection, barricading them. On the doors were stenciled stars with lines representing wings, a shooting star crashing to town. Sentries guarded the trailer park entrance.

Jimmy's squad car was parked at the Stuff 'n Pump. The sheriff parked behind it and jumped out. "Jimmy, what the hell's going on here? I thought I told you to secure the crime scene?"

"Whoa, Uncle Lee," Jimmy said. "I did. These

Army guys showed up after you left. Dude, they had these papers, yelling about 'proper jurisdiction' or some shit. What was I supposed to do? They had papers."

"They're not Army," John corrected him. "They're Air Force."

"Bro, what's up?" Jimmy said. He stuck his hand up for a high-five. John ignored it. "So, you were talking to Rosa last night. She's one fine piece of poonanny. I've been trying to get up in that for a minute now."

"Goddamnit, Jimmy!" the sheriff said. "You should have radioed in, stalled them until I got back. I'd drag you out to the desert and tie your balls to a goddamn cactus if you weren't my goddamned nephew. Now, watch how a cop is supposed to act."

"So, seriously, bro, you hit that? You give her a Tijuana Toilet Seat?" Jimmy asked, his question reminding John that he'd never see Rosa again, and that some people who would didn't deserve to.

The sheriff stomped toward the tent. John made sure the sheriff was out of earshot before turning to Jimmy, saying, "You remember that guy in the bar, right?"

"Yeah, dude, he was fucked up."

"You ever talk about Rosa like that again, I'll rip your fucking arms off. Got it?"

John didn't remind him that it was Charlie and his friends who beat up the man, and that John was unconscious when it happened. He just walked away, leaving Jimmy standing alone by the cars.

John weaved his way through the crowd. They had surrounded the sheriff and were asking him why armed men had yanked them from their homes. The sheriff tried to be diplomatic, saying he'd get to the bottom of it, but became impatient, agitated, and pushed his way through them.

John and the sheriff squeezed their way to a strip of yellow caution tape that blocked the street. They bent underneath it and stepped into the empty road in front of the tent's entrance. The walls of the tent were smoked, but blurred images moved behind them. A circus of muffled voices accompanied electronic beeps.

A young soldier was posted by a metal barricade in front of a slit in the tent, guarding the entrance. They tried walking past him.

"I'm sorry, sirs. I can't let you pass." The kid stared straight ahead, into that space, the empty source of his courage. He was a few years younger than John, but John sensed the age difference, like the extra half-decade he'd lived gave him a natural authority over the kid.

"I'm the goddamn sheriff. Are you telling me you're not gonna let me through? This is my goddamn town."

"I'm sorry, sir. I have my orders." His rifle shook in his hands, slightly.

"Do you see this badge?" The kid stared straight

196

ahead. "Look at it!" The kid glanced at it, moving only his eyes. "Do you know what it means?"

"Uh." He finally looked up at the sheriff. "Yes, sir, I know what it means, but, uh, sir, I have my orders. I can't let anyone through."

"To hell with your orders!"

"Sheriff." John put his hand on the sheriff's shoulder. "There's no need to yell. I'm sure we can work this out. Airman, I understand you're just following orders. Maybe it would be best if we spoke to your commanding officer. Why don't you find Colonel Hollister? Tell him John Abernathy and Sheriff Masters would like a word with him."

The sheriff gave John a subtle but curious look.

"The motel room," John said. "Remember?"

The sheriff nodded.

The kid sighed, relieved. He said something into his walkie-talkie, held it to his ear, deciphering squawking, the secret language of airwaves. He didn't question how John knew Colonel Hollister. It wasn't his job to question.

"The colonel will be right with you, sirs," he said, a receptionist with a rifle.

John leaned over the metal barricade, closer to the tent. Behind the foggy plastic, men in hazmat suits ran to all the trailers, holding devices to everything, outdoor furniture, trash, reading residual energy from various types of radiation, then making notes on iPads. One walked out with a box full of Leadbelly's dirty magazines. He put it in a van by the tent's entrance. On the van's side was another logo: NASA.

"Mr. Abernathy, how good to see you again. I'd like to say I'm surprised." Colonel Hollister walked toward them, his tan arms swinging. He wore an Air Force uniform, minus the jacket.

"But you anticipated me coming out here."

"I told you, we're not over."

"You Colonel Hollister?" Sheriff Masters asked when the colonel stopped at the metal barricade separating them. A young soldier with a battered and swollen face stood behind the colonel, carrying an attaché case.

"That's correct," he nodded.

"You wanna tell me what the Air Force is doing at my crime scene?" Sheriff Masters asked, pointing to the tent-covered trailer park.

"This isn't your crime scene. This is an official military investigation and, as such, is under our jurisdiction." He crossed his arms and smirked, stiff with false authority, enjoying the metal leaves on his shoulders.

"Like hell! I know a few things about military investigations. The only way this could possibly fall under your jurisdiction is if someone in the military was involved. Now, I know for a fact that no one in that trailer park's military. So, why don't you tell me how this falls under your goddamn jurisdiction?"

"Corporal McGillis," Colonel Hollister said,

glancing over his shoulder, "please show Sheriff Masters and Mr. Abernathy the letters from the State Attorney General, the governor, and the president."

"Let me see those goddamn letters," the sheriff said. Corporal McGillis pulled a few papers from a folder in his attaché case. Sheriff Masters snatched them from him, his hand extending over the barricade.

Sheriff Masters offered the letters to John, but he brushed them away. He was interested in something else.

"How'd you get those bruises?" John asked Corporal McGillis.

The corporal started to step forward. His swollen left cheek, shaded yellow and green, hid a smile. It caused his left eye to squint and close. He cracked his mouth to speak, but Colonel Hollister interrupted him.

"Don't answer him, Corporal. Mr. Abernathy, Corporal McGillis's appearance is none of your concern. Neither you nor Sheriff Masters have any authority to question my men. Now, Sheriff Masters, are you satisfied with the documentation?"

"Well, everything looks on the up and up. I'll have to verify these."

"Leadbelly must have been pretty important if you're going to all this trouble," John said.

"Gentleman, I have an investigation to oversee,"

Colonel Hollister said, turned and began walking away.

"You know, Colonel, something's missing," John said. "When you came to my room the other night, there were two men with you. I don't see them here."

"What are you talking about?" Colonel Hollister returned to the metal barricade separating him from John. It was lightweight and unanchored, and could be easily tossed.

"Last night Sheriff Masters arrested your two men in connection with the murder of a kid outside Truth or Consequences. He was a reporter for the *Enquirer*, was supposed to interview Leadbelly." John didn't look around the street or at the tent. He stared into Colonel Hollister's eyes, watching the lines and wrinkles around them twitch.

"And?"

"I find it odd that this kid gets killed, now Leadbelly's dead. And you've been here the whole time."

"Was that a question or an accusation?"

"Why did you have Leadbelly's place under surveillance?"

"Mr. Abernathy," Colonel Hollister said, his voice remaining steady, but agitated, "the desert is a dangerous place, occupied by elements that don't like questions, or people being where they're not welcome. I'm sure Sheriff Masters can tell you all about New Mexico's criminal underworld. And their body count. Or perhaps, since you're employed by that ridiculous tabloid, you're convinced there's something conspiratorial going on, government agencies operating secretly, but the truth, Mr. Abernathy, the truth is, and I suspect this is what your young reporter discovered..." Colonel Hollister lowered his voice and leaned closer, "People die in the desert all the time."

The colonel pivoted to walk away. Then he turned and said, "Besides, who said those gentlemen are still the sheriff's guests?"

Sheriff Masters rolled up the documents, slapped them against the railing. He jogged to his car like a retired bull rider with bad knees, looking over his shoulder, getting more upset with each look, watching Colonel Hollister calmly walk inside the tent.

"Jimmy, go call your cousin and find out the legality of these jurisdiction papers." He tossed the documents at his nephew.

"Which cousin?"

"The goddamn judge! Which one do you think?" Sheriff Masters threw his hat on the ground and kicked it. "And pick up my goddamn hat!"

"And you," he said to John. "Why didn't you raise hell about getting into Leadbelly's place?"

"They weren't going to let us in, no matter what we said." John leaned in, lowered his voice like he was sharing a secret. "You see that kid's face?"

"He was beat up pretty good."

"He matches the description of the kid that got into it with Leadbelly the other night at Levi's."

"Leadbelly was probably scared shitless they'd come looking for him."

"Looks like they got to Leadbelly before he could leave town."

"Why the hell would they kill Leadbelly, then start an investigation like this?"

"I'm guessing they're covering up something bigger than an Elvis photo."

An explosion inside the tent. Smoke filled it like a fortune teller's crystal ball, spirits from the other side trying to make contact, or a parlor trick. Men in hazmat suits rushed into the street, screaming at everyone to get back.

The people in the street ran from the flames, house shoes flapping on the asphalt, or tried to get into the tent, into their homes, either to help put out the fire with garden hoses or to save photo albums, scrapbooks, and other family memories. Sheriff Masters and Jimmy ran to the middle of the crowd, ushering people away from the trailer park.

John checked for Colonel Hollister. He and his men stood on the opposite side of South Grand, away from the smoky trailer, away from the Stuff 'n Pump, watching the smoke occupy the sky. Seeing that they were distracted, John sprinted toward the tent.

John fought against the ragged house robes and plastic hair curlers congesting the street, slid past the steel barricades, the military vehicles, NASA vans. He slipped through a slit in the tarp. Smoke plumed from Leadbelly's trailer, filling the upper half of the tent. A Ford Econoline cargo van, its side door open, was parked in front of Leadbelly's. John ran to it, crouching, one sleeve covering his mouth and nose. Tripping on a can of paint thinner next to a trailer, his sleeve slipped from his face. He expected to choke on the fumes, but he breathed freely in the thick and oxygen deprived atmosphere.

Cardboard boxes were stacked in the van. He tossed the lids back, looking for something he'd missed the other night, something that might explain the Air Force's interest in Leadbelly. And Rosa. Most of the boxes were filled with trash, food wrappers, unread mail, women's phone numbers. John flipped open another box. Leadbelly's wall photos, the ones labeled 'Area 51' and 'Los Alamos'. Digging through aerial shots of military bases, John found more photographs. Not photos linking Leadbelly to the Air Force. But of something else.

Photographs of John.

John leaving his mom's place last Sunday. The photo was dated and labeled in the same hand as the aerial shots. John graduating high school, playing catch in the front yard, his mother watching from the porch, John in junior high, going to a Halloween party as Colonel Nathan Norris from *Cape Canaveral.* He still had the outfit. Leadbelly even had a photo of John kneeling behind a tree and photographing Randall Neilson getting slapped by his girlfriend at Genesse Mountain Lookout four nights ago. John had heard a cracking sound that night. He thought it was tree limbs breaking, but it had been Leadbelly moving to get a better shot.

He kept digging, and found pictures of his grandpa. Pictures going back sixty years. His grandpa as a young man, standing on the porch of a small home, his arm around a young, pregnant woman, John's grandma.

And buried underneath these were pictures of another man. John recognized him from dreams he'd had every night since childhood, since the man disappeared. They were pictures of his father. Photos John had never seen. His dad as a child, then a teenager, and as an adult. And photos of John and his dad. In one photo, John is sitting on a Transformers Big Wheel, laughing, while his father is pushing him down the street. His father is laughing and smiling, playing with his young son. With John.

The last time he saw a picture of his father outside of his mom's billfold was his sixth birthday, when, in an ice-cream-cake-induced rage, he threw out all the pictures of the man. That night, he heard his mother go to the trash and pull them out. The sound of the metal lid being lifted, the framed pictures scraping against Coke cans, juice boxes, and snack cake wrappers made him roll over and cry into his pillow. How could his mother still love someone who'd left them? who'd denied a child a lifetime of his love? How could he not have been there for his birthday?

John gripped the photos. He crumpled them, then smoothed the glossy pages' ridges and depressions, his hand accidentally brushing over his father's face. He wanted to wad them up, step on them, crush them until they were nothing, not even a memory. He wanted to save them, put them in simple, black frames and hang them in the living room next to pictures of family vacations and graduations. Holding the photos, he experienced eighteen years of anger and regret and yearning. But mostly, he felt paranoid. Leadbelly, or someone, had been following him and his family, photographing them over the decades, and he'd never suspected.

John scanned the trailer park, trying to catch the glint of sunlight off a camera lens, hidden in rusted sheds or behind tipped trash cans or in windows with broken screens. He laughed at his sudden paranoia and wondered if this was what the people he photographed felt like when they saw pictures of themselves dressed as pandas, having three-ways with people dressed as giant tacos and grinning dolphins.

He searched the box, looking for some reasoning behind the collected images from his family history. At the box's bottom, he found it.

A book.

The leather cover was faded, stained, and split along the spine, but the binding still held. John opened the first page and read: *Contained within is the personal journal of Archibald Abernathy, chronicling the years 1862-1901.*

John recognized the name from the genealogy project he did for Sidewalk Stencil 204, spray painting his family tree all over Pearl Street. It was a branch whipping him in the face. Archibald Abernathy, John's great-great-great-grandfather.

Leadbelly had kept the one-hundred and fifty year history of John's family, the journal and photos, hidden among dirty clothes, empty beer cans, pornography.

A loud pop behind him. Glass breaking. The blast forced him against the van and to the ground. Green flames from Leadbelly's trailer windows burned holes in the tent. The photos flew from John's hand and were scattered on the ground like discarded big top ads from his Survey of Dadaist Circus Sideshow Posters 101. John scooped up the photos of him and his dad, put them and the book under his shirt, and zipped up his hoodie. He tossed the rest of the pictures in the box. There were some pictures he'd like to keep, photos of his father as a child sitting on his grandfather's lap. His grandmother would want them. But there were too many photos, and John couldn't keep them all. No one could. He put the lid back on the box and lifted it from the van's floor. John faced Leadbelly's burning trailer, the green flames rising from the windows and caressing the outside walls, and heaved the box inside.

The cardboard box quickly caught fire. It blackened, shrinking under flame. Satisfied no one would see the pictures again, John put one hand in his hoodie pocket and held the book and photos in place. Even though he was breathing freely, he covered his mouth with his other sleeve and blended in with the distracted crowd.

John and Sheriff Masters leaned against the sheriff's car and watched NASA scientists run to their vans, wanting to save as much data as they could for later study, like it was a once-in-a-lifetime find, while Colonel Hollister stood in the turn lane, the gap between the dotted yellow lines dividing South Grand Avenue, watching the fire consume Leadbelly's trailer, the Air Force's crime scene.

And suddenly, it was over.

The fire burned itself out. The whole thing lasted a few seconds. Leadbelly's trailer was the only one damaged.

"He burned his way out of Las Vegas again," John said. He would have laughed, but journal and photos pressing against his stomach reminded him that there was something more urgent than trailer park arson.

Crossing South Grand, Colonel Hollister motioned for his men to get back in the tent and see if they could salvage scraps from the trailer's skeleton. The wreckage still smoldered, but the fire was out. A hole had been burned in the tent's roof. Its edges were shriveled and peeled back, having retreated as it blazed.

"John," Sheriff Masters said, "what the hell's going on here?"

"I don't know," he said. Elvis, Leadbelly, what he'd found in the burning tent, John didn't know how they fit together. As much as he hated to admit it, there was someone better qualified to help them. "But I think I know someone who might."

"Yeah?"

"Mrs. Morris," John said, shuddering. He'd hoped to return to Denver and Mrs. Morris would be nothing more than a funny story to tell at bars or parties. Instead, he'd have to risk returning to her home of collectibles and bondage paraphernalia. "The woman who took the photo of Leadbelly, I talked to her when I first came to town. She seemed to be an expert on Elvis. Among other things. She might know some oddball Elvis theories, something that might help us out."

The sheriff turned to the wreckage. Smoke still rose from the holes in the tent, but men in protective suits were inside, inspecting the charred frame of Leadbelly's trailer. One of them held a small, black box, wires falling from it.

"Alright then, let's go see what this Morris woman knows."

"You think there's anything to what the colonel said about the two from last night not being in your jail?" John asked, getting in the car, knowing that the men from the bar were far away, someplace outside of Sheriff Masters's shrinking jurisdiction.

"God help us if there is." The sheriff removed his Stetson and placed it on the dash. He picked up the radio. "Shirley, you there? How're our two guests doing?"

"Didn't Jimmy tell you? They checked out last night. Someone came in with a court order. Came from pretty high up, too. Had to release them."

"Lemme guess, it was a military man, right?"

"How'd you know?"

"'Cause we're up to our asses in goddamn military men. Have you heard from the sheriff in Truth or Consequences?"

"I talked to him this morning. He said they have an open homicide investigation regarding some poor kid who went and got himself shot in the desert, but no leads."

"I think our two biggest leads just flew the coop," Sheriff Masters said, putting the radio handset back in its mount.

John rolled down his window, let his elbow hang out. Warm air filled the car as they drove away, leaving the Air Force to clear the confusion Leadbelly created.

Unzipping his hoodie, John removed the photos and book from under his shirt.

"What are those?" the sheriff asked, looking over.

"Something I pulled from one of the boxes they were taking from Leadbelly's." John guarded the pictures, putting them between random dates in the journal. "Let me ask you something. You said his place was a mess, right? blood everywhere?"

"If I had to guess, I'd say that it'd been tossed."

"Leadbelly had something they wanted." John's fingers rapped against the book. "Colonel Hollister's had Leadbelly's place under surveillance for a while, since Mrs. Morris took his picture. I think he got impatient, sent those two from last night to toss Leadbelly's. Leadbelly walks in on them, they kill him when he doesn't talk. Then they go to the bar looking for Rosa."

"He had Leadbelly's place under surveillance? You didn't think to tell me this?" The sheriff jerked the car right, onto New Mexico Avenue. "You know how much trouble you coulda saved me?"

"I didn't think they'd...I thought I could get Leadbelly to leave town, avoid something like this."

"Goddamnit, John, if there's anything you're keeping from me, now's the time."

"Nothing that pertains to this case." John moved the book to his right, between the seat and car door. He didn't know what was in it, or how it connected him to Leadbelly, or why Leadbelly had pictures of him. He knew he'd tell the sheriff everything. Once he'd figured it out.

CHAPTER EIGHTEEN

The journal was written on yellow paper. The black ink had faded, and now the words were light blue.

February 22, 1862

I just returned from my meeting at the White House. I was quite surprised when I received a letter from President Lincoln requesting a meeting, but I was more surprised at the nature of the discussion and its participants.

Secretary of State William Seward met me at the White House doors and ushered me into a private sitting room where a woman sat before a fire. Of course, I knew who she was, Mrs. Mary Todd Lincoln, the First Lady. She wore a black dress and matching bonnet. In her hands was a small lithograph. I couldn't see who the lithograph depicted, but I knew by the way she held it, it was someone important.

Without turning, Mrs. Lincoln told Secretary Seward to leave us. He nodded and backed out of the room.

Mrs. Lincoln turned and faced me. She was short and stout. Her dark hair was pulled tightly behind her head, exposing her round features. Her mouth was severe and down-turned. Her eyes were bloodshot and looked as if they had been aged by several personal losses.

She reached over and put the lithograph on the mantle next to a flickering lantern. It was then that I could see its image. It was of a young boy in a dark suit. His light hair was neatly combed. He had an expression on his face that said he hated standing still. I had read the papers and knew who the boy was, and why Mrs. Lincoln was in mourning.

She saw me looking at the lithograph and said it was the second child she'd lost; then she asked if I had any children.

I was stunned that the First Lady would address me so casually.

I told her that I did not have any children. She suggested that I should have as many as I could, so they could find new ways to break my heart every day.

The conversation made me uncomfortable, so I asked if President Lincoln would be joining us, and referred to the invitation, although it was vague in nature. Mrs. Lincoln said the president would not be joining us, that the death of Willie, that's what she called their son, had taken a heavy toll on him.

She then veered the conversation in an unexpected direction. She was rambling and mostly incoherent due to grief, but I followed her as best I could. Mrs. Lincoln said her son was still with her, that he was with all the other spirits the White House attracts. She said their late son Willie had visited her during a dream, and told her to find me, or more specifically, someone like me, and to send me on a quest.

I told her I didn't understand what she expected of me. Mrs. Lincoln simply said that we lived in troubled times. She handed me some pages and asked that I read them.

They were entries from a journal written by a Colonel Azeriah Standish stationed in Indian Territory. He described an attack on his garrison by unknown creatures that resembled men, but turned into animals when approached. Colonel Standish said the attack was over quickly, but when he looked at his pocket watch, over six hours had passed. Everyone was unharmed, but all their food and horses were missing.

When I had finished reading, a faint smile spread across Mrs. Lincoln's tired face. She was excited and asked me if I knew what Colonel Standish had discovered. Spirits, she said, not letting me answer. Mrs. Lincoln then startled me by saying she wanted me to go and find them.

I wanted to protest, instead I asked why I was chosen for the task, and suggested that there might be someone more qualified for this expedition.

She said I was chosen because I was an attorney, like her husband. I replied that my abilities as an attorney were questionable. In fact, I hadn't won a case in over a year, and had recently lost my license to practice law.

Mrs. Lincoln ignored me and called the steward to the door. She said Secretary Seward would have all the details regarding my mission. Then she proceeded to berate me until I left the room.

The young man escorted me to Secretary Seward's office. Mr. Seward started by apologizing for having to send me on what he considered to be a fool's errand, but with the war going on, President Lincoln felt they needed to explore every possible advantage, no matter how obscure. He then proceeded to tell me what was expected of me. He told me President Lincoln wanted me to go west in search of the spirits mentioned in Colonel Standish's journals, and to convince them to fight for the Union. He gave me the journal entries and money to buy supplies. He said I was supposed to send correspondence to them when I could, and then sent me on my way.

John ran his hands through his hair and groaned. He bookmarked the page with a photo of his father playing tee-ball.

"So?" the sheriff asked. "What's in the book?"

"When I figure it out, I'll let you know."

"Everyone's got a right to their secrets, and I'm trying to respect yours, but goddamnit, John, if this leads to something..."

"I'll let you know before that happens."

* * * *

They pulled up to Mrs. Morris's house, walked up the gravel driveway past the Pinto and camper. John shuddered with each step, recalling her dry hands searching his body, her tongue forcing its way into his mouth.

"Sheriff, do me a favor. No matter what happens, don't leave her alone with me."

"You scared of an old woman?"

"Something like that." John put his hands in his pockets and drew his elbows close to his body.

They were halfway to the house when Mrs. Morris threw open the front door and ran toward them.

"Mr. Abernathy! Sheriff Masters! Oh my, this is

exciting! You'll have to forgive my enthusiasm. I saw you walking up the drive and I couldn't help myself, I had to come out here. Oh, I'd been dreaming of seeing you again, Mr. Abernathy." She lunged toward John and hugged him. His arms at his side, John pulled his head back, wincing as she put her cheek on his chest.

The sheriff cocked his head to one side, mouthed, 'Okay?'

"So, did you find him?" Mrs. Morris asked, releasing John. "Did you find my Elvis Presley?"

"That's what we've come to talk to you about, ma'am," the sheriff said. "Maybe we should go inside."

"Yes, yes. Let's go inside," Mrs. Morris repeated, shaking with excitement. "I've just made some lemonade. Would you boys like some?"

"We would love some, ma'am."

They followed Mrs. Morris into her house. John saw the Elvis bowtie in the glass display case, steam cleaned. Mrs. Morris coughed and winked, startling him. He didn't want to be in the congested living room where Mrs. Morris had attempted to seduce him. Having been there before, he knew what to expect, from both the room and from Mrs. Morris. John ran his hands through his hair, determined that no matter what she did or said, he wouldn't unravel, and defiantly marched into her sitting room like he was immune to Elvis fever.

But at the sight of the room, the Elvis

memorabilia decorating every wall like an interior designer's nightmare, Sheriff Masters skidded to a stop at the door. John imagined the sound of screeching, stacked leather boot heels and black boot prints across Mrs. Morris's entryway. The sheriff gawked at the keepsakes and collectibles, wide-eyed, his mouth hanging open. Then he turned to the fireplace, to the painting of naked Elvis with a comically large erection hanging above it. Unable to contain himself, the sheriff bent over and laughed, slapping John on the back.

"Whew, that is something," he said catching his breath, wiping a tear from his eye.

"What do you think of my collection, Sheriff?" Mrs. Morris asked from the kitchen. She poured lemonade from a glass pitcher, decorated with Elvis singing into a microphone, into matching glasses. She put them on a tray depicting Elvis in a cage, being lowered into a pool of sharks.

"Well, it's something, ma'am. I'll definitely say that. I thought places like this existed only on talk shows. I never woulda guessed we had something like this in our here town."

"I've spent a lifetime collecting everything I can, but I think the picture I sold your newspaper is my new prize."

"Not the painting?" the sheriff asked, pointing to the black velvet. "That seems like a prize to me."

"Oh yes," Mrs. Morris said, smiling. "I do love that painting. Sometimes I stare at him for hours."

"Sure," John said. "All you do is stare."

"So, I'm so excited. Tell me all about him. Is he a nice man? He seems like such a nice man," Mrs. Morris said, carrying the tray into the living room.

"Well, Mrs. Morris," John started.

"John," she interrupted, "after everything we've been through? You know you can call me Elizabeth. You could even scream it if you'd like."

"Well, Elizabeth," John said with a perturbed wince.

The sheriff put his hand on his knee and squeezed it, trying not to laugh.

"About the picture," John continued, like the sheriff wasn't struggling with hysterics, "I'm sorry to say it wasn't Elvis."

She almost dropped the tray, spilling some of the lemonade.

"Oh, pooh. I'm so sorry to hear that. I was really hoping it was him."

"I know you were. The good news is there was an Elvis connection."

"Oh, do tell." Her face beamed as her spirits were lifted again. She handed them two glasses of lemonade. The sheriff guzzled his. John sniffed his first, checking for roofies. He set it on the coffee table, pushed it away from him, the ice rattling against the side of the glass.

"Turns out the man you photographed was an Elvis impersonator," John said.

"An impersonator? Well that explains everything.

What exactly did he do? Did he tell you?"

"He didn't say much, just that he ran a chapel in Vegas, officiating marriages."

"Oh my, a religious man doing good works." She held her hands over her heart.

"That's Leadbelly, Patron Saint of Hasty Marriages."

"So, is this man, this 'impersonator', around? I'd love to talk to him, maybe bake him some cookies."

"Unfortunately, ma'am," Sheriff Masters said, "it appears that Al Leadbelly, well, it appears that he met with some foul play."

"I'm sorry, I don't understand what you're telling me."

"Ma'am, sometime last night this Leadbelly fella was murdered."

"Oh my goodness!" Mrs. Morris collapsed into her chair. An Elvis throw pillow fell to the ground. She dutifully picked it up, brushed some dust off, and clutched it to her chest. "This is shocking news. Do you think this had anything to do with my picture? I'd hate to think that my photo was responsible for that poor man's death."

"You don't need to worry about that, ma'am. We believe this is unrelated to your photo."

"You'll have to forgive me. This type of thing doesn't happen everyday. I'm sure you're used to it in your line of work, Sheriff, but it's new to me."

"Fortunately, ma'am, it doesn't happen to me everyday, either."

"That's actually why we came to see you," John said.

"Is that the only reason?" Mrs. Morris asked, crossing her legs.

"We were hoping you could help us out." John ignored her, determined not let her ruffle him, at least not in the way she wanted.

"I'd be happy to help, John, in any way I can. And I mean any way," Mrs. Morris said, her finger rimming her glass.

The sheriff smirked at John.

"Uh, yeah," John said. "So, this morning, after Sheriff Masters discovered Leadbelly's trailer, he came and got me. When we went back, the Air Force and NASA had commandeered the crime scene, investigating as well. Now, can you think of any reason why the Air Force or NASA might be interested in an Elvis impersonator?"

"Well, of course I can. I can think of quite a few reasons."

Mrs. Morris went into the next room. John leaned over, checking to see if she was bringing out another bowtie. Instead, she came back with a shoebox full of books.

"Each one of these books offers insights into the world of Elvis Presley and his dealings with the United States government, but this one..." she pulled out an old paperback with yellow pages and faded spine, "this is the only one that talks about the Air Force or NASA."

Mrs. Morris handed John a tattered book, but wouldn't let go, biting her upper lip. John quickly yanked the book away, making Mrs. Morris squeal quietly. He set it on her Elvis coffee table, illustrated with a scene from *The Elvis Presley CBS Mystery Hour*. Elvis is walking down a haunted mine shaft, flashlight in hand, leading a group of beach-goers in the search for buried treasure, unaware they are being followed by a ghost pirate. John slid the book over and showed the sheriff the title.

Elvis and the Extraterrestrials.

"In this book," Mrs. Morris said, "the author talks about how Elvis is tracking extraterrestrials for the Air Force."

"Extratawha?" Sheriff Masters asked.

"Extraterrestrials. Aliens from another world."

"I'm sorry, and I don't mean to be offensive, ma'am, but are you telling me that Elvis hunted aliens for the government?"

"That's alright, sheriff." Mrs. Morris grinned. "I honestly don't expect you boys to believe me. I know I must seem a little eccentric, what with all my collectibles, but yes, that's exactly what I'm saying."

"Whew," the sheriff exhaled, crumpling into the couch.

"You were telling us about the book," John said. He squinted at the sheriff, wondering if he really believed what Mrs. Morris was saying.

"It's by an expert on extraterrestrials, Professor

Zeke Gentry. I'm surprised you haven't come across him in your line of work, John."

"We probably haven't crossed paths yet." And John wondered if Mrs. Morris knew what he really did, climbed on trashcans to photograph a straying husband with a belt around his neck, tugging the belt with one hand, pleasuring himself with the other, while watching an eighties cartoon about an all-girl rock band, would she leave him alone or propose to him?

"Well, you really should meet him. He's quite remarkable. Anyway, in his books, he reports that Elvis met with government officials in early 1960's. They showed Elvis the Roswell spacecraft and recruited him into a top secret branch of the Air Force, where he was trained to defend the Earth against hostile aliens. And in 1970, President Nixon gave Elvis a special badge allowing him access to all levels of law enforcement. Sheriff Masters, I'm sure you received a memo about that."

"That was a while ago. It's hard to remember everything that crosses my desk."

"Well, Elvis became the Air Force's secret weapon in the fight against aliens."

"Elizabeth, do you think there're aliens in Las Vegas?" John asked.

"Of course I do."

Sheriff Masters leaned in, putting his elbows on his knees, paying attention to every word Mrs. Morris said. John furrowed his eyebrows at the sheriff, questioning why a stoic cowboy, the embodiment of the American West, was so willing to believe in something so ungrounded.

"You see," she continued, "the aliens have focused their attention on the American Southwest."

"It is prime real estate," John said.

"Roswell's not too far from here. I'm sure Sheriff Masters can tell you all about that. Los Alamos Research Facility is not too far away, either. That's where they take apart the alien spacecraft and see what makes them work. You know, John, Roswell holds a UFO festival every summer. You should attend this year. We could come together."

"Uh, thanks for the invite. I'll, uh, I'll give it some thought," John said.

"Believe me, I'll be thinking about it, too."

"Anyway," the sheriff said, clearing his throat, "you were saying, ma'am, about Elvis."

"Yes," she resumed, "it was the government's idea for Elvis to be stationed in Las Vegas so he could keep an eye on things for them. The concerts were his cover. Professor Gentry believes the aliens found out Elvis was spying on him, so he faked his death. Now Elvis is collecting data on aliens for the government, but that's really all I know. Professor Gentry hasn't published a book in a while."

"Ma'am, why do you think the Air Force was out here today, then?"

"I'm not really sure. Maybe the young man was working with Elvis. Oh, my." She sat up quickly.

"Do you think the person who killed this man wants to kill Elvis?"

"That's very unlikely," John said. "It was probably something totally unrelated."

"I hope you're right, but I think you should talk to Professor Gentry, anyway."

"What do you mean, ma'am? 'talk to Professor Gentry'?" the sheriff asked.

"Why, didn't you know? He lives just outside of town. On a ranch. I can get you his address, if you'd like."

"Yes, please," the sheriff said, leaning forward, hands on both his knees.

Mrs. Morris came back with a small slip of paper.

"Here's Professor Gentry's address, and here's a copy of his book to read."

She slipped the address in like a bookmark and handed John the paperback with both hands. When he took it from her, Mrs. Morris stroked the back of his hand with her dried fingers. John yanked his hand away, like the friction from her fingers would light his skin on fire.

"You know where that is?" John asked the sheriff, giving him the slip of paper.

"Yup, it's east of town. It'll take little awhile to get there."

"Good thing I brought a book," John said.

"Ma'am," the sheriff said, "thank you again for all your help."

"Oh, don't mention it. I'm always glad to help,

especially if it involves my Elvis. And John, come back anytime you'd like. We can continue our conversation from the other day." She wiggled like a burlesque dancer with a plastic hip.

John shivered.

"Conversation?" the sheriff asked, walking outside.

"Yeah, she likes speaking in foreign tongues."

They walked down the dirt driveway to the sheriff's car. Mrs. Morris watched them from her picture window, curtains clutched.

"Sheriff," John said, "I'm sorry for bringing you out here. This was a mistake. Mrs. Morris doesn't know what's going on. She's just worried about aliens sneaking around doing God-knows-what to some farm animals."

"Seems like you're more worried about her doing God-knows-what to you."

"You don't know the half of it." Mrs. Morris stared at John through the window, smiling. "I mean, look at her, she's so excited. She knows she's just become part of Elvis folklore. She's probably getting ready to blog about it."

"Hell, she just might be checking out your ass," the sheriff joked. "I don't know about her not being helpful. She did tell us about this Gentry fella. Seems like a good lead to me. Besides, I gotta feeling this is gonna get real interesting."

"Sheriff, be honest with me, do you believe what she said about aliens? Because inside..."

"Hell no!" He looked east, away from the mountains. "Well, maybe a little. You telling me you don't?"

"You kidding? Of course not. It's just something people buy into because they don't want to admit that this is all there is." John pointed to a pink house across the street, its collapsing car port, a light blue pick-up with a brown door parked on the street.

"You know, I got a lot a questions need answering. Hell, you should hear the calls we get. Strange stuff. People seeing floating lights, hearing children laughing in the middle of the night."

"Kids out past their bedtimes, that is scary," John said.

"Makes me wonder if everyone in town's nuts or there really is something out there. Besides, if this Professor Gentry has an inkling as to what the Air Force is doing here, well, I think we should hear him out. He could blow this whole case wide open."

CHAPTER NINETEEN

They drove east, away from town, the slip of paper with Professor Gentry's address propped on the dash between air conditioner vents blowing cool air in opposite directions. John skimmed through the journal, looking for something interesting, anything that could help him find a link between everything that he'd experienced since coming to Las Vegas. He was looking for clarification.

September 5, 1862

> The most interesting thing happened in Lamar County, Texas. I was walking around the town of Paris when I came across an old Indian sitting in front of the trading post trading skins for dental work. I struck up a conversation with the man and offered to buy him a drink. I purchased a bottle of whiskey, and the old Indian, who went by the name Jonathon Deerfoot, and I sat behind the blacksmith stable drinking until the early hours of the morning. I eventually asked him if he'd heard any legends or tales of spirits walking the earth. He looked at me and said those people were dangerous and I would be wise to leave them be. I tried my best to convince

him to tell me where to find the spirit-men, but, not being much of a drinker, I had become intoxicated, and my words stumbled over each other. Mr. Deerfoot looked at me gravely, as if peering into my soul. He took another liberal drink of whiskey and started laughing. He said I should head west into New Mexico Territory, to the town of Las Vegas, and search at the foot of the mountains.

Eventually, I passed out. When I awoke, I was in my bed at the inn were I was lodging. When I asked the innkeeper how I got there, his response puzzled me. He said I came in shortly after dinner and had been there all evening. I inquired about Jonathon Deerfoot. The innkeeper responded by saying I had returned alone. I searched the town for Mr. Deerfoot, but no one had heard of him, not even at the trading post.

John took off his glasses and rubbed his eyes, trying to grind aside the coincidence that both he and his great-great-great-grandfather had traveled to Las Vegas, New Mexico to investigate a legend that had its basis in blind obsession.

October 23, 1862

Yesterday, I arrived at a small town, at the foot of the mountains, called Las Vegas. I entered the saloon, seeking room and board. Even though I was in a US territory, the men in the saloon were mostly Mexican, and a few, Indian. Being the only English speaker, I attracted immediate attention.

I attempted to strike up a conversation with a Mexican gentleman standing at the bar. He gave me a peculiar look when I said that Jonathon Deerfoot suggested I visit this town. He informed me he'd never heard of him and walked away. Seated men whispered. They watched while I had a small dinner of potatoes and pork and went to bed.

That night I was awakened by the sound of footsteps outside my room. I rose and looked for my Remington Model 1858, but it was not in its holster. I heard the doorknob twist and saw the door open slowly. The barrel of a revolver peeked through a sliver of light from the hallway. Two shots were fired. I grabbed my chest, expecting wounds, but there were none. Instead, the man in the doorway fell dead. The shots originated from the corner of my room. I looked over and saw the Mexican gentleman from the bar. He tossed me my revolver and told me to pack my things. I thanked him, and then asked why I should trust him, even though he had apparently just saved my life.

He looked at me and said Jonathon Deerfoot had sent him. That was all I needed to hear. Jonathon Deerfoot had sent this man to protect me.

Although it did occur to me that I mentioned Jonathon Deerfoot's name earlier that evening, I decided to go with him anyway. It was either that or attempt explaining the circumstances surrounding the man's demise to the constable, if there was one.

I started for the door, but my new friend stopped me, motioning to the window. I crawled onto the roof. We walked to a ladder he had placed against the back of the saloon and climbed down. At its base was my wagon. My new friend had liberated my belongings from the stable. My horse was old, the wagon cumbersome, and I feared our escape would be brief. My colleague told me not to worry, that our exit was already secured. At the time, I did not know what he meant, but I quickly found out.

We headed northeast, out of town. In the rear, I heard horses chasing us. Gunshots exploded behind us. I ducked my head and grabbed my ankles, trying to become a small target. My new friend whipped my elderly horse, trying to compel it to move faster.

Suddenly, from behind us, I heard ghastly noises, like a menagerie had been loosed on our pursuers. Their horses neighed and snorted in fear. The riders shouted, trying to regain control of their horses.

My new friend told me not to worry anymore. He said that the horses had become so disoriented that it was impossible for the posse to chase us. I sat upright, thanked him again for his aid, and introduced myself.

He said his name was Oscar Ramirez. I asked him if he really knew Jonathon Deerfoot. He said everyone knew Jonathon Deerfoot. The Territorial government considered him an outlaw, and that's why those men chased us. They thought I was a co-conspirator.

We traveled for several hours. The sun was rising over the desert to the east. Oscar Ramirez nudged me. I looked up and saw a small settlement by a little body of water. As we got closer, I could make out small houses. Tents surrounded the lake.

We dismounted from the wagon and walked through camp to a small building near the water. It was empty except for a man sitting behind the desk. I recognized him immediately. I had found Jonathon Deerfoot.

I introduced myself to Mr. Deerfoot, saying I had been sent by President Lincoln to implore him and his men to fight for the Union. I was about to deliver an impassioned speech, when Jonathon Deerfoot stood and walked over to me. He put an arm around me and started laughing. He said they wouldn't be fighting any wars, but there was something I could do for them. I was confused. He said not to worry, that I would understand everything in due time. He invited me to stay and enjoy their hospitality.

Oscar Ramirez took me to a tent by the lake which was to become my home. My belongings had already been arranged inside. I tossed my jacket on the canvas cot and walked outside to survey my new surroundings. The lake was very inviting. It wasn't very large, and I could see land on the other side and the mountains in the distance. Men were net casting off canoes and some were hauling their catches back to shore.

Feeling thirsty, I walked down to the water. I knelt and scooped some water with my hand. It was cool, and stung my dry, cracked lips, and soothed my throat as it slid down. I drank another handful, and then another. The more I drank, the more I wanted. Eventually, I succumbed to my thirst and submerged my head in the cool water. When I couldn't drink anymore, I lifted my head and coughed for air.

I collapsed with joy on the grassy bank of the lake. My head was soaked and my belly was full of liquid. And I laughed, not at myself, or anything, really, but rather at life. For the first time in a long while, I felt alive. These people were fisherman, farmers, not Mrs. Lincoln's spirit army. My mission was the fool's errand Secretary Seward suspected it to be, and I did not care.

When I sat up to let the sun dry my face, I was approached by a mysterious creature. Its silhouette blocked the sun. I held my hand above my eyes and shielded myself from sunlight, but still couldn't make out what was before me. Then it bent down, revealing itself to be the most beautiful woman I had ever seen. She smelled like lavender on a spring morning.

I tried to introduce myself, but stammered repeatedly. Finally she spoke, saying that she'd come to invite me to breakfast on behalf of her father, Oscar Ramirez, and that she was his daughter, Louisa.

At breakfast, I sat next to Oscar Ramirez, who was to become my benefactor. I was to go to him if I needed anything. I planned on visiting him often, although it would be to visit his daughter, Louisa.

December 18, 1862

I had been living in this new community for a few months and was trying to learn as much as I could about them, but so much remained a mystery.

My afternoons and evenings were spent with Louisa. She apparently taught astronomy. She would tell me about the constellations, how far they were from Earth, how their light took millions of years to reach us, and how those stars no longer existed. In the evening, she would teach the children about celestial bodies. She pointed out one in particular, Sagittarius, telling them to look to it and to wave when they felt alone, that someone was waving back. I thought it was mere whimsy, but the children took the lesson to heart, waving to the night sky.

One evening, a young girl named Rosa Jimenez approached us. She asked me if I wanted to marry Louisa. I had the sneaking suspicion that others had been discussing this topic. I told her that, yes, I did indeed wish to marry Louisa. Rosa became very excited. She jumped up and down and ran back to the village.

After dinner, Louisa and I walked hand in hand by the lake. The sun had set and stars shot across the sky. I told her I intended to ask her father for her hand. She smiled and put her head on my shoulder, saying that would make her very happy. I kissed her. Louisa sighed and we spent the rest of the evening making love under a meteor shower.

That night, I was woken by the sound of an animal growling outside my tent. I grabbed my pistol and pointed it at the tent's entrance. I am not a brave man, but Louisa was sleeping next to me, and I was not going to let anything happen to her. I summoned what courage I could and got out of bed. I opened the flap of the tent and walked outside.

Standing outside my tent, I looked around, the pistol shaking in my hand. My ears throbbed with the sound of my heartbeat. My breath, quick and heavy, floated aimlessly in the cool night air. In the black night, a set of red eyes approached. I was about to fire, when I grew suddenly calm. My breath slowed, as did my pulse. My hand stopped shaking and I lowered the firearm.

A mountain lion walked out of the shadows. It growled and hissed as it approached. It paced back and forth in front of my tent. Then it raised itself onto its hind legs. Its snout receded and its hair shrank. The front paws split, forming five fingers. However, the most jarring transformation happened to its hind legs. The mountain lion's knees dislocated, moving forward with a loud, popping sound, forming human legs. In a matter of seconds, the beast had transformed into a man I knew very well: Jonathon Deerfoot.

Jonathon Deerfoot addressed me, saying it was time he answered my questions. We walked in silence to the one-room building I'd been in when I first came to the village. Clothes were bundled on the desk. Once dressed, Jonathon Deerfoot sat behind the desk, putting his elbows on it, and folding his hands. I sat in a chair opposite him.

I thought Jonathon Deerfoot intended to discuss my desire to marry Louisa, but I quickly realized there were other matters requiring discourse.

He told me his people's history. He said they were colonists from another world who had arrived here one hundred and two years ago. They traveled across the galaxy instantaneously by opening a hole in space, bridging the distances. They were required to leave most of their technological devices behind, including the device that helped them bridge space, and, as a result, were stranded here until the next wave of colonists arrived. However, he added, what foreign machinery they were able to bring enabled them to make the desert hospitable by manipulating and reshaping the natural landscape.

I wondered what else they could do.

He sighed deeply and said that before they left for Earth, his people were given certain abilities that aided in colonization. They could alter their appearance to resemble the indigenous life of whatever planet they were colonizing. They could heal from wounds and had learned to slow their aging process. Jonathon Deerfoot confessed that he was roughly three hundred years old. He also said that they could communicate telepathically and could send their minds anywhere they chose, that they could even affect our dreams, which is how he was able to visit me in Texas, and how they were able to convince the Lincolns that the ghost of their late son wanted them to send someone to find a spirit army, but they couldn't control the minds of others. Instead, he said, they were given an advanced pheromone system, enabling them to release pheromones that affect our moods, making us calm, afraid, or amorous, all with merely their scent.

I asked him why they had chosen Earth to colonize. Jonathon Deerfoot said they chose planets where the indigenous population was still in its technological infancy. These planets were easy to infiltrate because the inhabitants hadn't developed the mechanisms to detect the colonists, and that by the time they did, his people were already positioned to take over.

I asked if he intended to make war on humanity. He told me that I misunderstood him, that they didn't colonize through violence, the way we had been colonizing the West. They colonized through an involved, selective breeding process, creating a new species that would eventually replace humanity. However, the process took time, and it was often centuries before they prepared a world for the next wave of colonists. They had colonized thousands of planets this way, and it brought peace to many troubled sectors in the galaxy.

I asked him if humanity should have a choice in the matter. He asked me which would I prefer, peace, or the destruction of the planet. I told him, if those were my options, then I'd choose peace, but there are some who will not make that concession, that their independence is important to them, even if it means their demise.

Jonathon Deerfoot said there will come a time when the planet's population is connected telepathically, and that this connectivity will help them realize that they are not isolated groups, separated by land or language, religion, or access to resources, but that they are one people, the inhabitants of a planet whose unified efforts toward their advancement are stronger than a few, loud voices demanding autonomy. He said this is why they chose to colonize Earth, so that one day we will understand the peace that comes from unity.

And then I realized that my initial assessment of our conversation was correct. We were discussing my desire to marry Louisa. Jonathon Deerfoot wanted me to mate with Louisa so that our children would be the first generation of a new species.

I asked him why he chose me for this. Jonathon Deerfoot said when they initially visited the Lincolns's dreams, it was to convince them to send someone who his people hoped would be suitable for crossbreeding. After my visit to the White House, they visited Mrs. Lincoln again. When she told them she'd sent me to find them, they searched my mind while I slept and found I was someone who was relatively intelligent, with a gentle temperament, ideal qualities for a crossbreeding candidate.

I asked if Louisa knew about their plan. He said she did. I then asked if she altered her pheromones so I would fall in love with her. Again, he said she did, but quickly added that Louisa volunteered for this mission because she loved me, that she fell in love with me the first moment she entered my mind, and she only used the scent because she was unsure that I would reciprocate her feelings.

I told him she didn't need to do that. I would have fallen in love with her regardless, and added that I will love her until I die.

Jonathon Deerfoot smiled and walked me outside.

My wagon was waiting for me, stocked with enough supplies to last several months. Louisa sat on the bench seat, looking beautiful. She had a flower behind her ear.

I pulled myself onto the wagon, next to my bride. There was no official ceremony. Louisa told me that their culture did not require formalities, that devotion of the heart was enough for a union.

We decided to ride north to Denver City, in Colorado territory. On our way out of town I asked Louisa if she would miss her family. She looked at me and said that they would always be with her and she could visit them anytime she wished. I asked her how she could do this. She replied by tapping the side of her head and saying, the same way she fell in love with me.

John flipped back a few pages and found it buried in a paragraph. Her name made the surrounding scribbles inconsequential. He overflowed with joy and hope, anxiety and inadequacies. He read the section again, making sure he'd read correctly.

Rosa Jimenez.

Archibald had written her full name.

John put the journal away as the sheriff turned onto I-25, an interstate road running north-south, separating town from wasteland. But the road had failed to keep decay from consuming homes, mobile or otherwise, and parts of town had broken and drifted into endless desert. History decomposing.

"This is where the world comes to die," John said.

They turned east, onto Highway 104, then onto a dirt road, and stopped in front of a rusty fence, waist-high, with thin, iron bars running its length. It looked fragile, like an autumn leaf breaking between fingers, red flakes ready for ground. The old gate was sealed with a chain and a rusty, unbolted Masterlock. John got out, opened it. The hinges screeched under pressure.

They followed bald earth for a few miles, unsure if they were on a road or were lost, two more victims of the desert. Then, on the horizon, a growing blackness absorbing everything, grass, light, dirt.

Professor Gentry's home.

From a distance it shined like black steel. As

they drove closer, they saw that it wasn't steel, but old tires, steel radials.

Stopping in front of the tire wall, they got out of the squad car. Professor Gentry hadn't built a home, he'd built a fortress. Out of used tires, staggered and mortared. The wall was over twenty feet tall, at least fifty yards wide, running in a circle, like a structure in John's Found Object Architecture 103 textbook.

John put his hand on it and pushed a little, testing its sturdiness. He could climb it like he did the trees in Cheesman Park when he was younger and his mother would take him there for weekend picnics of baloney sandwiches, Shasta lemon-lime soda, and off-brand pudding pops, and tell him stories about his father, hoping John would grow to love the vanished man based on her recollections and not recent events. Instead, John would run and climb the oaks and maples, escaping story time. John slapped the tire wall and decided against climbing it. Whatever hermit lived on the other side was hiding from something, possible everything, and they needed his help.

"So, how do you think we get in?" Sheriff Masters asked.

"Knock," John joked, pointing to another iron gate that led inside, only this one looked new, a crisp, metal barrier. It was the height of the wall and solid steel. On the left side of the gate was a small speaker with a little red button with the word

'Press' on it.

The sheriff pressed it. Nothing happened.

"I knew this was a waste of time," John said, walking back to the car, convinced that Mrs. Morris intentionally gave them the wrong address so he'd be forced to go back to her home, and she could tell him about her dream Roswell getaway, an all-inclusive vacation including crotchless spacesuits, alien themed sex toys, and scrapbooking.

"Hello," said a crackly voice from the speaker.

"Uh, hello," the sheriff said.

"You have to...button...talk."

"Oh, okay," the sheriff said. He pushed the button and began speaking. "Hello, Professor Gentry? My name is Sheriff Masters. I'd like to ask you a few questions."

"There's no...here by...name. Please...away."

"Professor Gentry, we'd really like to ask you some questions about Elvis and the government."

"Like...said, there's no one...name. Please...away. Thank you."

"Professor Gentry, Mrs. Morris seemed certain you were the guy to talk to. Could we please come in for a moment? It'll only take a second."

"Mrs. Morris? Why...you say so. Get...your car...park next to..."

The speaker buzzed and they heard sound of iron gears turning, like a giant watch winding. The large iron gate slowly opened, revealing a hill covered in dry New Mexico grass, brown and dead.

A small mobile home sat on top of the hill like an old man in a beach chair watching alternative news reports on his phone. Aluminum-foil-wrapped bars barricaded windows. Several satellite dishes of mixed sizes were planted on top of and around the home. They were pointed skyward, receiving transmissions. A stone path led from the bottom of the hill to the trailer.

"Jesus. This place looks like a meth lab," John said.

"Where the hell did he say to park?" Sheriff Masters asked, driving through the gate, scanning the brittle weeds and compressed rubble in the lot.

"I don't really think it matters. Just park over there." John pointed to an old, beat-up Chevy pick-up rusting at the foot of the hill. They'd hiked halfway up the path when the door opened.

A large head with thick gray hair emerged from behind the screen door. A dense beard climbed his cheeks, covering over half of his face. Pop-bottle glasses guarded the only hairless skin. His eyebrows, like fuzzy pipe cleaners, swept across his forehead as he scanned his yard, suspicious of something that wasn't there.

"Professor Gentry?"

"Sheriff Masters?" he asked. "Were you followed?"

"No."

"You sure?" He scrutinized the yard sealed in Goodyears, Michelins, Firestones, and other brands.

"Yeah, I'm pretty sure."

"Yeah, right. They always follow. Who's that with you?"

"John Abernathy, Professor. Nice to meet you," John said, attempting to compensate for whatever phantom threat had put Professor Gentry on edge.

"Abernathy?" Professor Gentry stepped onto the yard. He was short, around 5'3". Thick, black hair poked above the collar of his black t-shirt like weeds next to a fence. "Son of a bitch."

"*Cape Canaveral.* Nice." John pointed to Professor Gentry's black t-shirt. The logo and setting of the popular sixties TV show was printed on it.

"You know, I used to work for the actress that played Lieutenant Megan Strata. She had a pair of Bichon Frises. Adorable animals, but noisy. They barked at everything."

"What exactly are you a professor of?" John asked.

"Elizabeth didn't tell you? Good. I knew she could keep a secret." His eyes darted between Sheriff Masters and John. "I'm not a professor of anything. I'm a dog walker."

"A dog walker?" John said, thinking he shouldn't be surprised that Mrs. Morris would trust a phony professor over common sense.

"But you wrote that book?" the sheriff said.

"I was Elvis's dog walker. He called me 'The Dog Professor.' I used it on my books so the fans would know it was really me, not some imposter. Let's get inside. I'll explain everything. Elizabeth sent you to me because there are things you need to hear."

"Yeah," John said, "I know what she wants me to hear."

"Now, we can stand out here all day while they listen to us." Professor Gentry pointed up. Instinctively, they followed his finger. "Don't look. Or you can come inside where it's safe."

Sheriff Masters turned to John and shrugged his shoulders as if to say, 'We came all this way, might as well.' Professor Gentry ushered them in. He grasped the aluminum handle next to his door and climbed up the steps. Standing in the doorway, he surveyed his dirt and rubber yard one last time before closing his trailer's door.

Unlike Leadbelly's trailer, this place was spotless, like a laboratory. The kitchen appeared to be ordinary, a yellow stove, tan linoleum, plastic cabinets designed to look wooden. However, the living room refused to be unremarkable. A series of monitors hung from the walls, displaying a live feed of the outside wall, the endless desert beyond.

Professor Gentry offered them seats at the kitchen table.

"So, you know Elizabeth?" He smiled and gazed past them. "She does the most incredible thing with her tongue."

"Aagh, I don't want to hear that," John said, convulsing.

"She starts by taking out her false teeth."

"Professor Gentry," the sheriff interrupted, sounding official, "Mrs. Morris told us you were the man to talk to about Elvis."

"Well, it depends on what you want to know. You want the propaganda, the endless lies fed to you since birth? Or would you rather hear the truth, the truth they don't want you to know?"

"Who's 'they'?" Sheriff Masters asked.

"The government, of course," Professor Gentry said, pounding his fist on the kitchen table. "They've been trying to silence me for years. Why do you think I moved all the way out here? To keep them out, to keep them from spying on me."

John had run into Professor Gentry's type before. Whether they were passing out flyers on his college campus, at the farmers market trying to get signatures for unnecessary legislation, or feeding pigeons in the park while wearing a tinfoil hat, they always believed that there was a mammoth conspiracy moving and shaping society, machinations that only they could see, and that it was their duty to educate and recruit everyone they met to their cause. At first, John humored them, listening, nodding, pointing out obvious holes in their logic, but he got tired of hearing comments like, 'but don't you see', or, 'you just don't get it', or, 'you're all sheeple'. Now when he encountered someone with an irrational conspiracy theory, he either ignored them or walked away. To John, all

Professor Gentry needed was a tinfoil hat.

"Now," Professor Gentry said, leaning back and folding his hands across his stomach, covering the image on his t-shirt of Kennedy Space Center floating through the Milky Way, "why don't you tell me what this is about?"

"Mrs. Morris took a picture of a man she believed was Elvis. I was hired to come down here, investigate it. Turns out he was just an Elvis impersonator. Said he was leaving town, didn't want any trouble. Apparently, he was murdered before he could leave."

"Murdered?" Professor Gentry leaned forward, his hands on each side of the table, anchoring himself like his curiosity defied gravity.

"I'm not surprised. It's not the first time they've killed to cover up the truth."

"That's not the strange part," Sheriff Masters said. "When we got to his place, it was crawling with government types, Air Force, NASA. What does NASA have to do with Leadbelly or Elvis?"

"Unbelievable." Professor Gentry shook his head, and slapped the table with both palms. "You two have stumbled onto the biggest conspiracy in modern times and you don't even know it. Let me tell you something. There are scientists out there who correctly believe we're not alone in the universe. They've spent careers searching the cosmos for intelligent life. Then, there are those who believe intelligent life has been searching for us. What's more, they're all part of a clandestine branch of the Air Force, a very secretive unit, whose sole mission is to study alien life both in the skies and here on Earth. They're trying to keep the existence of extraterrestrial life a secret, while at the same time attempting to weaponize their findings."

"And how do you know all this, Professor?" the sheriff asked.

"I was Elvis's dog walker. He'd go out with me when I'd walk Brutus, Snoopy, Baba, Sherlock. I walked all of them. He told me everything about the government and UFOs. He even showed me some of his journals, the field reports he filed for the Air Force."

"He trusted you with all that?"

"People trust their dog walker more than their babysitter. But Elvis, he was one of them, a government agent. In 1960, after he was discharged by the Army, Elvis was recruited by an Air Force officer named Major Hollister."

"He's a colonel now," John said. "He was at Leadbelly's trailer today."

"I walked his dog when he came to Graceland, a piece of shit toy poodle named Astro. Can you believe that? He's looking for little green men and he names his dog Astro. What a dick. Anyway, he recruited Elvis into the Air Force, personally overseeing his training, turning him into an 'intergalactic covert operative', that's what Elvis called it. Colonel Hollister, he said Elvis was his greatest achievement. Let me show you something."

Professor Gentry scooted out from behind the table. He waddled through the kitchen, past the tan cabinets that were coated in plastic mimicking wood, and toward the bedroom. At the bedroom's accordion door, he peeked over his shoulder at John and Sheriff Masters like they were going to steal his locker combination, and cracked the door partly, creating just enough space for him to squeeze through, then closed it behind him. There was shuffling behind the door. He returned from the bedroom, flipping through the pages of a folder. Professor Gentry pulled out a piece of paper and slapped it on the table. A series of numbers was written on it. Several letters were circled and 'Wow!' was written next to them.

"Looks like a number puzzle," John said, remembering his unfinished puzzle in his hotel room, regretting not working on it.

"In a way, it is," Professor Gentry said. "Every minute of every day, we send radio waves into space. SETI, you know what SETI is, right? They assume someone out there's doing the same. So SETI listens for radio waves, or, more precisely, their interns and PhD candidates do. For years they listened, hoping to hear something. Mostly what they heard was static, white noise, patterns like these." He moved his hand over the page, gesturing at the patterns of ones, twos, and threes.

"But, on August 15, 1977, they heard this." He pointed to a group of letters circled in red ink. Next to the letters, one word had been written that accurately summarized the astrophysicists' sentiment toward this find: 'Wow!'

"This signal made everyone at SETI lose their shit."

"Is that the technical term?" John asked.

"They'd been trying to talk to the stars for years. And now, someone was talking back. The SETI guys did their math thing and determined the signal was sent two hundred years ago from a star in the constellation Sagittarius. Now, this is the part of the story that changed my life. The very next day, August 16, 1977, Elvis Aaron Presley died."

CHAPTER TWENTY-ONE

"Think about it. Someone up there," Professor Gentry said, pointing toward his popcorn ceiling, "talked to someone down here, and the very next day Elvis died. This isn't a coincidence. And I'm not the only one who thinks that it isn't."

"In your book, you say Elvis faked his death," John said, repeating Mrs. Morris's comment. He hadn't read Professor Gentry's book. He'd been reading something else.

"His fans weren't going to buy a book saying Elvis was dead," Professor Gentry said, shrugging his shoulders like suggesting Elvis was still alive was a sound marketing strategy. "One thing I learned from Elvis, you have to know your audience."

John shook his head. Professor Gentry was no better than *The National Enquirer*, using folklore to sell copy.

"After Elvis's death, Colonel Hollister became obsessed, paranoid. This was all anyone was talking about at Graceland at the time. No one there can keep a secret. Like me, Colonel Hollister figured both Elvis's death and the Wow! Signal were related, but he took it one step further. He believed both events were part of an alien invasion plot of the United States, that they intended to cripple our psyche by eliminating cultural icons, starting with Elvis Presley."

"Alright," the sheriff said, "what's all this gotta do with Leadbelly getting murdered?"

"For years Elvis collected data on alien activity. During our last walk, he told me he was worried an alien contingent had learned he was spying on them. Colonel Hollister had Elvis's manager increase the amount and function of his body doubles. Everyone thought the doubles were due to Elvis's increased drug use. That's what they wanted everyone to think, but it really had to do with the danger he was in."

"Elvis told you everything about his investigation, about aliens?" John asked. He had been holding the journal on his lap since they sat down and John brushed his thumb along the pages' ratted and tattered edges.

"Yup."

"Did he tell you about this?" John set his great-great-great-grandfather Archibald's journal on the table, delicately slid it to the middle. He only showed them the book, not the pictures. He left them under his seat in the car.

"You're kidding me." Professor Gentry held the book, caressed its cover. "Where did you get this?"

"It was in Leadbelly's trailer."

"I guess this is that moment where you tell me what the hell that thing is," Sheriff Masters said, looking over at John.

"The journal of Archibald Abernathy," Professor Gentry said. "I thought it was a myth."

"What the hell does a diary gotta do with Leadbelly?"

"Not Leadbelly," John said. "Me. Archibald Abernathy's my great-great-great-grandfather."

"You know your great-great-great-grandfather's name?" the sheriff asked.

"School project."

"This journal is the key to understanding the alien invasion," Professor Gentry said. "Have you read any of it?"

"Parts," John said. He told them what he'd read so far, Abraham Lincoln, Archibald, Louisa, the extraterrestrials, Las Vegas. "Sorry I didn't tell you about it earlier, Sheriff. I didn't know what to make of it, how everything fit together."

"And what do you think about you being part alien and all?" the sheriff asked.

"It's just a piece of paper. It doesn't mean anything." The connections existed, but they weren't fastened together, unable to convince John that he was anything more than a puzzle maker.

"The journal," Professor Gentry said, standing and pacing the linoleum, "Elvis told me all about it when we'd walk his chimp, Scatter. Walking dogs is one thing, but a diaper-wearing chimp...That journal, he'd talk about it like it was the Holy Grail or the Rosetta Stone, something that would help them find an edge in their battle against the extraterrestrials. I never thought I'd live to see it."

"When we showed up, that's how you knew my name." John realized it was also how Colonel Hollister knew his name.

"The Abernathy name is infamous in some circles. All because of this journal." Professor Gentry jabbed his finger at the journal before turning and continuing his circuit. "Archibald Abernathy regularly sent copies of his entries to the War Department like President Lincoln asked, but after a while, he just stopped sending them. Your great-great-great-grandfather kept really detailed journals, so it was always assumed he continued chronicling his life. President Roosevelt, not FDR, the other one, Theodore, he issued an executive order authorizing the secret service to seize it, but Archibald's house burned down the day of his funeral. Everyone thought the journal was lost in the fire."

"The land where the house was, it's a Party Store," John said. Everything Professor Gentry said contradicted what John had learned about his family history, how the Abernathys migrated to Denver looking for a new life, how Archibald's fate became a parable for making sure the stove was turned off, not wanting to lose the family fortune in a fire. Although the present-day Abernathy fortune consisted of student loan debt, late rent, and credit card bills.

"When I was in Leadbelly's trailer, I saw a bunch of photos on the wall. For Los Alamos and Area 51. Surveillance photos." John left out the pictures of him as a kid.

"He must have somehow become aware of Elvis's connection to the government and was secretly investigating."

"Maybe he read your book," John said.

"And he discovered something he shouldn't have, probably the journal, and was assassinated for it, but where did he find it?"

"Wait? If Elvis read a copy of the journal…"

"He'd quote it to me while I'd scoop dog poo," Professor Gentry said.

"Then Colonel Hollister gave it to him." John had read another name in the journal, one that held immediate significance for him. "Rosa! Archibald mentions her. It said she was just a kid then."

"If it's in the journal…" Professor Gentry said.

"Then Colonel Hollister believes it."

"And your Rosa is in danger."

CHAPTER TWENTY-TWO

On the way back to town, John's foot bounced against the floor mat. He kept thinking about Rosa, what she knew, what she didn't tell him. He thought about seeing her again, and wondered whether she'd be happy to see him. He hoped that she'd embrace him, let him hold her, run his fingers along the narrow muscles in her lower back. He doubted that would happen. She'd probably be awkward and uncomfortable, subtly hinting that he should leave. Still, he needed to see her.

He read an entry near the journal's end. Professor Gentry stuck his head between the front seats, trying to read over John's shoulder, but John ignored him.

July 23, 1867

> *After years of trying to conceive, Louisa and I finally succeeded. Fortunately, several of her relatives had journeyed from New Mexico to help with the delivery. I say fortunately because the birthing was so unusual that a normal doctor would have been hard pressed to continue after the first child was born.*

Two days ago, Louisa gave birth to six children, two boys and four girls, in succession.

After the delivery, I walked over to a chair and collapsed. The experience exhausted me. I could only imagine what Louisa went through. From the chair, I looked around the room at Louisa's mother and aunts. They shared similar features, the shape of the nose and jaw line in particular. I thought they shared these similarities because they had the same parents, but looking at them I realized it was because they were like my children, born mere minutes apart.

Louisa's mother and aunts decided it would be best if they took five of the children with them to New Mexico. Louisa and I agreed and kept the oldest boy. We named him Dominic Oscar Abernathy and swore never to tell him about his siblings.

"Learning anything useful?" Professor Gentry asked, leaning over John's shoulder.

"It's just a book," John said. "It doesn't mean anything."

"Then how come you keep reading it?"

September 3, 1901

I cough more often than I care to admit. The nurse comes running when she hears me caught in a fit. My body becomes spastic and uncontrollable, but the soothing presence of the young woman helps. She reminds me of my beautiful Louisa. I miss her. She still visits me in my dreams, but I am becoming senile and I think it hurts her to see my mind deteriorate. She left twenty years ago. It was a mutual decision based on the need to protect our son. I knew it would end soon enough when I started to show my age and she remained as beautiful as the day we met. I'll never forget that warm, sunny day. On my fiftieth birthday, we ventured into the mountains for a weekend retreat and I came back alone. I told everyone that there had been an accident, but Louisa turned into an eagle and flew south to her family and our other children. I often wonder what of Louisa is in Dominic. He has never shown any sign of the abilities she possesses, but that doesn't mean they are not there, lying dormant.

Sheriff Masters's siren could be heard in the plaza as they turned off the highway, a faint chirping that grew louder with each block, until the two-toned alarm filled the square, forcing cars to pull to the side of the road and pedestrians to run onto sidewalks.

The plaza looked normal, with the exception of the people staring at them, whispering to each other. John searched the crowd for Colonel Hollister or his men. He sighed and relaxed in his seat, not seeing anyone looking like they worked for the Air Force, the clean shaven faces, the crew cuts, the heavy artillery. They might have been through already, searched the plaza, or they were still cleaning up Leadbelly's fire, but they weren't there now, and John hoped that meant Rosa was safe.

The sheriff parked in front of Rosa's Restaurante, leaving the car in the middle of the street. John sprinted to the restaurant's glass door.

"Where's Rosa?" he asked, surprised that he wasn't out of breath. The high school girl who worked last night was back, doing the lunch shift.

"She's not here."

"Well, where is she?" John asked. She glanced at the sheriff.

"It's okay, darling," the sheriff said. "No one's in trouble. We just need to know where Rosa is."

"I don't know. She called in saying she was taking a vacation, that she'd be gone for a while."

"How long?" John asked.

"I don't know, she didn't say."

"No, how long ago did she call?" John asked, grabbing her arm.

"Sometime this morning, before we opened," she said, taking a step backward, clutching the menus in front of her chest.

"What about Jose?" Sheriff Masters asked. He put his hand on John's shoulder and John stepped back, bumping into a chair, looking at the scuff marks on his shoes.

"He's not here either. He called in saying he was taking a vacation, too."

"Has anyone been to her house, checked on them or anything?" John asked.

"Yeah, Jed, the line cook, lives with Jose. He said he took them to the bus station this morning. Uh, he shouldn't be back there."

While they were talking, Professor Gentry had

slinked into the kitchen. He held a lid in his hand, inhaling the smoke from a steaming pot as it lingered above the stove.

"Professor!" John yelled. "Get out here! We gotta get to the bus station!"

He ambled out of the kitchen eating chips from a small, paper bag.

"Really?"

"John, I don't get into town that often."

"That's obvious."

The bus station was a blue art deco building on the corner of New Mexico Avenue and West National Avenue, a few blocks from the Plaza. The building's edges were rounded and a neon Greyhound sign extended above the entrance. White wings stretched from the sides of the building, shading travelers who waited for the two buses that could dock there and currently one idled. It reminded John of an image from his Survey of Great Artistic Movements Expressed as Public Transportation Buildings textbook. The sheriff trotted to the counter, asked if Rosa and Jose had bought bus tickets. The attendant told them they boarded the bus for Albuquerque at 9:30 a.m., twenty minutes after she'd left the motel.

"Has anyone else been by asking about them?" John asked, through the hole in the glass partition that separated them from the attendant.

"You're the only ones," the attendant said.

"She's probably fine," the sheriff said to John as

they walked through double glass doors and into the parking lot. The hiss of hydraulics. "They were halfway to Albuquerque when we were at Leadbelly's this morning."

"Albuquerque," John said, looking south. A Greyhound left the station and headed toward the highway.

"Tell you what, the sheriff in Albuquerque's a buddy a mine. I'll give him a call, see if one a his boys can run down to the bus station, see if Rosa made it."

"Thanks, Sheriff, I appreciate that."

The sun reflected off the exiting bus's windows. It was an intangible, bright ball, existing only in reflected image. But it was real enough to blind.

"Goddamnit," John said, shielding his eyes. "If Rosa was worried about something, why didn't she talk to me?"

"Maybe she was protecting you."

That morning, when she'd said goodbye, she was distant, pushing John away. But the way she kissed him, the longing, she seemed torn.

"That hadn't occurred to me."

They heard muffled departure times announced and turned as Professor Gentry ducked into the bus station. He loitered by the entrance, then sprinted to the bus station's diner and packed his jacket pockets with napkins and ketchup packets.

"You should take Professor Gentry to your station," John said, "show him the jail cell that guy was in last night."

"Ha, I would, but I don't want him bothering the rummies in the drunk tank. I'll get Jimmy to take him home."

"What are you thinking?" John asked.

"I'm thinking this is gonna be another one a them unsolved cases." A fast food wrapper drifted across the empty bus lot. It brushed the sheriff's boot. He leaned over to pick it up, but a gust of wind blew it underneath a Honda Civic.

"I don't know. Someone once told me it's not over."

"You know, I try to do my job best I can, but I just ain't equipped to handle people like Hollister."

"I know the feeling," John said.

"So, how much longer you gonna be in town?"

"Not sure. I got the motel room another night. Figure I'll leave in the morning."

"Wanna ride to your car?" the sheriff asked, thumbing to his squad car parked in the handicapped space.

"I think I'll walk. It's not that far."

"All right, then. I'll pick you up for dinner?"

"Sounds good," John said. He wouldn't be at the motel. Rosa had absconded to Albuquerque, and John needed to find her, protect her. As soon he was packed, he'd leave, dropping a note for the sheriff at the front desk. It would be an impersonal goodbye, a big city goodbye. But it would have to do.

He shook Sheriff Masters's hand and walked

down the street to the plaza. Halfway down the block, John heard the sheriff yelling and reeled around, and laughed as the sheriff tried to shove Professor Gentry into the car. The professor was like a dog that had escaped from its yard, running everywhere but home.

CHAPTER TWENTY-THREE

John checked the bullets in his gun and reinserted the clip. The faded cloth interior of his Saturn absorbed the metallic snap. He was parked down the block, on the corner, and had been watching the motel for over twenty minutes. But it was empty. Nothing moved. He set the gun on the passenger seat, next to the journal and photos.

The journal. It was the most dangerous object in the car. Scribbled by an ancestor, it completely rewrote John's history. At first he thought it was preposterous, that he was the latest product of an alien breeding program. He had an expensive degree that said he knew how to pursue clues and solve puzzles, and, pondering the evidence and events of the past few days, he reached a disturbing conclusion. He gripped the top of the steering wheel, rested his head on his hands, accepted that the journal and everything in it was real. A tear dribbled down his cheek. As more tears flowed, John lifted his head and laughed, feeling sorrow and relief, because everything he knew about himself was false.

John sniffled and wiped his eyes and slowly

drove down Baca Drive. He scanned the road as he crossed Grand Avenue, looking for anything that seemed unusual or artificial, a suspicious car, an unnaturally empty street, or Professor Gentry walking a diapered monkey.

He pulled into the motel parking lot and the pain in his stomach returned. It was stronger, like his intestines were twisting. John clamped onto his stomach and bent over, accidentally slamming his foot on the gas. His car careened through the parking lot, heading toward the motel room door. John braked hard, stopping between two parking spaces, spilling the gun and book onto the car floor. He decided, if the sheriff asked, he'd tell him that it was a strategic move, meant to confuse anyone who was watching, make them think he was lost or drunk, a pretty easy sell for a town where half the billboards advertised DUI attorneys.

John picked the gun and book off the car floor, grateful the gun hadn't gone off, shooting him in the foot. He scraped up the pictures. The photo on top. John is opening a Christmas present, an inflatable Godzilla that he could punch and wrestle. His mother wanted to get him a Pound Puppy, thinking the giant lizard would be too terrifying for her young child, but his father insisted, saying John needed to learn that what he thinks are monsters are really just obstacles to be body slammed and pile drived. John lodged the photos in the book, surprised that seeing a photo could cause him to relive something as cool as getting a blow-up Godzilla. He carried the book and photos to his room, pulling out his key.

But at the door.

He stopped.

It was cracked a few inches.

But he'd locked it before he left, tugged it a couple of times to make sure.

The curtains were drawn. A soft lamplight shone through the crack. The maid's cart was a few doors down, parked in front of an open room.

John took out his gun, put his back against the wall. Turning his head slightly, he smelled the crack. He didn't know why he did it. It just seemed natural, instinctual. The scent confused him. He expected the room to smell like cleaning supplies. Instead, it smelled like peanut butter and bananas. There was only one person who ate that combination, a person who was supposed to be dead.

John tucked the journal and photos in the front of his pants, zipped up his hoodie.

With his back to the outside wall, he slowly pushed the door open. Keeping half his body hidden behind the wall, John spun and pointed the gun inside. A man sitting on the bed, watching TV, eating a sandwich. The sequins on his one-piece jumpsuit flickered like the nighttime neon on the Vegas Strip.

"Leadbelly," John said, lowering his gun. "Jesus

Christ. We thought you were dead."

"Now, man, why would you think a thing like that?" Leadbelly asked, taking a bite of his sandwich. The bruises and swelling from the bar fight were gone. The skin on his face was smooth and the color had returned from the greenish-yellow of contusions to the tan of the Memphis Delta. Every hair in his pompadour had been intentionally arranged. His sideburns were focused and had been trimmed, ending right at his earlobes. And Leadbelly looked exactly like the King.

John holstered his gun and closed the door. "Because you went missing and your trailer was covered in blood. The sheriff even came out here."

"Yeah, I saw y'all leave this morning. Decided to wait for you to get back." He took another bite.

"You've been here all day watching soaps?"

"Well, man, not exactly." The toilet flushed.

"Who's in there?" John put his hand on his gun. The bathroom door opened and a heavyset Mexican woman in her mid-fifties walked out, buttoning her housekeeping blouse, smoothing and putting bobby pins into her dyed, black hair.

"Adios, Señor Elvis," she said.

Leadbelly stood. He grabbed her around the waist with one arm and pulled her in, the sandwich still in the other hand. He leaned in, kissed her, then curled his lip and said, "Thank you. Thank you very much."

She clutched her shirt and staggered out of the

room. John heard her vacuuming the room next door through the wall.

"Man, Carmilta's a big fan," Leadbelly said, taking another bite of his sandwich.

"On my bed? Really? On my bed?"

"Don't worry, man, she changed the sheets."

"Well, that makes it alright," John said.

"I told her you'd say that."

"I spent all day trying to figure out what happened to you, and now I find you've been here with what's-her-name."

"Carmilta. Man, she's a very sweet lady. Did I mention she's a big fan?"

"On my bed? And please tell me you weren't wearing that suit the whole time."

"Oh, this," Leadbelly said, smoothing some sequins on his chest. He tucked his thumb under the bedazzled lapel like a farmer whose cash crop was nacho cheese. "Man, this here's my traveling suit."

"Where're you going?"

"That's what I came here to talk to you about, man. My transportation has kinda, well, burned to the ground."

"You talking about your trailer? I was there. My clothes still smell like a burnt leisure suit."

"Yeah, well, I need a ride outta town."

"If you think I'm giving you a ride anywhere..."

"You looking for Rosa, man? She didn't go to Albuquerque."

"How did you..." John recalled Rosa sleeping on her side, the sheet slipping from her naked shoulder.

"We're going to the same place, man. All I need's a ride." Leadbelly placed his open palm over his heart like he was pledging allegiance to polyester, cheap beer, and unprotected sex. John sensed a rare sincerity radiating from Leadbelly, like he was projecting his earnestness. Even though John knew he could trust Leadbelly, his day had been dominated by riddles.

"Alright," John said. "You want a ride out of town? Tell me why the Air Force was at your trailer. What do you have on them?"

"The Air Force? Man, they're the sonsabitches I been running from. Been running since Vegas."

"They're the ones you borrowed money from? They're the reason you burned your chapel?"

"Yeah, man. It's like you said," Leadbelly said, taking a bite of his sandwich, "I owed them some money and now they've caught up to me."

"You're going to have to try harder than that. What do you have on them?"

"They're blackmailing me, man. Trying to."

"They're after you," John interrupted, "because you have something they want. This." He pulled out the journal. John didn't toss it on the bed or put it anywhere Leadbelly could reach it. He held it, waved it, the photos flapping between the pages. Taunting Leadbelly with the journal, John felt tranquil, admitting a truth about himself, the journal, its implications, and he was agitated that the only person who could explain it to him was an Elvis impersonator.

"Oh, man, I thought I'd lost it," Leadbelly said. He relaxed a little. "I'd a been in a heap a trouble. But you got it, man. That's a good thing."

"You sure? 'Cause I know how you got it. You took it from Archibald's house the day of his funeral, right before you burned the place."

"How did you know, man?"

"It's your M.O. Every time you run, you cover it up with a fire. You burned your trailer, your chapel, and Archibald's house. Archibald's house, the land where it used to be, it's a Party Store now."

"Yeah, man, maybe they'll have a fire sale."

"Not funny." John waved the journal. "Are you in here? Does Archibald mention you?"

"Briefly," Leadbelly said. "I'm his son, man, the one that was raised in New Mexico. Your great-great-uncle."

"Are you kidding me?" John grabbed his hair and looked at the ceiling. A crack in the plaster cut through it.

"Sorry, you had to find out this way, man. I wish I could have been there for you, taught you how to play guitar, how take off a girl's bra with one hand."

"The important stuff, right?"

"I just wish things coulda been different. Hell, if

they had, I coulda sang at all your birthday parties."

"You were already there." John threw a picture at Leadbelly. John is sitting at a table, crying as he blows out the candles on a cake shaped like a giant six.

"Hey, man, don't be cruel."

"Really? You're quoting songs now?" John said, rolling his eyes. "This is just great. My great-great-uncle's a fucking Elvis impersonator."

"It's not like that, man. I was one of Elvis's body doubles, from '69 to '77, all the way to the end." Leadbelly finished his sandwich and wiped his hands, brushing crumbs onto the carpet.

"That's why you look like him? so you could spy on him?"

"Yeah, man. We found out he was spying on us. So, a group of us became his body doubles."

"And being aliens, you were the perfect body doubles, copying his hair, voice, everything, right?"

"Yeah, man, all us body doubles were Sagittarians. Man, it was glorious." Leadbelly looked at the curtains covering the window, cloaking them from the empty parking lot.

"Sagittarian? You all were into astrology, too?" John asked, thinking about the horoscopes just below the crosswords, and how he ignored their manufactured prophecies.

"It's who we are, man, where we're from, you and me."

"Bullshit. I'm nothing like you. I don't play dress-up. I don't pretend to be something I'm not."

"You sure about that?" Leadbelly nodded to the table, to John's blank crossword.

"That's you. You and all the body doubles, dressing up like your hero Elvis Presley, living off his scraps because you couldn't make it on your own. Then he died and you went into hiding 'cause you couldn't take it."

"After Elvis's funeral, man, we all knew the Air Force would come for us. So, man, we decided to make a run for it."

"Did they know you were aliens?" John asked. He squeezed the journal and the cover squeaked.

"Not sure, man. One a my buddies, he started getting these phone calls, real scary shit. So, man, we decided to take off."

"But they didn't know where you were, not until you fucked up and let someone take your picture. You even posed for it, waving to God-knows-what. And the Air Force got everything they needed from the reporter, right before they killed him. Then they put your place under surveillance. Followed you, found out about Rosa."

"Yeah, man, I kinda fucked up."

"Who told her to sleep with me?"

Leadbelly's head jerked back. "Man, that's not really for me to say."

"The fuck you can't." John threw the journal at Leadbelly. He caught it, gently held the artifact.

John charged him while he was distracted. He grabbed Leadbelly's lapels, swung him around, slammed him into the wall.

"Did Jonathon Deerfoot tell Rosa to sleep with me?"

"Man, you're worrying about the wrong thing."

John reared back to punch Leadbelly. His hand started to ache. The aching grew into biting pain as the bones in his hand pushed their way to the surface, breaking through his skin, wrapping around and shielding each finger and joint until his fist was gloved by an exoskeleton.

"That's awesome, man." Leadbelly smiled.

"Fuck you." John punched Leadbelly. He'd never punched anyone before and was surprised at how it felt. He smiled, exhilarated, but his smile faded as the adrenaline ebbed and he turned away, feeling guilt, shame at hurting someone. Even if it was Leadbelly.

"Oh, Jesus. Are you alright?" John asked, his hand on Leadbelly's shoulder.

Leadbelly leaned over, his hand propped against the wall, its textured wallpaper slightly peeling. He straightened up, laughing, blood running from his nose to his chin.

"Alright, man, alright." He held up a hand in mock surrender. The blood retracted, crawling past his lip, returning to his nose, healing.

"Why didn't you do that the other day? after the bar fight?"

"I had to be convincing, man," Leadbelly said.

"I'm sorry," John said, staring at the bones covering his hand. "I didn't mean..."

"Did you see what you just did, man? with your hand?"

The bones shrank back into John's flesh. The splits in his skin sealed, as did any doubts John had about his ancestry, his present. It was the final piece of evidence that the journal and everything in it was real. He rubbed his hand, checking to see if it was softer, or would crack at his touch.

"Man, you're embracing your Sagittarian side. That's great."

"Not if it means hurting people." John sat on the bed, wrinkling the newly straightened comforter. Slouching, he looked at his hand, flexed his fingers. "This isn't who I am."

"This part of you, man. It can be whatever you want it to be. It can be amazing."

"I don't want any of this." On the small table by the window. A pad of unused graph paper. His voice lowered to a whisper. "I just want to do my puzzles."

"Man, tell you what," Leadbelly sat next to him, "you get me outta here and I'll tell you everything you want to know. Rosa, the pictures you took from my trailer. Man, I'll even tell you about your dad."

"Fuck him," John said, an automatic response, then added in a whisper full of suppressed curiosity, "What do you know about my dad?"

"More than you, man. That's for sure." Leadbelly slid out a photo that was tucked in the journal's pages, looked at it and grinned. "You look just like him, you know."

"Fuck you." John's eyes watered up. He always assumed his dad was living in another part of the country with another family, and another son. Then his dad would visit him in dreams and try to convince John that he was the most important person in his life. Talking to Leadbelly, it occurred to him that his dad might be out there, hiding, and the only person who knew where to find him reeked of bananas, sex, and cleaning supplies. The police station number was printed on the hotel's phone along with a pizza delivery place and other emergency numbers.

"Shirley? Yeah, this is John Abernathy. Is Sheriff Masters there yet?"

The sheriff came to the phone. "John, what can I do you for?"

"Well, how can I say this, our friend came to visit me?"

"Our friend?"

"Yeah, you know the one. He's here with me right now. Wants to see you."

"Oh. Okay, I'll be right over."

John scrolled through his call history, not wanting to dial the next number.

"Rex Grant, please. Tell him it's John Abernathy."

"John. What have you found out?"

"Rex, how would you like an exclusive with an Elvis body double?" John didn't need to sell the story. Rex Grant would have jumped at anything Elvis.

Leadbelly raised his hands, shook his head, objecting.

John put his hand over the phone and whispered, "Don't worry. I'm just bluffing."

John told him everything, the alien conspiracy, the Air Force's involvement, even the Elvis connection. He could see Rex drooling on the other end of the phone, envisioning old women lined up at the supermarket, issue in one hand, a couple of dollars and a pint of mint chocolate chip ice cream in the other.

"Here's the catch, Rex, you gotta get us outta the state. The Air Force'll lock up Leadbelly the minute they see him, and you'll be out a story."

"Hold on, John, I'm looking at a map right now. Can you get to Santa Fe?"

"Yeah, I think so."

"If you can get to Sante Fe, I can meet you there with a chartered flight to L.A."

Rex Grant told John to take back roads in case the Air Force was watching the highway. He suggested which roads to take, planned their route. John wrote them down and hung up.

John quickly texted Rooftop, telling him the case had taken an interesting turn, that he'd be a few more days. Rooftop wouldn't mind. A few more days meant more money. John debated telling him what was really going on, but knew what his response would be, that John should drive to Denver and leave everything in the hands of the police. John knew that leaving wasn't an option, that there was nothing for him in Denver, nothing that could help solve the Sagittarian conundrum. Only Leadbelly could help him with that, and he'd given John another incentive to help him. He'd promised to tell John about his father, and to take him to Rosa.

John went to the window, peeled back the yellow curtain. The lot was empty. Every now and then, on the road, a truck going nowhere.

They heard the sheriff's siren down the block. He sped into the motel parking lot, parking next to John, taking up a couple of spaces. Leadbelly and John ran out the door, not giving him a chance to get out of his squad car.

"What's he doing here?" John asked as Professor Gentry got out of the car.

"I thought he and Leadbelly could talk about Elvis."

"I know you." Professor Gentry stared at Leadbelly, pointing his stubby finger.

"Professor Gentry. Al Leadbelly," John said, introducing them. "He was an Elvis body double."

"We met a couple a times at Graceland, man," Leadbelly said.

"Where're we going?" Sheriff Masters asked.

"Santa Fe," John said. "*Enquirer's* gonna meet us there. I told them about Leadbelly, the Air Force, everything."

"Man, that's not our main worry," Leadbelly said. "We gotta get past the Air Force."

"In that case, John," the sheriff said, "we're taking your car. It'll attract less attention. Gimme the keys. I'll drive."

Sheriff Masters went to the back of his squad car and popped the trunk. "John, get over here." Sheriff Masters strapped on his gun belt. He pulled a Remington 870 12 gauge shotgun out of the trunk and handed it to John. "You know how to use this?"

"Yeah, I think I remember." John rubbed his shoulder, recalling the bruise the kick of a shotgun can give a skinny teenager. And smiled remembering Rooftop's bribe of an Xbox if John promised not to tell his mom.

The sheriff handed John some shells.

"Good. Load it in the car."

CHAPTER
TWENTY FOUR

The sky around the trailer park was pink and blue against the brown desert and rusted portable homes. Although barricades still sealed Alamo Street, the road around the entrance to the trailer park, blocking residents from returning to their homes, the tent that had covered it was being dismantled, folded and collapsed. The soldiers that had guarded the tent and protected the crime scene were packing their gear, checking their ammunition. The sliding doors of vans filled with boxes, artifacts taken from Leadbelly's trailer, were being slammed shut. Standing next to a Hummer, arms crossed, Colonel Hollister admired the crisp and efficient movements of his men.

They'd arrived early that morning, the science team and the platoon, when the sun barely hovered above the ground and the sky had begun to brighten. Colonel Hollister requested them after he received an alert in the middle of the night that the local sheriff's office was running the fingerprints of one of his operatives. He immediately sent Private Ramsey to Leadbelly's trailer to check on the old drunk, see if he was passed out. Colonel Hollister watched through the monitors in their converted command center as Private Ramsey rushed from the trailer, shrieking. When he returned, breathless, talking about blood and a dead body smell, although it was only cheap cologne and dirty clothes, Colonel Hollister thought about John leaving Leadbelly's, how calm he'd been. He scratched his head. He was actually beginning to admire the Abernathy boy. At least he didn't embarrass himself like this.

Colonel Hollister called Los Alamos and requested everything he'd need to initiate the next phase of his investigation. He almost giggled when he hung up the phone, excited that a dead lead had been revived, his investigation renewed. He felt rejuvenated, like an aging artist that had rediscovered their love for creation.

When his authorization came, Colonel Hollister dispatched Private Mulworth to fetch his men from the town jail. The story of how John Abernathy had interfered with the retrieval of Rosa Jimenez, hospitalizing the other operative, was told to Colonel Hollister as he ate a bowl of microwave oatmeal. He took a bite and burned his mouth on an uncooled chunk of apple when he saw Sheriff Masters run from Leadbelly's trailer, even though a convoy of Hummers and cargo vans had just exited I-25, was turning onto South Grand.

After a long day, with some unexpected fireworks, his men should've been returning to their families. But, as Colonel Hollister knew, their job was never over.

"Sergeant Portersley, are your men ready?" Colonel Hollister asked, shouting over the engine noise. He held an iPad, glancing at the image of a map.

"Yes, sir. The men are loaded up." Sergeant Portersly said, dragging his finger along a scar that ran next to his ear, from his blond crew cut down to his jaw, an unconscious habit. He had served in Afghanistan before being transferred to Colonel Hollister's unit, and thought protecting an underground research facility, pacing on the green and white tiled floor beneath neon lights, beat the hell out of getting blown up in the desert.

"And you have the coordinates?" Colonel Hollister asked.

"Yes, sir. You're sure the target will be there?" A few ambushes on Afghani mountain roads due to bad intelligence caused him to question his commanding officers. It's one of the reasons he was transferred. The other reason, the reason Colonel Hollister requested had him, was his predisposition for malice and persecution.

"Our intel is reliable."

"With all due respect, sir, you're not really giving us much to go on."

"You have all you need," Colonel Hollister said, glancing at his map.

"The men have questions, sir," Sergeant

Portersly said, hooking his thumbs under his body armor. "If we could just get a little more information about the target…"

"You're dismissed, Sergeant."

"Just telling us where to go isn't…"

"Dismissed." Colonel Hollister glared at him.

"Yes, sir."

Sergeant Portersly stamped over to where some of his men were lounging next to their Hummer. He yelled at them, telling them to step it up, that they were moving out shortly and didn't want to be left behind.

Colonel Hollister tapped the iPad against his leg. He couldn't tell the sergeant how he got his information, how he knew John Abernathy and Al Leadbelly would be leaving town, what route they'd be taking, or the significance of either man. All Sergeant Portersley needed to know was where to stand and whom to shoot.

Al Leadbelly.

It had been years since Colonel Hollister had heard that name, not since the days when he visited Elvis in Graceland, sweating in the shade, or when Elvis lived in the suite at the International Hotel, the room smelling like stale cigarette smoke and air conditioning. Leadbelly would stand next to Elvis, whispering jokes about chocolate pudding and pussy. Elvis would laugh hysterically, because he loved both of those things. Usually at the same time. That was how he got close to Elvis, dirty jokes. But he stayed close because he was reliable, talented, always there, ready to step in if needed.

The first time he met Al Leadbelly was on August 6th, 1969. Colonel Hollister was just a major then and Elvis had finally convinced him to let him spend more time in the field investigating alien activity. Elvis had just finished his dinner show at the International Hotel in Las Vegas and was interviewing body double applicants, singers, actors, and regular people who resembled Elvis, to perform in his place. He'd seen several singers that day and didn't like any of them. Some were too short, fat, bald, sang off key, couldn't do karate, didn't like Southern food, drove Lincolns instead of Cadillacs, didn't know any of Elvis's songs, wore bad wigs that would spawn rumors that Elvis wore a toupee to hide his drugs in, were missing three fingers on one hand, had burns on half their face from blacking out next to a radiator, or even worse, didn't know who Elvis was. Reducing Elvis's expectations. Elvis had pointed out a table full of women during his first show to the stage manager, had backstage passes sent to them along with shots of Southern Comfort. They were waiting in the hall and Elvis wanted to take them to his suite before his next show, but he had to listen to another hack from Buttfuck, Nowhere butcher 'Jailhouse Rock'.

Then Al Leadbelly strutted into the dressing room. He complimented himself in the mirror, patting his hair into place. Major Hollister wanted to kick him out, but Elvis saw something familiar in Leadbelly, the inexplicable charisma, the irreverent way he asked Major Hollister to get him a French dip sandwich, that he wasn't intimidated by the most famous person in the world, and that Leadbelly didn't wait for an invitation to sing. He belted out 'Heartbreak Hotel' with all the awkward gyrations, hand gestures, and perspiration of a grown man trying to recapture his youth. Leadbelly stopped after one verse, then suggested that if they wanted to hear more, they'd have to pay him. Major Hollister moved to throw him out, but Elvis stopped him, saying Leadbelly was perfect, just what they needed. He even suggested that Leadbelly do his midnight show. Major Hollister started to protest, but Elvis hurried past him, to the group of women in the hall. He put his arms around them and walked off, telling Major Hollister not to wait up. Leadbelly sat in Elvis's chair, opened a beer, and called for the next impersonator.

Leadbelly performed Elvis's midnight show flawlessly, wearing Elvis's white herringbone suit, a perfect fit. He even hired seven more body doubles, convincing them he was Elvis. Over the next couple of days, he helped Elvis hire the other four body doubles. Standing next to his Hummer, Colonel Hollister wondered if Leadbelly knew the other body doubles, if the whole thing was a set-up so they could get close to Elvis. Or maybe it was that years of working covertly had made him paranoid.

But that wasn't what truly bothered him. It took him years to admit it, but he was actually envious of Leadbelly and the other body doubles. He had trained Elvis, nurtured him, treated him like a son. And that was the problem, by being a father figure to Elvis, he could never be as close to him as he would have liked. Their relationship would always be two-tiered, master and apprentice, teacher and student, commanding officer and top-secret-operative-that-spied-on-extraterrestrials. They could never be equals. Not like with the body doubles. They gave Elvis what Colonel Hollister never could, someone to party with, someone who mirrored Elvis in every way, shared his self-destructive need for drugs and women, the need to get as fucked up as possible every night. As much as he hated to admit it, Colonel Hollister wished that person could have been him, but that never would have happened. Even though Elvis loved him like a father, Colonel Hollister was not cool. He was still just a square.

Colonel Hollister strapped on his gun belt. He tightened it, feeling the pistol's weight on his right hip and leg. He checked his clip, made sure there were enough rounds. He'd only need one.

"Sir," a man said. He stood behind Colonel Hollister.

"Lieutenant Grant, out of the office at last," Colonel Hollister said, putting his gun back in its holster. "Your first field assignment. Are you ready?"

"Yes, sir," Lieutenant Rex Grant said. "I just wanted you to know that I appreciate the faith you've shown in me." The other men wore desert camouflage, browns and tans, but Lieutenant Grant wore a dark blue suit and a thin black tie. He adjusted the Half Windsor knot.

"Well, you deserve it. We wouldn't be here if it weren't for you."

"It was luck, sir. That's all." He was still young, early thirties, but his hair was turning gray. He ran his hand on top of it, combing it forward.

"Nonsense. Luck is just a word used by people with no initiative. You showed what you can do with a little responsibility. We haven't been this close to winning the war since..." At his feet, a pothole had cracked and eroded the street. It had been patched with asphalt and tar, patted down with a shovel. A black lump in the road.

"Sir?"

"This is a great night," Colonel Hollister said, putting a hand on Lieutenant Grant's shoulder. "Just remember that. Whatever happens, whatever you see, this is a great night."

"Yes, sir, I will. Anyway, I just wanted to come over here and thank you for the trust you've shown in me." His thumb brushed the tips of his nicotine-stained fingers.

"And the promotion doesn't hurt either."

"No, sir, it doesn't." He tried to smile, but kept his mouth closed. He whitened his teeth with each cleaning, but they were starting to stain.

"You'll find that now, with your clearance raised, you'll start to see the world differently, like you're looking through a window that has just been cleaned."

"That's very poetic, sir."

"You would know. You're the writer. Now, the Abernathy boy, he doesn't suspect anything?"

"How could he, sir? To him, I'm just someone who sells gossip at the supermarkets. He has no idea what I really do."

"Then he won't know what's waiting for him."

"And you're sure he's who you've been looking for?" Lieutenant Grant searched the pockets of his tailored suit for a pack of cigarettes.

"I made a promise to his father that I'd leave his son alone, assuming his son stayed out of New Mexico, but he's here now, and with Al Leadbelly, so I have no choice. Now, go get ready. We have a car to catch."

Lieutenant Grant hopped in a Hummer that was loaded with armed men and smelled of gun oil, gasoline, and sweat. He lit a cigarette, blew the smoke out an open window, and draped his arm outside, his hand tapping the thick metal door.

Colonel Hollister knew Lieutenant Grant would rather stay with the science team, cataloging the various articles of debris they excavated from

Leadbelly's trailer, but it was important for him to see the effects of his work at *The National Enquirer*. Colonel Hollister had been to his office, seen the cubicles, the old desktop computers, *Potato Chips That Look Like John Travolta Vol. 12* wall calendars, novelty coffee mugs shaped like alien heads or covered in middle fingers that comprised Lieutenant Grant's work life. He'd walked past the rows of enlisted men who had been rejected from *Stars and Stripes* magazine for various minor offenses, usually wanting to publish stories about celebrities and their breasts. These young men, with their desire to exploit and belittle public figures, were sent to Lieutenant Grant to become the writers behind *The National Enquirer's* greatest stories and headlines, selling the public on the importance of cloning mermaids and convincing its readers that the ghost of John F. Kennedy haunted a porn studio. It seemed to Colonel Hollister that every time he walked on the beige carpet between the gray, plastic walls, the men giggled at a recently written headline like it was an inside joke. And the punch line was that they weren't writing headlines or poorly edited articles to fulfill their journalistic calling. The reason they laughed as they created absurd stories about the sex scandals of celebrity pets and fad diets of South American shamans was because they were serving their country by providing a distraction, not from the monotony of hollow jobs or indifferent families, but a distraction from the work that Colonel Hollister was doing.

And Lieutenant Grant was one of the best, although that wasn't his real name. Rex Grant was a pseudonym given to every editor-in-chief of *The National Enquirer*, past and present, and the current Rex Grant was a top graduate of the Air Force's Psychological Warfare Academy. He had an uncanny knack for giving the public just enough truth and just enough fiction, causing them to draw the wrong conclusions. Anytime he needed proof of this, Colonel Hollister went online and searched 'conspiracy theories', and was pleased that he never saw his name.

The science team was packing up, getting ready to take everything they'd found in Leadbelly's trailer to Los Alamos to study it for the next fifty years. Several of them were collapsing the poles that held the tent over the trailer park. The plastic had already been folded and stored.

The crowds that had left were returning. Most of them had gone to bars or cookouts, been picked up by family or friends. The two that stayed, an older woman in a sea foam green housecoat and a ten-year-old boy, left alone all day with reality TV as his only entertainment, had called their neighbors, telling them to come home. They were angry and anxious, wanting to get into their trailers, wondering why they were forced from them so early.

Colonel Hollister ignored the clamor and protests of the half-drunk people in the street. They would never know what he did for them, all the work that went into protecting them. He accepted this long ago, the anonymous life, destined to be a small star on a large, gray wall. All that mattered to him was that Earth was safe.

Colonel Hollister hoisted himself into the Hummer and shut the door. The window was down, but he kept his elbow inside. Pink and blue clouds floated in the dusk. Soon it would be dark, and Colonel Hollister would have Al Leadbelly in custody and John Abernathy on his knees with a gun to his head. It was shaping up to be a good day.

CHAPTER TWENTY FIVE

John silently loaded the shotgun in the passenger seat. The walnut stock, buckshot shells. The black metal reflected the fading sunlight, streaking the barrel orange.

The sheriff took a circuitous route to the interstate, avoiding the burnt corpse of Leadbelly's trailer. He drove through town, opting for side roads and residential neighborhoods instead of the major thoroughfares. To John, all the houses looked like Mrs. Morris's, dilapidated.

The sheriff turned onto Hot Springs Boulevard and nudged John, pointing to a house. "Hey, John, guess who lives there? Rosa."

"Really?" John tried to seem disinterested, concentrating on loading the gun, but he glanced at her home, trying to quickly memorize every detail. Rosa's two-story brick home. Green shingles. A white storm door. New concrete steps leading to a front deck supported by white columns. A large, ceramic pot on the deck. Something grew deep inside it, but John didn't see it.

Professor Gentry leaned over to Leadbelly, said, "John just found out he slept with an alien last night."

"Hey, John," the sheriff said, "I hope you don't have asteroids on your rocket. I don't think we got any radioactive penicillin in town."

"You know, man, it might be worse than that," Leadbelly said. "Hey, John, I gotta a telescope, man. We could check to see if there's any rings around Uranus."

"You know," Professor Gentry said, "Uranus is a gas giant."

The men in the car were significantly older than John, but they laughed and joked, having discovered a way to temporarily return to their adolescence.

"Whatever," John said. They didn't understand what his night with Rosa had meant, that it was the first time in his life that he'd known the tranquility that can be gifted from someone, and that he could give it back.

The sheriff looked at Leadbelly in the rearview mirror. "So, Al, I went by your place this morning, saw all that blood. Gave me quite a scare."

"Sorry about that, man. I needed to throw some people off my trail."

"Where'd you get all that blood?"

"One thing you learn working Vegas, man, is how to put on a show."

"Yeah, that Hollister fella seemed pretty steamed you were dead."

"Man, that kid I beat up the other night, he said

Hollister'd been looking for me for years. I guess he finally caught up to me, man."

"Hey, I gotta ask you," Sheriff Masters said, "what was it like working for Elvis? I mean, was it all drugs and women? And why the hell are you wearing that jumpsuit? You look like a goddamn shiny peacock."

"Oh, this? It was the only thing I had time to pack. Besides, man, it has a special purpose."

"Yeah, what's that? Does it call the mothership?" The sheriff laughed, slapping the steering wheel.

"Something like that, man," Leadbelly said. "Being an Elvis body double was fun as hell. There were twelve of us. Man, there were nights when Elvis was too messed up to perform. He'd get drunk or high, and we'd take turns doing his shows for him. Man, a couple of us would travel with him. One stayed in Memphis in case he was needed at Graceland. A couple stayed in Vegas to do his nightly show. But that was just the first year. Man, after that, we didn't really see him much. He'd always disappear for a couple of weeks. When he'd be away, we'd do everything, man, concerts, interviews, run to and from the cars and hotels. But towards the end, man, he stopped traveling. Just hid out in his hotel room, drinking, popping pills.

"Man, there was one night I was about to go on for him. This was back in '74. I was going over the set list with the band and, man, Elvis came out with a pistol in each hand saying, 'I'm the King.

And the King's gonna get him some aliens. I know one a y'all's an alien, man. Now fess up or I'll start shooting. T.K.O.B., baby!' Man, Colonel Tom Parker had to run in with Elvis's security and tackle him before he could shoot anyone. They wrestled the guns away from him. Elvis stood up and kicked at us, then got in one of his karate stances and said, 'Don't mess with the King, man. Hot damn tamale, I need a sandwich.' Then, man, he collapsed right in front of us. Fell flat on his face."

Sheriff Masters started laughing, slapping the steering wheel. "Holy shit! That's funny. Why did he think one of you was an alien?" Leadbelly began tapping his foot.

"Because he is one," John said, surprised they hadn't figured out Leadbelly's secret. "How do you think he's stayed so young?"

"You put me in the back with an alien?" Professor Gentry scooted all the way against the door, as far away from Leadbelly as possible. "Are you crazy? You know what he'll do to me?"

"Man, don't worry. I'll save the brain sucking till we get to Santa Fe." Leadbelly winked at John.

"You're joking, right?" Professor Gentry put his head between the front seats. "He's just joking, right? He's just joking?"

"Hey, Leadbelly," the sheriff said. "Where were you when Elvis died?"

"I was in Memphis, man. All us body doubles were. He wanted us all there for some reason.

Maybe 'cause he had just announced a vacation, or something. I was downstairs shooting pool when his girlfriend found him. Man, that's why people thought they saw Elvis at the funeral. It was one of us."

John watched the road ahead as they left town, the spaces between buildings and homes growing, then empty desert. The sheriff turned onto Highway 281 off of County Road 23. Pink and orange colored the sky to their right. To their left, blackness sucked daylight, leaving only small, bright specks. A few stars showed, while the rest waited for the sun to leave the sky. The highway narrowed into a shoulderless, two-lane road, cutting through the small family ranches and dead grass. They passed an old, red pick-up driven by a man with a white beard, wearing faded overalls. He tipped his hat as they passed. John nodded back. And there was only the car, the men riding inside.

And the journal.

When John first read it, part of him hoped it was a hoax, like the photo, and he could return to Denver and gawk at a blank crossword. Another part of him longed for it to be authentic, the part that spent his allowance on comic books and had lunchroom debates over which was a better super power for seeing women naked, x-ray vision or invisibility. He trembled with elation and terror. This was not a tiny alteration, like getting a haircut, but a cataclysm that would affect every aspect of his life. John rubbed his hand, the skin that had split and then smoothly sealed, the final proof that the book, its cracked, leather spine, was real. But John had found something else in Leadbelly's trailer, a connection between John and Leadbelly that extended beyond family.

"We need to talk about the photos you took," John said, turning to Leadbelly.

"Man, I always knew I'd be the one explaining that to you."

"You photographed everything. Why?"

"Well, you see, when a man and a woman like each other, not forever, man, but for one night, and the man finds out that the woman likes to make home movies..."

"What?"

"They go back to the man's place, and one thing leads to another, and the man winds up taking some pictures of the woman naked, bouncing on a Pogo Ball."

"What the fuck are you..."

"Sometimes raspberry syrup's involved."

"I'm talking about these." John slipped the pictures from the book and flung them at Leadbelly. The photos flew to the back seat, landing on Leadbelly's shimmering suit.

"I guess this means those pictures of Wanda and me burned up. That's too bad, man. That Wanda was one cool chick." Leadbelly peeled the pictures from his suit, shuffled and sorted them.

"Why do you have those pictures of me?"

"Don't worry, man, all your questions will be answered soon. You're just going to have to trust me."

"You have them because...Wait. What?"

A bright flash. Glass reflecting the setting sun. Something clogged the thin highway ahead of them. John pulled the binoculars from the glove box. Two military Humvees blocked the highway. Two more waited in the culverts on either side of the road. Colonel Hollister stood between the two parked Humvees, watching John's Saturn sedan drive toward him through a pair of binoculars.

"It's the Air Force."

"They're behind us, too. Coming fast," Sheriff Masters said, looking in his rearview mirror. "Everybody, buckle up."

Sheriff Masters jerked the car off the highway, crashing through a small iron gate onto a dirt road leading into an empty field, putting a big dent in the front of the car. The Humvees followed. The sheriff yanked the wheel, leaving the road, driving into empty desert. A dirt cloud trailed them, obscuring the field behind the car, but through the dust, Humvee headlights shone, following close.

Leadbelly started pressing sequins on his oversized belt.

"What're you doing?" John asked.

"Calling for help."

The car bounced over small mounds and burrows.

John pressed his forearm against the roof of the car, trying to protect his head as his body jerked.

Lights to their right. The Humvees that blocked the road angled to cut them off.

A Humvee bumped them from behind. They lurched forward and the Saturn's back wheels left the earth, then bounced hard against it. The Humvee bumped them again. John braced himself, readying for another knock. But it never came. The headlights disappeared into the dust clouds, as the vehicles behind them slowed down.

Colonel Hollister had parked in the open field in front of them. Their headlights punctured the Saturn's windshield, blinding the men inside. Instinctively, Sheriff Masters slammed on the brakes. The car skidded, sending a cloud of dust into the cool desert air. John shielded his eyes from the high-beams and he saw soldiers, protected by open doors and parked vehicles, aiming their rifles at the stationary sedan.

CHAPTER TWENTY-SIX

"We only want Leadbelly," Colonel Hollister said into a megaphone. "Hand him over and you can go."

"John, we only have to hang on for a few more minutes," Leadbelly said, leaning between the front seats.

"Oh, we're fucked," Professor Gentry said, pushing Leadbelly out of the way. "John, we give them Leadbelly we're as good as dead. We're fucked."

"No one's going anywhere," John said, confident Colonel Hollister was just trying to intimidate them, like when he broke into John's motel room. John flexed his hand and smirked.

Colonel Hollister spoke into the megaphone again, "I'm only gonna say this one more time, hand over Leadbelly!"

"Eat shit, Colonel!" Sheriff Masters shouted, then chuckled.

"Yeah, that'll convince him," John said.

Colonel Hollister punched Corporal McGillis with his megaphone. He gestured to a soldier standing nearby.

"Hey, Sheriff," John said, "isn't that one of the

guys from the bar?"

"That sonuvabitch should be in my jail."

The soldier stepped forward and grinned as he raised his M4 assault rifle to his shoulder. He aimed it at the car, not like a movie villain with the rifle at his hip, or a handgun turned sideways, he held it at his shoulder, secure, like someone trained to kill.

"Get down!" John shouted, ducking under the dash. "Everybody get down!"

They flattened, shrank, crumpled among the litter on the car's floor, hoping they were fully hidden and that no part of them remained exposed, no matter how small a target it might be.

The soldier fired. Bullets shook the car, miniature collisions at five thousand feet per second. The Saturn sedan screamed as metal was ripped apart, sacrificed for Colonel Hollister's violent version of an Elvis obsession.

"That was just a warning!" Colonel Hollister said. "Next time, he'll take out more than your engine."

John peeked above the dash. The windshield was still intact. No bullet holes. Gray clouds floated from the front of the car, mixing with atmosphere, automotive souls escaping Earth. The sedan's front was destroyed, metal punctured by faster moving metal. Fluids, some green, some clear, leaked onto the ground, smelling like a chemical fire.

Rooftop and John's mom had bought the sedan for him as a high school graduation present, something for him to drive to Boulder and back. At first he was indifferent, the color and interior symbolizing weekend soccer matches and ten-percent-off coupons and PTA meetings. Over time, he grew to love the car for its normalcy, blending in at the shopping malls, an artist undercover in Middle-America. Looking at his wrecked car, John felt despondent, knowing he would never drive it to garage sales, flea markets, or comic book shops again.

"Holy shit! Is everyone alright?" Sheriff Masters asked, sweating, breathing heavily, like he'd wrestled a pig and lost.

The only time John had been shot at had been in video games, where health packs and cheat codes gave him extended lives. He raised himself onto his seat, shaking slightly, knowing there were no floating red crosses hiding between vehicles. The journal lay at his feet and John picked it up. He flicked a desiccated French fry from the leather binding and reminded himself of everything Archibald Abernathy had chronicled.

"Man, we just need a few more minutes," Leadbelly said. "Then my ride will be here."

"The cavalry isn't coming," Professor Gentry said. "We're fucked."

Soldiers rushed them from both sides, aiming M4's, standing like heavily armed statues. Calm and in control, Colonel Hollister approached the car. "In case you didn't notice before, you're surrounded. Drop your guns or be shot."

"John, Sheriff," Leadbelly said from the backseat. "Man, I'll go with them."

"Don't do it," Professor Gentry said. "This guy's our only leverage. We give him up, we're dead."

"It's alright, man. I'll be okay," Leadbelly said.

"What about me?" Professor Gentry asked. "I mean us."

"John here's my great-great-nephew, man. You think I'd let anything happen to him?"

"You really want me to answer that?" John asked. He tossed his shotgun out the window and raised his hands. "Alright, Hollister. We're coming out. Don't shoot."

A soldier opened the car door and yanked John out. They did the same to the sheriff, Leadbelly, and Professor Gentry.

"Get your goddamn hands off me," the sheriff said, elbows flailing as he was pulled from the car. "I'm the goddamn sheriff in this county."

"I don't know these guys," Professor Gentry said, as he was pulled from the car. "I was hitchhiking. They picked me up outside of town."

The soldiers answered Professor Gentry's protests by shoving him to the front of the sedan. John expected them to laugh or joke like schoolyard bullies hopped up on candy bars, Jolt Cola, and negligent parenting. Instead, they behaved professionally, quiet and courteous, as they ushered all four men to the front of the car.

One of the soldiers frisked John, finding the gun and journal hidden under his hoodie. He handed the journal to Colonel Hollister. The colonel smiled covetously, like it was a once-in-a-lifetime find.

"I've been looking for this for a long time," he said. "I'd seen the entries Archibald Abernathy sent the Lincolns. We found them buried in the National Archives. He stopped sending them updates when he arrived in Las Vegas. When he reappeared in Denver, agents were sent to retrieve his journal. Everyone thought it was lost when his house burned, but I knew better. I knew this was out here."

He stared at it, his eyes fixed on the fragile pages.

Watching Colonel Hollister turn the pages, the wonder in his eyes, John realized he never saw the sections of the journal written after Archibald arrived in New Mexico, the entries where he described his life with the Sagittarians, where he mentioned Rosa.

"And Rosa? how did you know about her?" John asked, glancing at the soldier from the bar.

"We'd been watching Leadbelly for several weeks, tracking his movements. He visited her quite often, sometimes at her restaurant, sometimes at her home. When you told me he'd left town, which, by the way, I knew you were lying, not very smart, I had to send my men to retrieve her, see if she had any information about him. I was sure she knew

something. I don't believe in coincidences, John."
Colonel Hollister gently turned the journal's pages,
touching only the corners, stopping on a passage
mentioning Rosa. "And apparently I'm right not to."
He read for a moment, then carefully closed the
book.

Rosa had a life before him. As John thought this,
the fever of envy burned in his chest. He knew it
was natural, that when you meet someone you
never really know their past, that it becomes
untangled the more you open up to someone, and
they open themselves to you. He had wanted to
learn all her secrets, discover everything he could
about her. He had even anticipated having that
awkward, 'how many have you been with?'
conversation. But Leadbelly? The thought of the
two of them together made him cringe and wonder
if he should get tested. He trusted that Rosa was
selective, had chosen him over the other men in
town, including Leadbelly. Still, he couldn't help
resenting the man in the sequined jumpsuit for the
shared experiences he had with her.

"Gentlemen." Colonel Hollister walked up to
them, holding the journal at his waist with both
hands. "Did you really think you could escape?"

The sheriff laughed like he just remembered a
joke and wanted to share it.

"Do you find something funny, Sheriff Masters?"

"Yeah," the sheriff said, smirking. "You need to
know something. Everything you've been doing, all

the cover-ups, that reporter kid's murder, they're about to be blown wide open. We're supposed to meet a member of the press in Santa Fe, and if we don't show, Leadbelly's story's gonna be published in tomorrow's paper."

"No, it won't," John said.

Between two Humvees, the click of a Zippo. Embers of a lit cigarette glowed, a small, orange circle in the darkness. John had never seen him before, but he knew who he was. The only person who knew their escape route.

"Why don't you just get out here?" John said, defeated. All his plans and hopes for escaping from town, the case, his job, were edited away to nothing.

A man, standing between two Humvees, stepped into the light. He wore a dark blue suit, casually smoking among starched uniforms.

"Rex Grant," John said, "the minute I saw the Hummers, I knew you'd sold me out. How long have you been selling information to the Air Force?"

"I didn't sell them anything," he said. "I work for them."

"John," Colonel Hollister said, "I'd like to introduce you to Lieutenant Rex Grant, head of the Air Force Special Services, Propaganda Department, specializing in plausible deniability, or as they're more commonly known, *The National Enquirer.*"

"You see," Lieutenant Grant said, walking closer,

taking a drag off his cigarette, "people want to believe there's more to the world than what they see, that something is being kept from them. My job is to give them a version that's just enough reality, just enough fantasy to keep them making the wrong guesses, distracting them from the work we really do."

"You used me. You lied to me," John said. He'd been betrayed by someone who created stories of snow monsters pitching in the World Series and conveyed them as legitimate news.

"Don't feel bad. We've been doing this for years, since Roswell, when we went by our original name, Majestic-12."

"I knew Majestic-12 was real," Professor Gentry said, like having his assumptions confirmed was a personal triumph.

"We had to change it," Lieutenant Grant said. He dropped his cigarette, twisted it into the dirt with his shoe. "It sounded too conspiratorial, like an actual government program. *The National Enquirer* sounds more credible, don't you think?"

"You used me," John said. "You used Rooftop."

"We needed an impartial third party to research the Elvis pictures, just in case we found one of the body doubles."

"You already found him, had people staking out his trailer."

"Colonel Hollister's men tend to be a little heavy handed." He glanced at the soldier who shot up the car.

"When you showed at Leadbelly's trailer," Colonel Hollister said, "I expected you to be a typical detective, a bottom feeder, but instead I got you. I got an Abernathy."

"So, did you trick me into coming down so you could kill me, too? like that kid in the desert? Has this whole thing been a giant set-up?" John asked, taking a step forward. A soldier put his hand on John's chest, attempting to restrain him. John knocked it away. Guns were raised at the edge of his vision, and John grinned and thought about how he could release a pheromone that would cause the heavily armed soldiers to make out with each other.

"John, I didn't know how special you are," Lieutenant Grant said.

"Special? I just write puzzles," John said. He stared at Rex Grant, wishing Sagittarians had laser vision.

"I don't have the proper clearance. And I never used your name in any of my reports. Colonel Hollister didn't even know I'd contracted you to investigate the photo. He only briefed me on you after you showed at Leadbelly's trailer."

"What about the reporter? Did you have a file on him, too?"

"The kid was never real. Talking on the phone, I knew you'd never come down here. So we fabricated the story, found some drifter, someone no one would miss, cleaned him up, dressed him like a college kid, shot him, and left his body by the road, somewhere he could be found. Local cops did all the paperwork, making him bait. You gave me everything I needed when you asked if I'd sent a reporter down here. Now that kid is dead because of you."

"You don't get to put this on me," John said. "I'm not the one that uses people. That's you." The blood from the bar fight had been washed from his fingers, but he still saw the man lying on the floor, blood seeping between the floorboards. Without realizing it, John wiped his hand on his pants leg. The solider next to him lightly tapped his fingers against his rifle.

"Well, Al Leadbelly," Colonel Hollister said. "I have you at last, the first one, his closest companion. It's been over thirty-five years since we buried Elvis and you haven't changed a bit."

"Really? Thirty-five years looking like that? That's not really something to be proud of," John said, cranky, like an old man on the bus needing a nap, but not wanting to fall asleep for fear that teenagers would draw dicks on his face.

"Did you think someone as special as you could stay hidden? Eventually someone would take your picture, send it to Lieutenant Grant. And we'd be on your trail again."

"Man, I knew you couldn't stay away."

"It's been a long time since we've seen each other,

Al. I have thirty-five years of questions and I guarantee you're not going to like how I ask them."

"You might want to get in line, man. I got a few ex-wives looking to do the exact same thing."

"Always joking. Just like Elvis."

"He had a great sense of humor, didn't he?" Professor Gentry said.

"Professor Gentry, it's good to see you again. Elvis really valued your insight, your trust. It's a shame you betrayed him, sold him out for a book deal. I'm sorry we had to discredit you. You gave us no other choice."

"You must not have worked that hard," John said.

"We were all working overtime those days, trying to figure out what happened to Elvis. How a man in his condition could die from a heart attack."

"His condition?" John said. "That coked-up asshole?"

Colonel Hollister backhanded John across the face. Blood ran from the split in John's lip, into his mouth. He leaned over. Spat. Colonel Hollister clutched John's hair and tilted his head back. Blood retreated back into John's lip. The cut sealed.

"Brilliant," Colonel Hollister said, releasing John's hair, pushing his head back. "I'm glad Lieutenant Grant called you, John. I really am. I'm going to really enjoy your autopsy findings. I've always been curious about how your kind actually works."

"It's a healthy combination of cynicism and PBR. But mostly PBR."

"Do you know what it's like to lose a child, John? Of course not, how could you? It's devastating, something you never get over. You're constantly wondering if there was something you could have done, questioning your parenting. If I'd only been there for him. Elvis was like a son to me."

"Yeah," John said, "a son on Quaaludes."

"In some ways he was more. So, I've been searching for answers," Colonel Hollister turned to Leadbelly, "searching for you."

"Whatever answers I can give you," Leadbelly said, "they won't bring him back, man."

"You're right. I know. But killing John Abernathy will help."

"Wait. What? Leadbelly?" John's head spun between Leadbelly and Colonel Hollister. John thought they only wanted Leadbelly, to dangle him above a pool of bionic piranhas and question him about Elvis, but seeing Colonel Hollister absorbing the moment, John finally understood that Leadbelly wasn't their only objective.

"John, you know who you are, man," Leadbelly said over his shoulder as two soldiers led him toward a Hummer.

John rubbed the top of his hand, where his bones pushed through his skin, right before he'd punched Leadbelly. It didn't feel any different, the skin, thin hairs, the veins and ligaments. It felt like the hand he'd used his whole life for everything from writing puzzles to zipping up his pants to turning the pages of Archibald Abernathy's journal. But his hand wasn't the same. He had watched its reconstruction, the bones breaking through the skin, gloving it, then receding. And it wasn't just his hand that had adapted. When he confronted Leadbelly at the lumberyard, and after the bar fight, John had worried that he was becoming something foreign and unrecognizable, but looking at his great-great-uncle being led away in handcuffs, John knew he shouldn't have worried, that Leadbelly was right. He knew who he was. He was the descendant of Archibald Abernathy and Louisa Ramirez. Part human. Part Sagittarian.

"Wait, I want Leadbelly to see this," Colonel Hollister said. "So he'll remember." Colonel Hollister motioned to the soldiers standing next to them.

"On your knees," a soldier, the one who had fought with the sheriff at Levi's, said.

"Like hell!" Sheriff Masters cried.

"I said, on your knees." The soldier rammed the sheriff's lower back with the butt of his rifle, forcing him to the ground, then did the same to Professor Gentry.

Another soldier smashed his gun into John's shoulder, forcing him to his knees.

"You ruptured my friend's eye socket," he said to John.

"You know that wasn't me, right?" John said.

"He'll never be able to go into the field again."

"That was literally a whole barroom full of people."

"Colonel Hollister wasn't going to let me come on this mission. He said I was too emotionally invested. I had to beg him for this assignment."

"I was unconscious for the whole thing."

"I wanted to be the one that put a bullet in your head. When I'm done with you, I'm gonna find your girlfriend and do the same to her."

The journal mentioned a town. Oscar Ramirez had taken Archibald there. It was where he met Louisa, and a young Rosa. And John realized that's where Rosa went, not to Albuquerque, but to a town that had been hidden for hundreds of years. A town where she could be safe.

"Hollister!" the sheriff shouted, offering a final argument. "I'm the local sheriff, the law! You can't do this!"

"I am sorry about this, Sheriff. I really am," Colonel Hollister said with insincere remorse. "I try to limit collateral damage, but you see, I'm fighting a war. We've been invaded, attacked. There have been casualties. I'm just trying to protect humanity."

John calmly looked up at Colonel Hollister, adjusted his glasses, and said evenly, "You are fucking crazy."

The mountains were silhouetted behind them,

palpable and ominous, like a housewife's premonition. The lights from the trucks shone in John's eyes. He saw outlines of the bodies of the men in front of him, and from behind him John heard the unmistakable click of guns being cocked.

John told himself to calm down, that he could do this. It would be just like when he punched Leadbelly in the motel room. Except that had happened automatically, like a reflex. He hadn't willed it. But that didn't matter. He was a Sagittarian. He could do this. He just had to concentrate.

The men behind them slowed their breathing, detached from the present moment.

John closed his eyes and concentrated on how he wanted the soldiers to feel, lethargic, content, exhausted, like taking a nap in the middle of the desert was the best idea they'd ever had. John focused on the scents associated with those emotions. He grimaced and grunted, focusing these precise feelings and pheromones outward, infusing the atmosphere with the aroma of transformed awareness. Then, thinking he'd succeeded, he sighed, and waited for the sound of unconscious bodies collapsing.

And he waited.

And waited.

"Gentleman," Colonel Hollister said, his calm and pleased voice slicing the silence, "fire at will."

John opened his eyes. Colonel Hollister stood

above him sneering, pointing a gun at John's head.

"Oh, shit."

CHAPTER TWENTY SEVEN

At the sight of Colonel Hollister aiming his gun at him, John knew he'd failed to release his pheromones. He sniffed the air around them. It smelled like gunpowder and automotive fluids and sweat, not like an enchanting aroma that would have caused trained soldiers to slip into a wilderness snooze. John sat back on his heels and dropped his head. His pheromones were their last hope of leaving the desert alive. He had failed.

John gazed past the colonel, to the stars behind him. This was the last time he'd see them. He wanted to absorb the stars, memorize their celestial positions. He suddenly regretted not taking Constellation Cross Stitch 203. He could have embroidered all the constellations in glow-in-the-dark yarn and hung them from his wall.

The stars flickered yellow, then red, back and forth like a freshly struck match. Old constellations burned.

Then they moved.

The stars moved, not straight across the sky like shooting stars, but in bizarre, zigzag patterns, floating back and forth in pairs, synchronized, sky-bound vessels passing, signaling. One pair, then two, then three. They moved erratically and John lost count of how many pairs streaked and darted above him.

And he wasn't the only one who noticed. Colonel Hollister yelled at his men to take cover. Soldiers ran behind Hummers, pointing their guns skyward. Most of them had seen combat in some Middle East desert, had been hardened by IEDs and stop-loss redeployments, but the sight of descending stars caused them to speak to each other in hushed uncertainties. John didn't see or hear any of this. He kept looking up, watching the lights get larger until they were the size of the moon.

Machineguns fired. Shells were ejected as new rounds were pushed into the chamber, fired in a futile attempt to shoot out the stars. The hot casings hit John's head.

John, Sheriff Masters, and Professor Gentry fell to the ground. The sheriff tried saying something, but John couldn't hear him over the gunfire. He motioned that they should get out of there. John nodded. They got to their feet and, bent over, ran to the Humvees.

"Were you hit?" Sheriff Masters asked him when they reached the vehicles. They crouched next to dusty doors and tires, shielded from the chaos.

"You?" John asked, shaking his head.

"I'm good. What the hell's going on?"

"I think it's Leadbelly's cavalry."

The soldiers, illuminated by Humvee headlights, fired their weapons skyward as the lights above them grew and encapsulated the vehicles, forming a dome around them.

"Can you see Leadbelly?" the sheriff asked.

"Yeah, he's over there." John pointed across the field of shell casings and astounded soldiers to the Humvees behind the John's car. Leadbelly was looking up at the sky, smiling.

"Let's get him and get outta here while they're all distracted."

They made their way around the back, to the other side of the circle, where Leadbelly stood. The soldier guarding him was in the middle of the vehicles, shooting upward.

"Leadbelly, Leadbelly." Sheriff Masters got his attention.

"Sheriff. John. Man, I told you everything'd be alright."

"Let's take one of these Hummers," Professor Gentry said, "get outta here."

"Naw, man, this here's my ride."

The lights kept getting larger.

The soldiers stopped firing and stood frozen, confused, staring up at the glowing dome a few feet above them. There was no wind. Everything was still. The only movement was smoke rising from lowered gun barrels.

Shaking his wrists, Leadbelly unlocked his shackles.

"You pick up a few tricks working Vegas, man," he said, handing Sheriff Masters the handcuffs.

"You get that from a magician?" the sheriff asked.

"No, man, the assistant." Leadbelly winked. "C'mon, man, let's get outta here. Unless you wanna hang out with these fellas."

They followed him to the destroyed Saturn. A pair of lights broke rank from the dome and descended into the ring of gun smoke. The light's source was a long, rectangular box, twenty-five feet long, ten feet high, and seven feet across. Windows were on the front and sides. Its rear lowered, leveled.

The box landed in front of them.

Along the bottom, large, metal spikes crept up the frame, six on each side. They climbed the walls, connecting the box to two large metal domes underneath. Between the RV and the metal domes, green lights glowed. On the side of the box were three windows and a door with a small window. Two tan stripes ran the length of its white frame, with one end of stripes meeting the word 'Indian' at the rear. The other end forming a 'W' under the passenger seat window.

'W' for 'Winnebago'.

The flying Winnebago floated just above the ground, not disturbing the earth underneath. The driver waved at them with a big, friendly smile. He looked just like Leadbelly, big hair, sequined jumpsuit. He honked the horn. The first few notes of an Elvis classic, 'You Ain't Nothin' but a Hound Dog', performed by car horn, ended the silence. The side door opened and hinged metal steps unfolded.

"C'mon, man," Leadbelly said. "Let's go."

They followed Leadbelly past bewildered soldiers gazing at the light dome or the flying Winnebago. John shook his head and chuckled. When he saw the lights encasing them, he thought their rescue would be a little more science-fiction, little green men in flying saucers, and a little less Reno-road-trip.

The journal rested on the ground near John's car, dropped by Colonel Hollister at some point, an ancient text awaiting discovery. And his gun. Several of the pictures were scattered next to it. John ran over, scooped them up. He shook dirt from the photos before putting them in the journal, then picked up the gun.

When John rose, Colonel Hollister stood between him and the Winnebago. Colonel Hollister still held his gun, but it was lowered. He looked tired, angry, like the fan of a second-place team. John walked to the RV, and as he passed Colonel Hollister, the defeated officer clutched John's arm.

"This isn't over," he whispered. "You think running will save you. I will find you."

John jerked his arm free, took a few steps toward the Winnebago.

"Your mother has her women's group on

Tuesday," Colonel Hollister said.

"What did you say?" John said, spinning around.

"They're getting ready for their annual fund raiser."

"You touch my mother..." John gripped and re-gripped the gun in his hand.

"I believe they're doing a flower show this year."

"You son of a bitch," he said, pointing the gun at Colonel Hollister.

The side of Colonel Hollister's mouth rose slightly. He tossed his gun on the ground. It landed against a small grass cluster, growing shrewdly between cracks in the earth.

John stepped closer to him, held the gun inches from Colonel Hollister's chest.

"There's only one way you can stop me," Colonel Hollister said, his arms outstretched, surrendering. "Only one way for this to end."

Colonel Hollister would never stop coming after him, never leave him or his family alone. He would track John to Denver, ambush him leaving work, or when he was in one of the city's dark and lonely corners, photographing a client's wayward husband dressed like Rudolph at a Santa-themed orgy. Or he'd go to John's home some night while his mother was alone, force his way in like he had at the hotel, and John would return to find his mother tied up, or worse. Rooftop, he'd fight back. But it'd be a short fight. His mom, Rooftop, everyone he'd ever cared about, they were all in danger. Unless John stopped Colonel Hollister here. Now.

John flipped the safety and moved his finger to the trigger. He took a deep breath. It would be easy. He could do this. It would be just like when Rooftop took him to the shooting range, firing at a silhouetted paper man. His finger twitched, then steadied. He squinted. But he didn't shoot.

A sudden tickle in his mind, like a hand had reached across the car rubble and stupefied soldiers and was massaging a sensitive part of his brain. He shook his head like he'd eaten ice cream too quickly, but the tingling lingered and evolved into a voice with all the stumbling pauses, added syllables, and slow drawl of the Deep South.

Leadbelly.

John glanced over to the RV. Leadbelly's mouth didn't move, but he still spoke, like a ventriloquist without a miniature companion. It was John's first experience with telepathy and he found it invasive and a little creepy, like Leadbelly was watching him shower.

Leadbelly transferred information about Sagittarian technology into John's brain. Not everything, but just enough to make John lower the gun and look at it like it was an obsolete weapon.

"This is why I will always win," Colonel Hollister said. "You don't have what it takes."

"You don't really understand what's happened here, do you?" John said.

"You can try to run, but I will find you. I will find

your family. Every last one of them."

"You just got your ass handed to you by a bunch of Elvis impersonators in flying Winnebagos."

"I will firebomb that little town."

"And they didn't even fire a shot."

"Turn the trailer parks into mass graves."

"So, here's what's going to happen. You're going to leave us alone."

"I will nuke the whole desert. Turn the sky purple. Wherever you're trying to hide."

"Me, my family, Leadbelly, everyone else in the journal. You're going to head back to Los Alamos and leave us alone."

"You think anyone will be able to tell the difference between the desert and a nuclear wasteland? I will find you, whatever it takes."

John motioned to Leadbelly.

One of the RVs, an old, two-tone Dodge Travco, descended, floated behind one of the Hummers. Three aluminum beams covered the square grill. The beams lowered and rested against the front bumper. A metal tube extended from the square and began to spin and glow.

A black circle formed in front of the Travco. It was twenty-four inches of nothingness, empty of light and matter and everything else that filled the universe. Wind rushed into the emptiness and the Hummer was sucked across the earth toward it. The end narrowed and stretched like dark green taffy, and it began to spiral into the void. The vehicle twisted and spun as it was drained away. And when it'd been sucked into the hole, the only thing that remained was the stretches of dragged dirt marking the failure of three tons of engine and armor against time-consuming gravity.

The darkness was pulled back into the metal tube, the tube retracted into the RV, the grill rose, and light and sound and life returned, replacing the emptiness.

"Was that..."

"A particle accelerator," John said. "Every RV has one."

"A sustainable black hole? That would require..."

"A shitload of energy. Now you know what you're up against. Anything you launch, send, try to detonate, will get sucked into oblivion."

"What are you proposing?" Colonel Hollister squinted.

"A truce. You stay away from us, we stay away from you."

"Usually these types of pacts work when both sides have some sort of deterrent, something keeping the other side from breaking it. What assurances do I have that you won't destroy us?" Colonel Hollister smirked like he had something more devastating than the breach of an event horizon.

"You have my word."

"The word of an Abernathy. Worthless. I have a better idea. You keep your black holes locked away.

In exchange, I keep your father."

"My father?" John stepped back, almost stumbling over a rock.

"We have him in a cryonic deep-freeze at our Los Alamos facility."

For most of his life, John had lived with the narrative that his father ran out on them, leaving his mother at the foot of the mountains to raise a son. It was a common story, a young father not ready for responsibility. A son who grew up unable to cope with the conflicting emotions that came from having someone who was supposed to love and protect him leave without even hearing a sobbing five-year-old's appeal. As much as he believed this version of the past, there was a place in John that always knew his father didn't abandon him. He'd buried it in his dreams, those nocturnal moments when his father visited and endured the coldness of a teenager who only knew how to deal with his frustrations by turning inward, obsessing over puzzles. But his father didn't just live in his dreams. Apparently, he'd been in Los Alamos most of John's life, frozen. John peered into Colonel Hollister's mind and knew he was telling the truth.

His father is in a tube, the ice-frosted glass, his blue face preserved by the cryonic chemical bath and Sagittarian DNA. Machines are monitoring the fluids and gases keeping him close to death. The facility's layout unfolds in reverse, the room, the hallway, elevator, stairs, lobby, the security guard everyone calls 'Bobby J', the sign on the glass door reading 'Wayland Accounting', the nondescript Ford Tauruses in Parking Lot A of a corporate complex called 'Aspen Meadows'. Colonel Hollister is going through various levels of security, thumb print, retinal scan, voice recognition, *Cape Canaveral* trivia, swiping scan cards, entering key codes, and John was sure those security measures would change and the passwords he'd just seen Colonel Hollister use were useless.

Snapshots of the search and capture of his father, the Air Force giving up hunting body doubles and switching their focus to Archibald Abernathy's descendants. Colonel Hollister is in Philadelphia, watching some of John's distant cousins repair water heaters and steal tools from the homes they are working in. He is in New Mexico, sitting in a Jeep, reading carbon copied excerpts from Archibald's journal. There is purple ink on his hand and he takes out a handkerchief and wipes it, but the paper is smudged. He is in Colorado, watching a film of John's dad rushing from a burning building with an elderly woman wrapped in a wool blanket. His arms and face are burned. The camera is handheld and palsied and when it zooms in on John's father's arm to record it quickly healing, the camera jerks and has to find him again, reframing him. His dad looks around and runs off screen. His father is leaving work and Colonel Hollister approaches him with three men. Threats are made and John's father agrees to go with them, offering himself in exchange for the lives of his wife. And son.

It happened quickly, decades were viewed in the time it took for a single electrical impulse to fire across the hemisphere of his brain. And John was back in his own mind.

If Colonel Hollister noticed John watching a montage of his memories, he didn't show it. He stared at John with an arrogant grin, the same grin he had when he approached John's father and took away whatever options he might have had at a future with his family, with his son. John understood that his father had to leave, sacrifice himself for John and his mother, creating the unintended consequence that, for the past eighteen years, John had been angry at the wrong person.

"This is all your fault," John said. "Everything we've gone through, my mom and me, all because...Goddamnit! This is all your fault!"

"So, is it a deal? You have your black holes and I have your father."

A few wild flowers grew among some rocks and shell casings, their thin and stringy stalks, their small bulbs hiding vibrant colors. They survived the boot and tire treads and arid climate and were beginning to open. Flowers in half bloom, providing a glimpse of beauty amid the desolation. They seemed out of place, but belonged there, having made an evolutionary bargain necessary for survival.

"And we leave each other alone," John said.

"We leave each other alone."

John knew Colonel Hollister had spent his life hunting extraterrestrials, and to have come this close, seeing them descend from the sky in rickety and rusted RVs, the perfect disguise, he wouldn't stop now. And John's father, all this time, locked away, frozen, visiting John in dreams, only to receive cold anger. John couldn't stop either.

They didn't shake hands. They just stared at each other for a minute, each man plotting, scheming, knowing the other was doing the same.

John ran to the Winnebago and jumped in. As they lifted skyward, John stood in the open door, watching the world shrink. Colonel Hollister stood in the middle of the vehicles, watching them rise. Off to the side, unaffected by the flying Winnebago, a man smoked. The faint glow of tobacco embers offered little light, but John saw the nose, mouth, chin of Rex Grant. He took a few more drags, then threw the cigarette on the ground and crushed it. He stepped deeper into the darkness between the vehicles. Disappeared.

CHAPTER
TWENTY EIGHT

They had been telling stories about Elvis for an hour and now it was the driver Ricky Handjive's turn. He was a body double like Leadbelly, and told them a story about Elvis in Hawaii. Elvis is drunk, naked, chasing a mongoose with a handgun while eating a turkey leg, or maybe the mongoose is chasing Elvis. Handjive didn't really remember.

"Can you believe that sonuvabitch?" Sheriff Masters asked, laughing as Handjive acted out the story's climax, where a drunk, naked, gun-toting Elvis straddled a palm tree.

John sat at the kitchen table, staring out the window. He wasn't interested in ancient stories of a drunken pop star. He was thinking about something more recent.

"Did you know Hollister had my dad?" he asked Leadbelly, who was seated across from him.

"No way, man," Leadbelly said.

"I thought you were all connected or something."

"He musta closed himself off from us before Hollister put him in the deep freeze."

"You can do that?" John asked, surprised. He set Archibald's journal on the gold-flecked, white

Formica table. It seemed incomplete, like an introductory textbook.

"Man, you're gonna learn there's a lot we can do."

The kitchen table seat cushions' coarse fibers, a plaid of interwoven greens, browns, and oranges, scratched against John's jeans as he slid across it.

The blinds on the window were up. They passed over a highway. The headlights of the few cars beneath them were the only lights, and John barely saw the surface, the thin road, the near-dead earth. The Winnebago veered away from the road and the world outside John's window became obscured by height and darkness.

"Where are we going," he asked, hoping Leadbelly was fulfilling his promise and taking him to Rosa, but he was doubtful. "And I don't want any of your mysterious shit."

"Mysterious shit?" Leadbelly smirked. He waved his arms at John like he was conjuring spirits. "John Abernathy, you have been whisked away, man. Into the great beyond," he said, sounding like a spooky fortune teller delivering the tagline from *Elvis and the Groovy Ghost.* John knocked Leadbelly's hands away. Leadbelly stuck them back up, waving in hokey eeriness. "Co-starring Ann-Margret."

"Ann-Margret?" Handjive spun. "Man, I gave her a Tijuana Toilet Seat."

The taillights of Winnebagos, Coachmens, and Holiday Ramblers glowed red in the black sky. A

Chevy with a Coleman Camper on their right. A green glow radiated from underneath each vehicle.

"Whew," the sheriff said from the passenger seat. "Would you look at that?" He leaned over the dash, gawking at a vintage trailer above them, the kind found on highways sixty years ago. A chrome bullet cutting through the flesh of a country.

"I know what you mean, man," Handjive said, patting the dash. "It's a combination of a diesel engine and good-old Sagittarian know-how."

"Where are we going?" John asked again.

"Someplace where we can be safe, man," Leadbelly said. "Just trust me."

John lifted his knees up, wrapped his arms around them, turned away from his sparkling relative, and tried to see past the reflection of their ship's interior in the window and into the void beyond, but all he saw was the image of his own face, the lines creasing his forehead, the bags behind his glasses, the fatigue of an epiphany, and he turned and stretched out across the kitchen table's bench seat, his back to the window and the Rockies, indiscernible from this distance and altitude. Even if they were visible, he couldn't look at them. They reminded him of Denver, his life there, and about how, even if he did return, he'd have to tell his mom about the journal, the Sagittarians, his father. How was he going to tell her his dad was alive? and frozen in a lab in New Mexico?

This isn't easy for me, you know. John didn't say this. He thought it. It was not an internal thought, meant for introspection. He directed it at Leadbelly.

I know, man, Leadbelly thought back.

My life was supposed to be art and creation. Me and my mom. Now I'm an alien fugitive, related to an Elvis impersonator.

Man, I told them I'd make a good role-model. Leadbelly smiled at this thought.

Where did you get those pictures of me? John slid the stack of photos across the table. They were fanned out, each blade a shard of the past twenty-three years.

I've been watching you.

What are we talking here, lurking in the bushes, or video camera in the changing room?

Not like that, man. I was looking out for you.

And my dad, my grandpa? did you take those pictures, too?

Your grandpa, yeah, but not your dad. I was in Vegas when he was born, man.

Why look out for us?

We're family, man. We look out for each other. That's what we do. Leadbelly reached across the table and put his hand on John's forearm.

The only person you look out for is yourself. John wrenched his arm away.

Leadebelly brushed some dust onto the floor, his pinkie ring scraping the table.

Someone told you to take those pictures. John

tapped the journal. Did Jonathon Deerfoot order Rosa to sleep with me?

Jonathon Deerfoot's dead. Leadbelly's thoughts and emotions blended and John felt his sorrow. Man, he died forty years ago. Someone else's calling the shots now.

You're just a giant piece of sequined ambiguity, aren't you?

What can you do, man? Leadbelly shrugged his shoulders.

I have a few ideas. John gripped the table with both hands, stared intensely at Leadbelly.

He thrust his mind into Leadbelly's, searching for answers, but hit a wall and was jolted back into his body like he'd been caught by the seatbelt and the driver suddenly slammed on the brakes.

Telepathy, man, Leadbelly thought, laughing inside John's head. I knew what you were going to try the minute you thought it. Gave me time to get my psychic defenses up. Good for you for trying, man. Don't worry. You'll learn how to do that stuff, too.

John rubbed his head with the palms of both hands.

"Who's worried?" he said.

The ground glowed in the distance. It started out small, like a beacon, but as they got closer, they saw it wasn't a solitary light, but a series of lights on a grid.

"We're coming in for a landing, boys," Handjive said.

Out the front window, the other RVs gently glided to the surface, landing beside hundreds of small boxes lined up side by side. Spaces, like roads, separated some of the boxes, while others were almost on top of each other.

As they got closer, the details on the boxes started coming into focus. Metal, plastic, fiberglass. Colored stripes adorned white backgrounds. Solid colors, blue, green, or silver, covered others. Entrances were sheltered by awnings, Christmas lights stapled to them. Some were just plain.

"It's a trailer park," John said, leaning forward, his hands on the back of the front seat headrests.

Handjive mumbled into his CB, the cadence of his voice sounding like he was introducing his back-up band. On the sparsely lit ground, surrounded by RVs, a glowing, blue rectangle appeared. Handjive swung the Winnebago over it, and tenderly squeezed it into the space, landing.

"Home sweet home, man," Handjive said, flipping some switches and turning off the motor.

Handjive climbed out of the driver's seat. He wore a sequined red jumpsuit like Leadbelly's, but with a Latin-tinged pattern, like one of the sombreros hanging in Rosa's.

"John," he said, sticking out his hand, "I'm real pleased to meet you. I mean that, man. It's a real honor."

John shook Handjive's hand. He glanced over at Leadbelly, a little confused, wondering what he'd told Handjive, disturbed that he had gained a reputation among Elvis impersonators. He didn't know if it was because of his lineage, being the current carrier of the Abernathy name, or if it was because Leadbelly had pictures of John outside a hotel room photographing a client's diaper clad husband tied to a pole while accountants wearing maroon robes and rubber unicorn masks flogged the husband with stale baguettes.

Leadbelly opened the door. Metal steps descended. John gathered the journal from the kitchen table and followed them into the cool desert night.

The only light came from the Christmas lights outside the mobile homes, and it took John's eyes a couple of minutes to adjust. The artificial lights made everything look crisp and shiny. Without them, it would have been a black and white world, no place for people who glowed on the Vegas Strip.

The park was also lit from above, by the stars. They covered the sky. John tilted his head back and spun around, gazing up in amazement. It was like the sky wasn't affected by the light pollution from the trailer park. The cosmos was fully exposed and every night the trailer park residents could see their place in the expanding universe. Growing up in Denver, John had never seen the night sky uncontaminated by all the lights employed to make the dark less terrifying. Even when he went into the mountains, he was close enough to the city that its glow dulled the brilliance above. Looking up, John shrank at the size of it, feeling empty and bare, aware of his insignificance. He spun around, trying to find a landmark, something to ground him. Like everyone who grew up near the Rockies, he turned to where the mountains should have been, but they were far away and their silhouettes were bumps on the horizon.

Handjive stepped from the RV, starlight bouncing off his jumpsuit, the cloak billowing behind him as he walked.

"Nice cape," John said.

"You like it, man?" Handjive asked. "Check this out." He grabbed the ends of the cape, held out his arms, and dropped to one knee.

"That's the showstopper right there, man. You're letting the crowd know you've given them all you got. And, man, the ladies love it."

"Ladies love a man in a cape," John said.

Behind him, the sound of rusted metal moving. Four of the metal spikes that connected the Winnebago to the glowing discs underneath detached from the sides of the RV. They peeled away and plunged into the ground, anchoring the Winnebago as it rested on its metal frame. The other mobile homes were the same way, floating above the surface, but fastened.

Gravel roads outlined the trailers, cutting the trailer park into the sections of a planned community. On the surface, it was like any other trailer park. There were open coolers by lawn chairs, broken stoves, hot water tanks, a tipped-over Weber Grill Master, outdoor TVs with aluminum-foiled antennas, orange extension cords running through open doors. There was only one thing that made it different from other trailer parks.

"Everyone looks like Elvis Presley," John said.

Elvis impersonators stood in dimly lit doorways. Some nodded or waved to Leadbelly and Handjive, but most stood and watched them walk down the street.

"This is Elvisville, man," Handjive said. "It's where all the Elvi live. It's outta sight."

"All Elvis impersonators are aliens?" John said. "Figures."

"At first we were," Leadbelly said. "Then it

became a fad, man, and the humans put on the jumpsuit. They started taking all the good Elvis jobs."

"Now, man, we just sit here in Elvisville, waiting," Handjive said.

"Waiting for what?" Sheriff Masters asked.

"The end of the world," John said, tightly gripping the journal.

They walked into the trailer park's square. The square was a small park from another part of the country where summer meant cookouts, fireworks, and tubing at the lake. John combed the soft grass with his fingers. He lifted them and smelled summer, green and sunshine, under his fingernails. The stationary oak trees rested. Their leaves were inverted, sleeping. John touched the bark. Thick flakes, papery, but solid. In the middle of the park, in front of the gazebo, was a giant granite statue of Elvis from the early years, when his gyrations caused teenage riots. At the far end of the park, an old woman sat on a bench. She looked like she was waiting for an army of pigeons to flap at her feet and coo, call for her to toss them torn squares of day-old bread.

Leadbelly stood by the tree, brushing grass with the toe of his boot. He flicked his head toward Handjive. Handjive tapped the sheriff on the arm and said something to Professor Gentry. The three of them disappeared between the trailers lining the park, joking about something John couldn't hear.

"Where are they going?" John asked.

"The woman on the bench, man," Leadbelly said. "You really need to go talk to her."

John knew who she was by the way Leadbelly acted, the reverential space given to her. But he didn't know her name.

"She's Jonathon Deerfoot's replacement, isn't she? the colonist supreme or whatever? Who is she?"

"Just go talk to her, man. That's all I can say."

The bench was on the far side of the park, under a large elm tree. A concrete path led to it, but John avoided it. He cut across the grass instead. The lights in the trailers turned off, leaving the lampposts in the park as the only light. When they'd landed, John had heard televisions, radios, now there was silence. And the sound of his Chucks squeaking on the dew dripped grass.

As John approached, the woman looked up. She was cocooned in a thick cardigan. It looked old, homemade. The off-white wool was frayed and fuzzy. The wooden buttons running down the front were chipped. Her dress flowed underneath it, ending at her ankles and the sandals on her feet. Deep wrinkles creased her skin. John could tell that black hair once covered her head, but now it was mostly gray.

"So," he said, sitting down next to her, "I'm supposed to talk to you."

"I'm glad you made it, John," she said, patting

him on the knee.

There was something familiar about her, but it was a distant familiarity, like John had met her years ago and she had meant something to him at the time. He tried to remember who she was, a forgotten grade school teacher, a friend of his grandmother's who baby-sat once, but the faces and people he recalled didn't match the woman sitting next to him, and he couldn't remember how he knew her, just that she was important.

"I have a lot of questions, you know."

"I understand you've started to unlock your Sagittarian side."

"I guess," John said, adjusting his glasses.

"When we came here," she said, turning to the park, "this land was nothing more than rocks and shrubs. Now look at it."

"You've turned it into another trailer park. Good job."

"People ignore trailer parks. They don't like to be reminded of what they could become. And we still have so much work to do."

"You mean there's work you need me to do. That's why I'm here, right?"

"Ricky Handjive wants to put in a water park. Can you imagine a water park out here?" She gestured to the trailers. The gesture was something from his memory, from his childhood.

"Why did you tell Rosa to sleep with me?"

"Where would we put the wave pool?"

"You can't just trick people into sleeping together."

"Why not?"

"What about love. Can't you just let people fall in love?"

"Do you love Rosa?"

"I want to. You fucked it up for me, telling her to sleep with me. Now I'll never know if it was real."

"There is so much you don't understand about us." She smiled and shook her head, almost mocking him. The way she looked at him, it stirred buried memories. It was a look that had been passed down through the generations, from his father, his grandfather. And beyond.

"I understand plenty, Louisa."

"But you don't understand telepathy," she said, smiling and shaking her finger at him like a disapproving school teacher. "When you graduated from college we began conspiring to get you down here."

"Like Leadbelly getting his picture taken."

"Last year we had Rosa probe your mind while you slept. She saw who you really are and fell in love with you. She's just been waiting for you to come to town. I know this has been hard for you, but think about how Rosa must feel. She didn't know if you'd fall in love with her."

"She's amazing! I would have...Doesn't matter now," John said, thinking about how he'd never see her again. He crossed his legs, folded his arms. His foot twitched involuntarily, keeping pace with the thoughts shooting through his head, the similarities between his situation and Archibald's.

Louisa took the journal from John, flipped through the pages.

"I still miss him. You probably think twenty years is a long time to be with someone, but when you've outlived them by a hundred years..." She read a passage, sighing. "I was going to go back and be his housekeeper, but Archie asked me not to. He said he didn't want me to see him as an old man, but watching his mind deteriorate was worse. They were going to name you Archibald. I thought it would have been a good name for you. Some names just fall out of fashion. It's a shame. It's a good name."

Louisa found a picture of John. He is in the front yard with a thick-ended, orange Wiffle ball bat. His father is pitching to him and John has just swung, missing the ball.

"You're a good boy," she said. "You turned out well. It wasn't fair, you being raised away from us, but you turned out well anyway."

"A lot of things aren't fair," John said, a photo of his dad sticking out of the book.

"You see those stars up there?" She pointed to a grouping of bright stars along the southern horizon. "That's Sagittarius. We're from a planet called Chi Sagittarii Prime, in the armpit of the constellation."

"Everyone has a favorite armpit." John studied

the constellation lit above him like a million fresh ideas. He turned to Louisa, the journal open on her lap. "Louisa, about the journal..."

"It's important you know your history."

"When Archibald talked to Jonathon Deerfoot, he wasn't really clear on how you guys got here."

"Archie was an intelligent man, but Earth's science hadn't progressed very far. So, Jonathon had to speak simply, in basic terms."

"Sounded like he was talking about a wormhole," John said, thinking about the *Cape Canaveral* pilot, where John F. Kennedy Space Center was sucked through a wormhole and into outer space.

"Think of the space around us, the subatomic space, like wrinkled aluminum foil. The smooth surfaces between the wrinkles are covered in tiny wormholes that lead everywhere in space. Long ago we developed the technology to latch onto one of these wormholes, expand it, and send objects through, seeding the universe."

"Because you're basically my grandma, I'm avoiding the obvious sex joke."

"We probed the holes."

"You're not making this easy."

"And found planets to colonize. It's how we found Earth. This is all part of our history, our culture."

"Like being obsessed with Elvis?" John looked at the statue.

"Like Sagittarius." She pointed to the constellation again. "We teach our children to wave to it at night."

"Why?"

"Because," she said, looking at John like he'd said something ridiculous, "someone might wave back."

Off in the distance, the last RV landed. The voices of the drivers were soft, but pronounced, in the silent park as they walked to another trailer, disappearing behind the click of a door.

"It's one of the traditions we pass to our children, a way of being connected to our home. It's a simple thing, but traditions always are. That's something you missed out on, our traditions, our mythology, our culture. If you had been raised with us, you'd understand it all."

She smiled. It was a superficial smile covering the machinery that had secretly moved around John all his life.

"Why do you wear glasses?" she asked.

"You're the second person that's asked me that."

"Can I see them?" She held out her hand.

John took off his glasses, handed them to her. Louisa folded them and put them in her cardigan pocket.

She held the journal in her lap, folded her hands over it. There was a benevolence about her, a grandmotherly quality that made John feel like he was wrapped in a warm quilt. Louisa cleared her throat and tilted her head, narrowing her eyes with menacing patience. She smirked expectantly.

Confused, John crinkled his forehead. He opened

his mouth to speak, but stopped. Something grew in his stomach. It was the same pain he endured when he drove into Las Vegas, only now it was deeper, magnified, and quickly overtook him.

John latched onto his gut with both hands, putting pressure on it, trying to suppress the pain. But he couldn't hold it back. As the pain grew, his stomach burned like there was a fire inside him that wanted to break out and blaze through the trailer park. John curled into a ball and fell forward, off the bench.

There was screaming. The noises sounded distant, like they were being shouted across a canyon. And John didn't recognize them as his.

Convulsions. Twitchings growing into a seizure. His body writhed violently against the concrete. Leadbelly's blurred image started running toward him, but Louisa held up her hand, stopping him. She left the bench and knelt above John.

She put his head in her lap, stroked his hair. John's skin exploded under her touch. He felt blood vessels pulsing in her hands, felt her skin loosen and absorb the moisture from his sweat, then tighten and dry. The identifying grooves on her fingertips, the dips and ridges, felt like a topographical map.

"There, there," she said. "It'll be over soon."

John didn't hear her say this. The severe pain deafened him. Everything beneath his skin burned, muscle, connective tissue, organs, nerves, marrow.

But mostly his mind burned, like the heat was melting every thought and associated synapse. The fire was so intense and complete that he couldn't remember a time without it, like it had existed from the day he was born, and was finally burning its way through him.

Then the agony ended.

Lying on the concrete, tears in his eyes, John felt physically different, not sick or hurt or that what he'd just experienced had damaged him. Instead, he was refreshed, aware of a boundless energy, making the world seem fuller, brighter, complete. His old self was gone, had been burned away, and in its place was something different, foreign, but comforting.

A new connectivity existed that wasn't there before, an expanded awareness. It was personal, intimate, like he was being gently caressed by a thousand hands, a thousand minds. He knew who they belonged to, where they were.

"I feel you," he said, wiping tears from his eyes. "I wish I had a better way to say it. But it's like I know where you are. Leadbelly, I know where he is without looking, what he's doing. I know where Handjive is and I haven't seen him since we landed. This feels...I know this feeling. I felt this before, when I first came to town." The stomach pains first appeared as he drove through Las Vegas, returning when he met Rosa and Leadbelly. Thinking back, John recalled other moments when he'd felt this sensation, instances when the streets were dark and empty and the hotel was vacant and he had sat on the bed, bent over, clenching the fabric and skin around his stomach, fighting the kinks and twists underneath. Sitting next to Louisa, John realized that in those moments he wasn't alone, that a Sagittarian must have been near. Watching him.

"Your Sagittarian side was reaching out, trying to connect with us, but you didn't know that, so you interpreted it as a stomach ache."

"There are nine hundred and twenty Sagittarians in the trailer park," John said, like a calculator. He flinched, as if waking from a trance, then added, "I don't know how I know that. I just do."

He knew the location of every Sagittarian in the park without looking. He felt them in his chest, his head, his body. There were three different types. One hundred and twenty-nine like Leadbelly and Handjive. They formed a border around the park, watching John. Two hundred and fifteen like Louisa. And five hundred and forty-two of another group. And within those groups there were the subtle variations of individuals, their essences like fingerprints.

But this awareness wasn't limited to just the Sagittarians. John also discerned Sheriff Masters and Professor Gentry, although it was more like the lack of feeling, a human emptiness among the Sagittarians.

John pushed himself from the grass, sat back on

the bench. A few tears still leaked from his eyes, obscuring his sight. He rubbed them away, and was surprised at what he saw. When he was twelve, John realized his vision was fading when the clues of his crossword blurred, but looking around the park, his world was clear.

"My glasses." John pointed to the black frames sticking out of Louisa's pocket. "They were what were holding me back? keeping me from my Sagittarian side?"

"If it were only that simple," she said, tucking them further into her pocket.

"Why did you ask for them?"

"So you wouldn't break them," she said, with a grandmother's certainty. "You had built a pretty substantial mental blockade. By accepting who you are, your past, your potential, you created a crack in that barrier. This allowed the Elvises to penetrate your mind while we talked and fully break the barrier down."

"I was penetrated by a gang of Elvises? That's what I want to hear after nearly blacking out."

The Elvis impersonators surrounded the park, keeping a respectful distance. A few wore their jumpsuits, but most wore ratted t-shirts and faded jeans. The only thing they looked like they were capable of doing was failing to pay child support.

"In the desert, when I read Hollister's mind? or at the hotel?" He inspected his hand, running his thumb over his knuckles.

"You were able to access a few of your abilities, what you'd read about in the journal, but you have been building a mental obstacle for twenty years. Breaking it down is not something you would have been able to do alone."

"That's why I couldn't use my pheromones in the desert. I get the whole 'mental obstacle' thing, but why did the transformation have to hurt so much?" John rubbed his stomach.

"Your body broke its genetic code. It ripped every double helix you have and then reassembled them, connecting them to your dormant Sagittarian genes. You were rewriting your DNA. Something like that is bound to sting. Don't feel bad. All our children go through this. Think of it as a right of passage, an initiation."

"When do I get my secret decoder ring?" John asked, thinking of American Cipher Discs as Jewelry 104.

"You alright?" Leadbelly asked, walking over from the statue. He sat by John on the bench. "You had me worried there for a second, man."

"Yeah, I'm fine," John said, rubbing the back of his neck.

The others that had come from their trailers stood at the edge of the park. They were out of earshot, but John heard their conversations. They formed a cushion of voices lining his head.

"I can hear them, up here," John said, tapping his head. He said to Leadbelly, "Like I heard you in the trailer."

"You don't seem overwhelmed," Louisa said.

"They just sound like background noise." John breathed, turning down the volume even further. "It's kind of comforting, actually, to not be alone."

"You catch on quick, man," Leadbelly said.

"When I was on the ground, I felt different types of Sagittarians, like subcultures. I felt more Elvises, like Leadbelly and Handjive. I could also feel the original Sagittarians, like you, Louisa. And I felt another group. They were like..."

Rustling leaves of the oak tree behind them. It was an old wind that had blown through the desert for centuries. John bent over, ripped up a single blade of grass. He let it fall, be carried on the gentle wind. It drifted into the park and landed in a green expanse.

"They're Hybrids, aren't they?"

"Did you think you were the only one, man?"

"We have almost six hundred thousand Hybrids in communities all over New Mexico, Nevada, and Colorado," Louisa said.

"Not Arizona?"

"You think we're crazy?" Leadbelly said.

"This is part of the colonization?" John asked, pointing to the journal on Louisa's lap. "What Jonathon Deerfoot talked about?"

"It's the beginning of the second phase," Louisa said. "We're gradually moving Hybrids into positions of power, local politics, attorneys, business owners."

"Like Rosa?" John smiled, thinking of her flowing between her tables.

"Civil servants, leaders in their communities. Eventually we'll move them on to national politics, replacing them at the local level with more Hybrids."

"You want a Hybrid president," John said, realizing the extent of their ambitions.

"We want all the world leaders to be Hybrids. They can create public policies and opinions that will make what's left of the human population welcome the next wave of Sagittarian colonists. This is where you come in. You'll live long enough to greet the next wave and watch this planet evolve into something it never could have expected."

"You want me to run for president? I'm not even registered to vote."

"I wouldn't ask that of you," Louisa said, "but you are an Abernathy and as such you do have responsibilities. You will lead us after I'm gone, guide us through the next phase of colonization."

"What about Leadbelly? He's your son."

"You think anyone'd take me seriously, man?" Leadbelly said, resting his thumbs on his oversized belt.

"Or your daughters?"

"They have other tasks," Louisa said, looking toward the Elvis statue. "But you, John, you will prepare the world, positioning Hybrids in areas where they can impact change, and help with the coming transition."

And all John's questions were answered, why they brought him there, why Rosa slept with him, why Leadbelly let himself be photographed, all so they could reshape him into their vision of the future, give him a new purpose, helping them bring about their new world. But the subtle manipulation made him uneasy. He didn't think he could function like Louisa and Leadbelly, sitting in the desert, moving pieces around, trying to make them fit. He knew he couldn't go back to Denver, be a private investigator with dreams of puzzle stardom. He accepted that. It made him happy knowing he'd never have to sneak around, photographing a client's husband naked on a tarp while insurance appraisers dumped buckets of lime green Jell-O on him. Still, he wasn't sure if he wanted this, being a Hybrid. He didn't know what he wanted. This was his private doubt, something he didn't want Louisa to know. He placed a wall around his mind, like the one he hit in the Winnebago, and hid his reluctance in a tiny box, tossing it into the same crevice where he buried his uncertainties about his puzzles. John folded his arms and looked away.

"Don't worry about that," Louisa said, detecting his doubt. "I'll be around for a long time."

The Elvises started walking into the park. John didn't look. He didn't need to. He sensed them getting closer, like he was inside their bodies, experiencing every footstep and breath and heartbeat required for several hundred Elvis impersonators to move.

He felt the human emptiness denoting where Sheriff Masters was making his way through the crowd. Professor Gentry followed, holding a woman's hand. John initially disregarded their conversation in Professor Gentry's home, but now, in a trailer park full of Elvises, it took on a new meaning.

"They sent you the Wow! Signal, didn't they? back in '77," John said. "It was some kind of message from colonist central or whatever, telling you they're coming."

"They gave us the date and time when the next wave will arrive. They'll be here in two-hundred years. We don't have much time. We have to start preparing."

"I have a question," Professor Gentry said, now standing at the front of the crowd. "The day after the Wow! Signal was intercepted, Elvis died."

"That was just a heart attack," Leadbelly said. "Not everything's a conspiracy, man."

"Even if it was a heart attack," John said to Louisa, "you still have a big problem. Hollister knows you've been watching him. He found Leadbelly's photos. I'm sure he's figured out the whole body-doubles-are-aliens thing by now. He probably thinks you actually killed Elvis. I made a deal with him. I'm not sure if he'll stick to it. But it should buy us some time."

"We're safe out here," Louisa said. "We've adjusted the atmosphere, obscuring us from the Air Force's satellites."

"It's not just that. He's got my dad."

Louisa turned, startled.

"You didn't know, did you?" John asked.

"When we lost contact with him, we assumed…" Weeds grew between the cracks in the sidewalk. They had been trampled by foot traffic, but still endured. Louisa brushed them with her Birkenstock.

"He walled his mind off, probably before they cryonically froze him."

"That would keep a mental barrier in place."

"Like what you did to me in the Winnebago," John said to Leadbelly.

"He should have told us, man. We would a gone out there and got him." Leadbelly's lip curled, jaw tightened.

"He was protecting me. If you rescued him, Hollister would have gone after me and my mom."

"So, he disconnected himself from us," Louisa said, folding her arms. "That poor man, alone and isolated. It's a hard and painful thing."

"But my dad wasn't alone," John said, remembering a lifetime of conversations with this father. "He's been talking to me my whole life. In dreams."

"He must have built a mental bond with you,

tethered his subconscious to yours. He probably started when you were a baby, while your mind was still forming. It's the only way he could talk to you while his mind and body were cryonically frozen."

"Then he knew Hollister, or someone, was coming for him?"

"Or maybe he just wanted to be close to you," Louisa said, patting his knee.

"I have to get him," John said, feeling the need to atone for eighteen years of hostility.

"Now that we know where he is, we'll send a team to do some reconnaissance. Don't worry, we'll get him back."

"My family, my mom, Rooftop," John said, jumping up from the bench. "Hollister will use them to get to me. I need to go back to Denver, make sure they're alright, get them out of there if possible."

"Your family will have a home here." Louisa nodded.

"And Rosa?" John asked.

"She's been asking about you, too. She's with her family…" Louisa rubbed the spine of the journal with her thumb, searching for the right words. "Taking care of some things, but you'll see each other again, soon."

John looked down and smiled. His cheeks flushed. When he drove into the desert with Leadbelly, he wasn't sure he'd ever see Rosa again, or if she even wanted to see him. But she'd asked about him, and that felt better than solving *The New York Times* Sunday crossword with a pen.

"Al, you and Ricky take John, Sheriff Masters, and Professor Gentry back to Las Vegas."

"I'd like to stay here, if that's alright?" Professor Gentry asked, his arm around an older, Mexican woman, one of the original colonists.

"You move quick," John said. "What would Mrs. Morris say?"

"Elizabeth and I have an open relationship."

"Very well. You may stay with us," Louisa said in her gentle way. "In the meantime, we'll contact the other Sagittarian communities and inform them about the recent developments."

Leadbelly and Louisa rose from the bench. Louisa hugged John. She put her hands on his face. "Hurry back to us."

"I'll get back as quickly as I can."

As the four men walked to Handjive's Winnebago, the sheriff turned to John, grinning like his mind was full of trouble.

"John, when we get back, let's drive around town. You can tell me who's human and who's not."

"You wanna kick the Sagittarians out of Las Vegas?"

"Shoot, if they're anything like Leadbelly and Handjive here, I just might kick all the humans outta town."

Handjive turned the key.

Nothing happened.

He tried again.

Nothing.

"So much for good-old Sagittarian know-how," John said.

Handjive smiled, a blend of comfort and seduction. He leaned over the dash, whispered into the air vents, then started singing to the Winnebago, "...and I can't help, falling in love with you."

Handjive turned the key again. This time the engine turned over, humming its own song. The metal spikes holding them to the earth detached and clamped to the side of the Winnebago, and they lifted into the early dawn.

"You gotta know how to talk to them, man, just like a woman." He continued romancing the mobile home, caressing the dashboard with his right hand.

They floated over the trailer park, the light of sunrise spreading across the desert floor. John propped his hands on the bed above the cab and surveyed the park out the front window. It grew the higher they rose above it and John saw just how sprawling and expansive it really was.

"Holy shit," he whispered.

When they landed, the park appeared to be smaller. Only a few trailers were lit, those necessary for landing, but against the morning light, he saw its immensity. Thousands of trailers covered several square miles of lifeless soil. A town established in nowhere. Empty spaces were spread throughout the park, awaiting absent trailers. And standing in the middle of it all was the Elvis statue.

"Check it out, man," Handjive said, pointing to the ground. Other Winnebagos dislodged from the surface, heading west and north. "They're gonna go have a chat with the rest of us, man. All the Sagittarians out there."

"You can't just talk to them telepathically?" John asked.

"Naw, man," Leadbelly said, sitting at the table, drinking a can of lite beer. "It's a distance thing. We gotta be within a certain radius or the whole dang thing won't work."

"What about dreams?" John asked. "I thought you could talk to them that way."

"Dreams are different, man. Your subconscious is more open, more receptive to telepathy. It's sunrise. No one's sleeping now. Besides, man, this is too important for dreams. Someone might misinterpret the message."

"I can see how a dream where a paranoid Elvis tells you to hide from the government can be confusing," John said.

"It's serious business, man," Handjive said. "We're gonna have to lock down the park for a while. Till we can figure this whole mess out. It's gonna be hard, man. No women."

"I saw women all over that camp," Sheriff Masters said. "Hell, Gentry found himself one."

"Man, we're either related to them or they're too old," Leadbelly said.

"Since when do you care about age?" John asked.

"When the women around here started turning four hundred, man."

"Hey, Leadbelly," Handjive said. "What do you say, man, after we drop these two off we make one last trip to Vegas. Do it up, Elvis style."

"I only got one thing to say to that, man, Viva Las Vegas." Leadbelly smiled, content and excited, like getting kicked out of Circus Circus and arrested for public drunkenness at the Fremont Street Experience was how he wanted to spend his last hours before being sequestered. Leadbelly and Handjive talked about all the off-strip casinos they wanted to visit, recalling previous booze-induced escapades. Listening to their stories, John chuckled and wondered if Vegas had a law against 'drinking while Elvis'.

Handjive piloted the Winnebago away from the park. As they flew away, John experimented with his new ability. He extended his consciousness as far as possible, testing its limits. He sensed the Sagittarians, the Hybrids, the Elvises fade like stars disappearing at sunrise, all except the two in the cabin with him.

As they got closer to the mountains, roads started cutting across the ground. John recognized I-25, the road they took to Professor Gentry's compound. They descended and, just for fun, Handjive flew over the plot of desert where the Air Force had ambushed them. John put his hands and face against the window, looking for his wrecked car, but it wasn't there. The area was totally clean. A sanitized desert.

Handjive hovered a few inches over an empty stretch of highway outside of town. Metal grinded, hiding the frame and the Sagittarian engine underneath the mobile home. Four tires moved into the wheel wells. Handjive smiled at his passengers and flipped the switch that lowered the RV onto the road. Caught by gravity, the Winnebago dropped to the ground, bouncing as it hit. The inside of the cab shook and John gripped the table, bracing himself.

Handjive turned the ignition key to the combustion engine, and where they expected to hear a motor turning over, they heard only a slight breeze blowing eroding sands. The Winnebago didn't start. He tried it again and again with the same results.

"Sorry, man," Handjive said. "I'd fly you into

town, but, man, we'd probably cause a riot."

"And Mrs. Morris would be leading the pack," John said, "swinging vibrators like nunchucks."

"Looks like we're walking," the sheriff said, rising from the passenger seat.

Stepping from the Winnebago into the culvert, brown grass tried to crawl up their pant legs. They said their goodbyes, and watched the RV convert back to flying mode. The metal frame grew from underneath, enveloping the tires, pulling them under the vehicle. The Winnebago floated for a minute then lifted skyward. They waved to their friends until the Winnebago disappeared, blending with the endless blue sky.

John held onto them with his consciousness as long as possible, seeing, feeling them disappear simultaneously. He searched the desert for alien life, but didn't feel any. They were out there somewhere. Just not near him.

"Hey, John. Check it out." The sheriff pointed up, smirked. "Elvis has left the building."

* * * *

The sun rose as they walked, reflecting off the road ahead of them. John squinted and a thin membrane, like a second eyelid, grew over eyes. A product of his Sagittarian heritage, it diffused the morning light.

Being in the trailer park, meeting the other Sagittarians changed John, showed him he was part of something bigger, older, part of a species that spread across the galaxy, reshaping the worlds they inhabited. John knew they had plans for him, beyond what Louisa told him, but he didn't care about their internal invasion, or the impending second wave, he just wanted to find Rosa and live a quiet life with her. He didn't think he was alone in his desire for solitude. When he was in the park, he'd heard everyone's thoughts, experienced their emotions. It was incredible, being connected to the Sagittarians, peaceful. His uncertainty, isolation, loneliness had vanished because he finally knew what it was like not to be alone. But he had felt something else, like the peace they shared was a thick crust covering another, equally prevalent emotion. They craved the unity that came with being connected to other Sagittarians, but they also coveted that human fragment that demanded reckless individuality, like Leadbelly and Handjive going to Las Vegas, trying to have as much fun as possible before the next wave of Sagittarians arrived. John thought these two desires would conflict, but he felt their symmetry and the contentment of everyone in the park, like they had learned what it really meant to be part Sagittarian and part human, something he was just starting to discover.

The sun beat down on him, was absorbed by the extra melanin secreted into his skin, and John felt its warmth and smiled. For the first time, John didn't have a detailed plan regarding his future.

When he was younger he'd dreamed and plotted out his life, college, writing puzzles for *The Denver Post*, a book deal that put his genre-bending work in the hands of the next generation of enigmatologists, talk shows, his own panel at Comic-Con, an Oscar winning biopic, but those fantasies no longer mattered. John's future was as open as the desert sandwiching the road. He wasn't sure what would happen to him, what he'd become. He just knew that whatever awaited him in the centuries ahead, he didn't want Louisa's job, to secretly organize a colonization effort from a trailer park in New Mexico.

John didn't share his thoughts with Sheriff Masters. Instead, they silently walked into town.

CHAPTER THIRTY ONE

The old gas station on the edge of town, its perfect view of nothing, was a relic from an era before nationwide infrastructure, when two-lane highways were the thoroughfares for cross-country shipping or family trips. Propped on posts next to the highway, an arrow pointed to the station. A red awning with neon lights augmenting it sheltered the two gas pumps, their gauges rolling like slot machines. Tires were stacked next to the front door. Metal signs for cola, beer, and motor oil hung in the window. The signs were dented and rusted, corroding them with the nostalgic quality that John loved.

John dropped his last few dollars on the counter, not looking at the cashier, but out the window behind him. The sheriff was talking on a pay phone. Beyond him, lifeless desert. John stepped outside with two beers and a bag of sunflower seeds. He heard the sheriff yelling at somebody. The sheriff slammed the receiver, started cursing.

"Goddamn Jimmy!" he shouted. "Stupid sonuvabitch! He found the car in the desert, all shot up. Thinks I got killed. Now he's got the NMBI out looking for me. What the hell am I going to tell everyone?"

"Tell them the truth, that we were abducted by aliens."

"Yeah," the sheriff said, "and instead of doing anal probes, they made us drink beer and eat hamburgers. They'll think I'm off my goddamn rocker."

"What? You think they'd believe we were anally probed?"

John handed the sheriff a beer, the opened bag of sunflower seeds. A red picnic table squatted in the sun next to the ice machine and, sipping his beer, the sheriff sat there. John straddled the bench seat and picked at peeling red paint.

"You know, they ransacked your room," the sheriff said, propping his elbows on the table.

"I figured as much," John said, popping a few sunflower seeds in his mouth.

"I guess they found Mrs. Morris's address." He sipped his beer. "She came home last night, found her place broken into. All her Elvis shit got destroyed. Made it look like teenagers. Jimmy was first on the scene, said there were broken plates and dildos everywhere. She's claiming the Elvis painting, you know, the one with his cock out..."

"What? She's got another one?"

"She's claiming it was stolen."

"Hollister's probably got it hanging in his office." John envisioned it hanging behind Colonel

Hollister's desk, his men suppressing their giggles when he'd order them to stand at attention.

"Goddamn Air Force. Worst part is, I can't prove nothing either."

"I think the world might be better off with one less painting of naked Elvis."

"Jimmy impounded your car. Your belongings are in the evidence locker."

"Everything?" John asked, pushing his sunflower seeds into a pyramid.

"Yup, including an envelope full of cash."

"That'll make Roof happy." John sipped his beer, looked at the road, trying to see its end. "Who's coming to get us?"

"Shirley. Should be here any minute."

The sheriff finished his beer and walked to the back of the gas station. Old train tracks resting a hundred years were overrun with dried grass, almost buried.

"Hey, John, bet I can throw a bottle farther than you can."

"You're on."

John hopped off the bench and trotted to where the sheriff stood. The sheriff dug the toe of his boot into the dirt. He took his bottle by the neck and tossed it at the tracks. John threw his, not waiting to see where the sheriff's landed. The bottles burst a few feet from each other, spreading shattered glass across the tracks. They laughed and argued over whose went farther.

A lone car on the road. The sheriff nudged John and started walking to the front of the gas station. A maroon station wagon with fake wood paneling pulled into the gravel parking lot, a ghost town stagecoach, a gray dust cloud in its wake.

"Lee, where the hell have you been? I've been worried sick," Shirley said when they opened the car doors. She was older, the sheriff's age. A floral print sprouted across her suit jacket. Freshly cut gray hair dangled around her ears. John slid into the backseat, next to boxes full of files that Shirley had taken home from the police station. John moved a box over, realizing that it was Shirley who kept the station from toppling.

"Yeah, I know" the sheriff said, grinning. "I'll explain everything at the station."

Shirley drove them back to the motel, scolding them like they were teenagers caught smoking behind the gym. The sheriff smiled at John, as if to say, 'Isn't she something?'

The motel parking lot was empty. From the outside, everything looked normal. The sheriff's car was untouched. An open sign hung in the lobby window. The door to John's room was closed, like he was out for the day exploring the town's historical landmarks.

"Lee," Shirley said, "you better get straight back to the station if you know what's good for you. And you, Mr. Abernathy, it was nice meeting you, but next time you come to town, leave the trouble in

Denver."

"Yes, ma'am," John said, not wanting to tell her that the trouble was already here, and would probably remain after he left.

"So, that's Shirley?" John asked as she drove out of the parking lot.

"Yup. That's the Missus. Twenty-four years this June. What you saw is tame compared to what I'm gonna get when I get home. Whew, be glad you're not married."

"Yeah, it must suck having someone who cares enough to worry," John said, thinking about Rosa and doubting he would ever experience that particular joy.

"You know it, buddy." Sheriff Masters slapped John's arm and watched Shirley drive away, smiling slightly, content.

"Don't worry about your stuff, now," the sheriff said. "I'll bring it over tonight. You want to get a beer later?"

"Sounds good, but I'm leaving soon."

"So, your job's done then, huh?" The sheriff put one of his keys under his thumbnail, cleaned out some dirt.

"Yeah, gotta get back. Take care of my mom."

"Your car's all shot up?"

"I figure I'll take the bus. It won't take me long to get back, probably a day and a half." John grinned at the sheriff, hoping he caught his joke about slow bus travel. Instead, the sheriff looked at the ground, silent.

"Well," the sheriff said. He moved a small pebble with the toe of his boot. It rolled away and he looked up, smiling. "I better get back to the station. Jimmy's probably got everything turned all back-asswards by now."

They shook hands, John thinking it was the last time he'd see the sheriff. He wondered, after all they'd been through, what Sheriff Masters thought of him. He didn't try to read his mind, leaving him his privacy. Instead, he just nodded, the sheriff nodding back. John hoped that after he'd left and the sheriff returned to his station and the quiet routine of his small town, that Sheriff Masters would still consider him a friend.

The sheriff got in his car, promised to stop by with John's things, again.

"Hey, check this out," the sheriff said, grinning.

He turned on his siren and sped down the street like he was heading to a bank robbery. John shook his head, chuckled.

When the sirens were a whisper, John pulled out his motel room key and stood in front of the door for a moment. He held the key by the thin part, tapped the fat end against his hand, feeling his palm withstand the key's weight. There was something inside the room, waiting for him, something he had to deal with.

He put the key in the lock and opened the door. The room had been cleaned. The bed was made, the carpet vacuumed. John smelled bleach and ammonia and pine perfume.

And he smelled himself, the stink of the activity of the past several days. He wondered if it would ever wash off. In the bathroom, John took off his shirt and splashed sink water on his face and chest. Jimmy had confiscated his luggage, his clothes, and John had to continue wearing his filthy jeans and sweat-soaked, comic book t-shirt.

On the table was something that hadn't been appropriated, his pad of graph paper. The barely-begun crossword puzzle. Blue, horizontal and vertical lines bisected on the pad. Words had been erased, written over, their letters sitting in the cells the lines created, imprisoned by John's misdirected imagination.

He picked up a pen, clicked it a couple of times, extending then retracting the ballpoint, like each click was a retort in some internal debate. But the argument was already over. It was won before he left with Leadbelly for the desert. John sighed. He clicked the pen one last time and, with two pen strokes, freely crossed out the puzzle.

He set his gun on the table. Relieved of the weight, John collapsed on the bed, the frayed plastic stitching from the polyester comforter poking him in the back, and quickly fell asleep.

* * * *

Later in the afternoon someone knocked on the door, waking John.

He opened it, drowsy, a little disoriented. Sheriff Masters stood in the late afternoon sun, his hands in his back pockets. Behind him, Jimmy and the motel manager, Ernesto, waited.

"I hope you don't mind, John," the sheriff said. "I told Ernie you were checking out. Asked him to come down here and handle it."

"I don't get it," John said, rubbing his eyes and yawning. "What's going on?"

Ernesto held the receipt close to his face, reading it, his forefinger guiding him. "Just sign here," he said, a smile wrinkling his tan face, handing John the receipt and pen. "Don't worry about the mess in the room, young fella. Carmilta's my cousin. She told me about your friend. We try to take care of our celebrity guests."

"Well," John winked at Ernesto, like it was their inside joke, "my friend said Carmilta took very good care of him."

"Good. I'll put it in her quarterly review."

"I think that's where Leadbelly put it, too."

"I brought all your stuff," the sheriff said. "It's out in the car."

John looked over the sheriff's shoulder at the squad car.

"The other car." The sheriff held out his hand. A set of car keys dangled from his fingers, augmented by a medallion with the Pontiac logo.

"Jimmy felt bad about overreacting. So, he decided to loan you his car for your trip home. Isn't that right, Jimmy?" Sheriff Masters glared at his nephew.

"Uh, yeah, bro. I'm real sorry," Jimmy said, looking at the ground like a little kid caught stealing change to buy Foreigner tickets. He wore a yellow t-shirt with a faded decal of a surfer. The sleeves were cut off. Wrap-around sunglass rested on his head backwards, like they were shading him from hindsight.

The car, a large, black two-seater with a flaming eagle painted on the hood. A custom license plate said 'Bandit'. It looked like something from John's history elective, Matchbox Cars of the 1980's 102.

"You're kidding me?" John said. "Is this what I think it is?"

"Dude," Jimmy said, his smile bright as fog lights, "that's a vintage 1977 Trans-Am. Like what Burt Reynolds drove in *Smokey and the Bandit*. Check it out, bro."

Jimmy showed John one of his exposed arms. Near his shoulder was a tattoo of Burt Reynolds's face with the collar of a red shirt and tan cowboy hat. A black Trans-Am was inked underneath.

Art school had prepared John for this level of obsession, his classmates dedicating their lives to an artist, band, or song. This fixation was embodied in a student exhibit comprised of trash from a famous rapper's hotel room. The highlight of the show was a piece made out of Chinese take-out boxes and hemorrhoid cream. John couldn't watch the rapper's videos, featuring bouncing cars, without laughing.

"So, I take it you like the movie?" John asked.

"Bro, this movie is my life. This car, dude, it's like a piece of American history."

"You don't need American history to go to Walgreens," the sheriff said.

Jimmy turned away from his uncle and toward the parking lot. He crossed his arms, making the tattoo of Burt Reynolds's face pout.

"Jimmy," John said, feeling sorry for him, "thanks for letting me borrow your car. It's really cool of you."

"Ah, no worries, bro," Jimmy said, sticking his fist out, waiting for a bump. "I'm just glad someone around here appreciates the classics."

John rolled his eyes, then gave Jimmy a fist bump.

"Just take it easy with her, okay. This bitch has a turbo-charged V8. You gotta watch her, bro, or she'll get away from you."

"So, no street racing?"

"No. Hey." Jimmy started laughing. "Dude, you almost got me."

"I'll get it back to you soon. A couple of days. A week at the most."

John's cooler sat on the Trans-Am's front seat, his bag on the floor. John unzipped his bag and started going through it. Everything was still there, even his cash.

John opened the cooler.

"Shirley made you some sandwiches," Sheriff Masters said. "And we packed you a couple of sodas."

John closed the cooler, caught the reflection of neon in the side mirror. When they arrived at the hotel that morning, the neon sign was off, but now it was dusk and the sign shone like it did when he'd checked into The Sagittarius Inn, arrived in Las Vegas, New Mexico, a town unmolested by coincidences.

"Ernesto, that sign, where'd you get it?" John asked, thumbing over his shoulder to the neon centaur.

"Oh, that thing," Ernesto said, pointing at it with his whole hand, fingers fused together by age. "It came with the place. I was gonna change it but it cost too much. Plus, the fella I bought the motel from said it'd attract a lotta good customers."

"You remember his name? the guy you bought it from?"

"Not really. That was a long time ago, back in '73. He was an Indian fella, I can tell you that much."

"Wasn't Jonathon Deerfoot, was it?"

"Yup," Ernesto nodded. "That's it. How'd you know?"

"I have family that knew him."

John thanked Ernesto for his hospitality, and thanked Jimmy again for letting him borrow his car.

"John, let me walk you to that car a Jimmy's," Sheriff Masters said. They walked to the driver's side, out of earshot of the other two. "I went by Professor Gentry's place this afternoon. The tire wall had been knocked down, the trailer was burned out."

"Meth lab. I knew it," John said, smirking. "He's out at the trailer park with his new girlfriend. I'll get word to him somehow, tell him to hide out for a while."

"Hey," the sheriff smiled, "when you get back from Denver, why don't you work for me. It's just a matter a time before Jimmy shoots himself in the foot."

"Thanks, but I think there's already plenty of work for me to do."

"Alright. Well, it's a standing offer. Just be safe driving home, okay?"

John got in the car. The windows were already rolled down and Sheriff Masters closed the door for him.

"Don't worry. I'll be fine," John said, putting the gun under the driver's seat.

"Alright. Hey, give me a call in a couple a days, when you figure out when you're coming back."

John turned the key. The engine of the 1977 Trans-Am vibrated underneath him, roaring like a defiant memory. It was why Jimmy liked the car. When it was dormant, the car looked like the punch line to a joke about New Jersey, but it hid a power only hinted at by the gold phoenix painted on the black hood.

John drove to the edge of the road and stopped and stuck his hand out the window, flipped them off. He stepped on the brakes and the gas at the same. The tires spun and smoked. Jimmy shouted something, but the squealing tires muffled his protest. Finally, John took his foot off the brake. The car fishtailed a little and John sped out of the parking lot, leaving two black streaks on the Las Vegas street.

CHAPTER THIRTY TWO

The road was empty, except for the occasional semi. The car roared under John and Jimmy's Judas Priest tape flipped sides as he sped past fence posts. A hawk circled above a field, searching for something invisible to John. He turned up the music, hoping thundering drums, crunching guitars, and a bird-like male falsetto would infuse him with a sense of badassery, make him feel aggressive and invincible. Driving away from the motel, watching the sheriff wave, seemed to drain him of his energy, and he began to yearn for Las Vegas, New Mexico in a way that he never longed for Denver, or Boulder, like it was where he really belonged, home. Everywhere he had lived, he felt out of place, whether it was growing up in Denver, going to art school, or working for Rooftop. John had assumed it was because he didn't have a father, even though his mom and Rooftop tried to compensate. But the reason he felt isolated was because he truly wasn't like anyone else. During late night dorm room sessions, ten kids piled into a room, passing a bong, the conversation constantly returned to how they always felt different from the other kids at their high school. In those moments, John felt a greater distance between them. Because, unlike the girl who blew glass vampires, or the guy who sculpted a clay Bob Costas with boobs, John truly was all the lonely and alienating adjectives his friends used to characterize themselves. He just didn't know how extraordinary he was.

John adjusted the rearview mirror. The town had vanished from it, finally blown to dust. On the empty highway, he had also been enveloped by the desert, surrounded by dried grass and barbed wire fences.

He had been driving for about a half hour when he sensed it. Sagittarians nearby. It was faint, not as strong as it was in the trailer park, but he still felt it, felt them. He pulled onto the shoulder, got out of the Trans-Am, and walked down the road, trying to find them, like a human divining rod searching the desert for an underground spring.

John walked through the culvert, toward a fence and the field behind it. A slight breeze carrying the smell of sage and dead grass. The sensation increased every second, growing in John, like they were getting closer. John didn't need to look for the Sagittarians. They were looking for him.

A fencepost had been uprooted and the barbed wire had been snipped and coiled. He stepped through the opening, then ran into the field. Brittle grasses snapped under his Chucks. Clumps of dry dirt broke and joined soil. John ran over yellow grass and rock to a spot far enough in the field that the road became a dark line against the golden ground. He sent his consciousness exploring, trying to find the Sagittarians that had caused his body to vibrate with awareness.

There were seventeen Sagittarians in the field. Their impression was different from Leadbelly's and the Elvises'. They felt like warm, red swirls. They surrounded him, but remained distant. John sensed them moving in independent circles, like they were pacing. Or stalking. Then one crept toward him.

The sky was cloudless. The sun was setting behind John, but the field was still lit and false, silver pools shimmered on the ground. From one of these mirages, something emerged. It was a blob breaking heat waves, gradually shaping itself into something resembling a human. As it got closer, John distinguished features, long hair, a dress, hips, a distinctive saunter.

Rosa.

She floated toward him out of the desert, out of a dream. He ran toward her and when he reached her, they paused awkwardly for a moment. John smiled and reached out to her, but pulled his arms back. Rosa looked at him, raised her eyebrows expectantly.

He clutched her dress and pulled her in and kissed her. She put her arms around him, kissed him back. Then she just hugged him, resting her head on his shoulder. He moved his arms, wrapped them around Rosa's waist, but they shook with excitement and he concentrated, stilling them. And gently held her.

She raised her head from his shoulder and smiled. Her smile filled John with a warmth and joy he'd never felt before, and he didn't want to let go of her, a once-in-a-lifetime find.

"So, does this mean we're boyfriend girlfriend?" he asked, looking into her deep brown eyes.

"That depends," Rosa said, "how do you feel about dating an older woman?"

"How much older are we talking? not four hundred?"

"How old do you think I look?"

"Not a day over perfect."

"You're so cheesy," she said. "I'm one hundred and sixty-three, if you must know."

"So you're a cougar?"

"I am not a cougar," Rosa said.

"I don't know..." John said, teasing. "You did seduce a younger man."

She rolled her eyes.

"So, seriously. Are we boyfriend girlfriend, or what?"

"What do you want us to be?" Rosa rested her arms on his shoulders and smiled up at him.

"You can't tell? I was practically all over you at lunch the other day."

"John." Rosa tilted her head. "I'm one hundred and sixty-three. Men have been hitting on me since the 1880's. Trust me, you were not all over me."

"That makes me feel better." A small yucca plant, the sharp brown leaves at its base, grew a few feet away.

"John, look at me." Rosa grabbed his head with both hands. "I came all the way out here to find you. You think I'd do that for someone I'd just slept with if there wasn't something more?"

"So, you've been with other guys?"

"Oh my God, John. Are you listening to me?"

"How many are we talking here? five, ten, twenty." John's eyes widened. "More? More than twenty?"

"I'm trying to tell you I love you."

John started laughing.

"You're such a shit," Rosa said, slapping his chest.

"I talked to Louisa," John said. He didn't want to bring it up, but there was something he needed to tell Rosa.

Rosa pulled away and turned her back to him. John put his hands in his hoodie pockets, stretching its front, making him slouch. He noticed Rosa was barefoot.

"You didn't need to do it, you know..." he said, "use those pheromones on me. I mean, I know Louisa asked you to. How fucked up is that, my great-great-great-grandmother has to hook me up.

Still, you didn't need to do it."

"I didn't want to," she said, biting her thumb. "I just wasn't sure if you..."

"Hey." John put his hand on her shoulder. "I wouldn't change anything, being with you. You know, so much of my life hasn't turned out the way I thought it would."

"John." Rosa spun. She folded her arms across her chest, put her weight on her right leg, raised one hip, the classic disgruntled girlfriend pose. "You're only twenty-three."

"Yeah, I know. Most people say that when they're like, I don't know, forty. But I'm saying it now. When I finished school, I thought I'd be designing crosswords for *The Denver Post* or something. When people asked me what I did, that's what I told them, that I was a puzzle maker. Even when I was sneaking around photographing people doing it, I'd tell myself, 'I'll be a professional puzzle designer soon and none of this will matter. It'll be a funny story for the talk shows.'"

"There are a lot of crossword designers on talk shows?" she asked.

"I was going to be the first. At least, that's what I told myself. Now I don't know. After everything that's happened, what I've learned. I'm not who I thought I was. And who I am is not what everyone wants me to be." John found the little box containing his hesitancies and misgivings. He added one more article to it before tucking it back in its nook.

"Who do you want to be?"

"All I know is when I look at you, you're the only thing that makes sense. In a weird, drugging-me-to-sleep-with-you sort of way." John moved to adjust his glasses, forgetting he'd left them in the trailer park. "I guess what I'm trying to say is, I love you. I fell in love with you the minute I saw you."

She smiled and put her arms around his neck.

"Okay, you can stop talking now," she said, kissing him.

"So," John said, "does this make me your boyfriend?"

"Actually, I think you're more than that."

"Huh?"

Rosa beamed at him.

"Something's different about you," he said. John reached out with his consciousness and was suddenly aware of more Sagittarians, not just Rosa, and not just the sixteen watching them. He put his hand on her belly. It was like a lake, a calm surface with hyperactivity underneath. Life working.

"Holy shit! You're pregnant!"

"Yeah." Rosa smiled. Even though her belly was flat, she rubbed it like she was in her third trimester, cradling what was gestating inside.

"Is it mine?"

"Yeah, silly. Who else's could they be?" Rosa said, nodding, her smile widening.

were called and a procession of Abernathys collected their high school diplomas. He saw his children marrying, having nonuplets of their own, John and Rosa eventually being like Louisa, several 'greats' preceding their names. Holding Rosa, feeling their children squirming inside her, John knew that a lifetime of exhaustion and worry, laughter and delight, awaited him. There was just one thing he had to do first.

"So, you're headed back to Denver?" she asked, looking at her bare feet.

"Just for a couple of days. I have to get my mom, grandma, and Roof. Louisa says she has a place for them in the trailer park. Then there's my dad. I gotta take care of that."

"You're going to rescue him?"

"I have to. He's my dad." John shrugged his shoulders.

"I'll come with you, help you find him."

"Louisa's already got people on that. You've got our kids to take care of." John put his hand back on her belly, wrapped one arm around her, and kissed the side of her head. He lowered his voice. "Don't worry, it'll just be a couple of days. Then we can just be together."

She wrapped her arms around him and kissed him.

"Hurry back to me."

"I'll be back as soon as I can."

John put his forehead against Rosa's and

whispered, "I love you."

Rosa leaned in, kissed him again, and whispered.

Rosa walked backward, her hand slipping from his. Her eyes glistened like she was verging on crying. She wiped her eyes then spun and ran into the desert. Louisa said Rosa had been waiting longer for them to be together than John had, for years, and now she'd have to wait a little longer. Watching her run away from him, John choked back his tears, and promised himself she'd never cry again.

He held onto her with his consciousness as she ran. She lifted her dress over her head and rolled it up. Holding the dress in her mouth, she transformed into a lynx and dashed toward the lingering Sagittarians. They circled around her several times and ran into the desert. Rosa turned her head toward John. She whimpered, then followed the Sagittarians into the desolation.

And she was gone.

The last light from the sun was vanishing. The sky, pink and violet. Twilight bloomed behind the Rockies. John followed this light to the road. He found the broken part of the fence and walked through, happy. He was going to be a father, Rosa a mother. And they'd do it together. He leapt over the culvert and skipped to the car.

John stood next to the Trans-Am and looked toward the blackening sky. Stars were beginning to pierce the twilight and the constellations' formations were becoming distinguishable. To the south, where Louisa had showed him, John spotted Sagittarius glimmering against the black backdrop. He turned toward it, and felt connected to the cluster of stars where his ancestors originated. And, standing in the empty highway, he raised his hand and waved to the constellation, confident someone would wave back.

ACKNOWLEDGEMENTS

Here's a very brief list of people who helped shape this book, making its publication possible. Kitty Honeycutt, Chad Douglas, Emily Alexander, Mark Gottlieb, Michael Neff, Alan Rinzler, Josh Mohr, Andrew Touhy, and the countless readers who provided invaluable feedback on this book, many of them I can't even remember. Without their insight, this book would not be the loose collection of fart jokes that it is.

To all my friends who've had to listen to me talk about this book. Again, there are too many of you to list, but you know who you are.

To my supportive family, Larry, Donna, and Daniel Adams, Frank and Sharon Malvoso.

And especially, Shelby, for, to put it simply, everything.

Made in the USA
San Bernardino, CA
03 May 2016